EYES OF
DOOM

RAYMOND LITTLE

ISBN: 978-1-940250-28-1

This book is a work of fiction. Names, characters, business organizations, places, events and incidents either are the product of the author's imagination or are used fictitiously. Any resemblance to actual persons, living or dead, events or locales is entirely coincidental.

Artwork by Jeff West

Interior Layout by Lori Michelle
   www.theauthorsalley.com

Printed in the United States of America

First Edition

Visit us on the web at:
www.bloodboundbooks.net

Also from Blood Bound Books:

Praise for Raymond Little

"Little's writing style is rich and controlled, yet it has an economy and a great sense of timing."

—Dead End Follies

"There are few writers who can capture the emotional resonance of multiple characters while also filling the pages with elaborate twists of circumstance and thrills, yet you have found your way to one of them: Raymond Little's *Eyes of Doom* chronicles the complex relationship between four friends who are entwined with a horror that follows them for decades, in this eagerly-anticipated debut novel by an ace of the short form."

—Eric J. Guignard,
fictionist, winner of the Bram Stoker Award,
and finalist for the International Thriller Writers Award

"It's ["Bow Creek"] one of the best short stories I've read this year. I had no idea who Little was before reading this, but he's officially on my radar."

—Benoît Lelièvre

For Julie Anne Little

PROLOGUE

2016—LONDON

OF **THE BRIDGES** that spanned the Thames, Waterloo had always been Vinnie's favourite. The supposed grandeur of Tower Bridge with its archaic and pompous entrance to a London that no longer existed could never compete. No, it had always been Waterloo Bridge, sleek and modern with its unencumbered view of the city, and Vinnie couldn't think of any other place he'd rather do it.

He rested one foot on the low stone wall that supported the three white rails and brushed a thin layer of snow off the uppermost one before swinging his leg over. A tune played in his head, an old one about the sun setting over the city, and he remembered a party at Jack's place. He was dancing with Sue, or maybe it was Jan—there were so many back then he'd lost track—and he'd been drunk or high. Maybe he was happy.

Vinnie raised his other leg up and over the bar and joined the small, silent boy on the wrong side of the railing, where he turned his back to the bridge and gripped the cold rail at his hips. Thick snowflakes drifted into the blackness below and he watched, hypnotized by their haphazard descent. He wouldn't cry. He hadn't cried since he was a kid, not for anybody, and he refused to waste tears on himself now in the middle of the night on Waterloo-fucking-Bridge. He didn't deserve them.

He looked at the boy. 'Is this going to hurt, Frankie?'

'Yes.' Frankie's eyes flashed red, and Vinnie returned his attention to the river, preferring to ignore what he'd seen. 'But it will be quick.'

Vinnie smiled at that. 'Quicker than life,' he said. His voice had a tremble not wholly attributable to the temperature. He felt Frankie's palm—as cold as his own—on the back of his right hand. 'I'm scared, Frankie.'

'Come on,' the boy said. 'It's easy.'

He released his hand from the rail and turned it to take hold of Frankie's.

'Now you just have to let go.'

Vinnie took a breath and tried to envisage something that might give him comfort in his last moments, but nothing would come. 'Oh, well,' he muttered, for lack of anything profound to say.

He gripped Frankie's hand tight and the two of them stepped off into the darkness.

PART I

1974—FOUR FRIENDS

1

'**O**H, BLOODY HELL.' Jack squinted at the clock as if it might somehow be wrong. He dropped his paint brush into the jar of water by his side with a splash that sent little dots of green in an arc onto his white underpants.

'Oh, that's just fucking great.' He ran barefoot across the cold lino to the big sink by the window and turned the tap on, which chugged and sputtered before releasing no more than a drizzle.

'What's going on?'

Jack glanced over his shoulder at his roommate, Maurice, red-eyed and pale-faced beneath a shock of shoulder length blonde curls.

'I've got a meeting with Hadley at eleven.'

Maurice sat up in his bed and fumbled with a cigarette packet. 'It's a quarter to.'

'I know.' Jack splashed water over his face and under his arms. He was in need of a shave, though too short on time for it. He'd been out of bed a couple of hours, but of course he just had to add a couple of strokes to his latest canvas. As usual, a couple of strokes were never enough.

'What you need to do—' Maurice lit his Marlboro and winced as the smoke hit his eyes '—is manage your schedule a little better.'

Jack wet his hair, glanced around, and picked a towel from the floor. 'Thanks. And to think they overlooked you for University Challenge.' He dried himself and ran back to the little rug at the foot of his bed, scooping up the clothes he discarded there the night before.

'I've got no classes today.' Maurice took a drag and blew a smoke ring. 'Fancy a little lunchtime livener in the Amersham?'

'After last night? You must be joking.'

'The best cure for a hangover is a pint. It's a scientific fact.'

Jack pulled on his jeans. 'You're on the wrong course,' he said to his roommate. 'You should have gone into the medical profession.'

'My skills are myriad. So how about it?'

'I dunno. I'll see how this thing goes with Hadley.' He buttoned his shirt and slipped his shoes on. 'I haven't any lectures, but there's some work I should be getting on with. I really need to stay away from the pub this week.'

'I'll see you there at one, then.'

'Maybe.' Jack grabbed his portfolio and opened the door.

'You haven't done your laces up, country boy!' Maurice called after him as he rushed down the staircase.

His digs were just two streets away from the university building which housed Hadley's office, and as he clomped over the pavement he regretted the decision to put on the platforms he wore last night instead of taking a few seconds to find his plimsolls. Jack checked his watch as he approached the campus—he was five minutes late already— and vaulted the small perimeter fence to take a diagonal short-cut across the lawn to the building. He took the steps two at a time to Hadley's first floor office and rapped his knuckle on the door.

'Come in.'

'Sorry,' Jack said as he entered. 'I'm a little bit—'

'Never mind, never mind.' Hadley was behind his desk amid a fog of tobacco smoke. He took the pipe from his mouth and looked up from the book he was studying. 'Good god. You look like you've been sleeping under a bush.'

Jack felt his face redden. 'Late night,' he muttered.

'Drinking and shagging, eh?' He motioned for Jack to sit opposite. 'Oh well, make the most of it. Everything was on ration when I was your age—especially the shagging.'

Jack smiled and relaxed. He'd been worried about being late, not because he was afraid in any way of Jeremy Hadley, but because he liked the man. Hadley was a good tutor and a respected artist, though he'd never quite made the big time of the London galleries.

'So, Mr. Porter. What have you been working on this term?'

'Portraits.'

Hadley raised his eyebrows. 'Style?'

'Traditional, that is to say, representative.'

'Hm.' Hadley returned the pipe to his mouth and leaned back in his chair. 'This is a bit of a departure from last year, if my memory serves me.'

Jack cleared his throat.

'Any particular reason for this drastic change in approach?'

'I felt I'd reached a dead end. What I've been doing this term feels . . . natural.'

'Yes. It sometimes takes a while to find one's niche.' He held out his hand. 'Let's have a look.'

Jack undid the string on his three canvases and placed them on the desk, along with a bunch of pencil studies. Hadley took the paintings and stood them on the floor against the wall to one side of the window before stepping back to study them. 'Hm.' He wandered back to the desk and leafed through the sketches. 'I see you've concentrated on just one model.'

'Yes.'

'Your muse, eh?' Hadley sat back down. 'The thing you have to ask yourself, and it's a very important question, is whether you are obsessed with your subject, or with painting your subject.'

9

'I am having a relationship with her.' Jack looked at the middle of the three paintings. Kate was sitting naked on the edge of a bathtub, backlit so that a sharp line of light silhouetted her figure. Her hair and eyes, both the darkest shade of brown, contrasted against her pale flesh. 'I find her fascinating. I've no real desire to paint anybody else.' He looked at his tutor. 'Is that a bad thing?'

'Not for your art, dear boy. But it could be very bad for you.'

Jack saw Kate standing outside the entrance to the ABC Cinema from the top deck of the bus as it turned onto the Elephant and Castle roundabout. The bus slowed, and he skipped down the stairs. As the bus passed her, Jack wolf-whistled at Kate from its open back while he clung to the white plastic-bandaged handrail.

'You shouldn't do that, you chauvinist,' Kate said as he stepped off. She held his collar and stood on tip-toes to kiss him. Jack felt her tongue dart between his lips for a brief moment, and tried to respond with his own. 'Too slow,' she said as she pulled away.

'I'll get you next time.'

'Come on.' Kate smiled and took his hand. 'It's about to start.'

The cinema was packed with Friday night crowds, and their seats were bad—way up in the right-hand corner so they were watching the screen at an angle. A grainy ice-cream advert was showing as they sat down, and Jack glanced along the aisle by his side to the fire escape at its bottom. Over his shoulder, just a few feet away, another emergency exit was lit by a dull green light from above. He leaned close to Kate. 'Did you get these seats on purpose?'

Kate concentrated on the advert and gave a slight shake of her head. 'No.'

Jack knew she was lying and loved her for it. 'There's really no need,' he whispered. 'I'm okay with—'

'Shh.' Kate turned to him and brushed her lips against his as the film certificate flashed on the screen. 'Watch the film.'

The film—*Young Frankenstein*—was good, and Jack found himself laughing along with Kate and the rest of the theatre at the comical absurdities. He'd seen the original Frankenstein movies on late Saturday night television and recognised the spoofed scenes, though he lost concentration in the latter half of the comedy as the palm of Kate's hand moved with a deliberate slowness along the inside of his thigh. Jack attempted to manoeuvre himself under her hand by slipping forward in his seat, and Kate giggled. 'I'm not going to toss you off in the pictures, you dirty old man,' she whispered.

A blue-rinsed woman in front of them turned in her seat and tutted at Kate before returning her attention to the film. Jack clamped his hand over his mouth and laughed in near silence, aware of Kate's shoulders jerking up and down at his side. On the screen, Frankenstein and his monster began to perform a duet of "Putting on the Ritz." When the cinema audience laughed, Jack and Kate let themselves go until tears streamed from their eyes.

'That was fun,' Kate said, later as they strolled to her house.

'Yeah, it was a good film.' Jack felt Kate's hand slip into his and he gave it a gentle squeeze. 'Are your parents home tonight?'

'Mum is.'

'Oh, well.'

They came to her house, a mid-terrace Victorian place with no front garden. 'You can still pop in for a while. Mum won't mind, she likes you.'

Jack looked at his watch. 'No, I'd better not. I don't want to miss the last bus. Plus I don't want to be there if your dad comes home.'

'Yes, maybe you're right.' Kate smiled. 'He hates you.'

'That's reassuring.'

11

'Don't take it personally—he hates all students. He also hates blacks, Pakistanis, queers, and communists.' She moved closer and stroked the thick black fringe from his brow. 'Most of all though, he hates boys with long hair.'

'And what about you?'

'Oh, I love boys with long hair.' She lowered her voice. 'I love you.'

Jack looked into her big, dark eyes and swallowed. They'd been together for five months, five glorious months as far as he was concerned, and it was the first time that love had been mentioned in what had been a frantically physical relationship. One corner of Kate's lips twitched in a nervous smile. 'You don't have to say anything.'

'No. I mean, yes, I want to.' He placed his hands on her hips. 'I love you, too.'

The bus ride back to New Cross seemed superfluous. He felt he could have floated all the way.

'What the fuck's up with you?'

Jack closed the door behind him and sat on the edge of his bed. 'Nothing.'

'Nothing? You're grinning like a fucking simpleton.' Maurice picked up a bottle of light ale and threw it across the small room, followed by the opener.

'Cheers.' Jack flipped the lid off and took a swig. The room was full of cigarette smoke and the electronic jingle of *Dark Side of the Moon* coming from Maurice's turntable. 'I thought you were going home for the weekend.'

'No need.' Maurice plucked an envelope from the mess of letters and magazines spread around him on his bed and waved it in the air. Jack could see the green edges of a bunch of pound notes protruding from its open end. 'My dad dropped by earlier.'

Jack laughed. 'Paying you to stay away now, is he?'

'Something like that.'

Jack kicked his shoes off and sat back against the headboard. As much as he liked Maurice he couldn't help feeling a little envious. Maurice's dad was loaded—he owned a scrap metal yard across the river in the East End—and he was immensely proud of his son for being the first member of the family to attend university. Maurice never had to take the bar work and casual labour jobs Jack had needed to get through the past couple of years.

'So, tomorrow night, my old son, you and me are going up west, courtesy of Maurice David Senior.' He frowned. 'You ain't made plans with your little bird, have you?'

'Er, no.' *She loves me.* He began smiling again.

Maurice got up and crossed to the record player where he turned the LP over. 'That's sorted then. You and me in our best togs out on the piss.' He walked back to the bed. 'Oh, I nearly forgot.' He rummaged amongst the paperwork. 'You had a letter, too. Here.'

Jack opened the envelope and pulled out the card. *An Invitation*, the wording on the front promised. He turned it over.

*You are invited to the 21*st *Birthday Party of Vincent Harris, please bring a guest.*

Underneath, Vinnie had written:

PS, Georgina and Matt are coming too, so make sure you turn up.

Jack felt goosebumps break out on his arms. They were once the closest of friends, but something in his stomach loosened at the thought of the four of them in the same room.

2

Georgina tucked the invitation behind her carriage clock on the mantelpiece and looked through the window onto the high street below. A pretty young blonde with a bright yellow guitar, probably a fellow student, was busking on the opposite pavement for the Saturday afternoon shoppers beneath an overcast sky. Georgina flipped the latch and slid the bottom half of the window up so that she could lean her elbows on the sill. The girl's voice was unusual—almost childishly high with a vulnerability that Georgina found rather haunting—and she was singing "Those Were the Days" in a cockney accent.

'They certainly were,' Georgina muttered, a rare sense of nostalgia for her childhood in Doom rippling through her. Despite all that happened she had some good memories of her childhood in the old village, especially of Matt, Jack, and Vinnie. She'd seen Jack only a few times in recent years, and Vinnie just once since starting at Canterbury.

The sun shone through a brief break in the clouds and warmed her skin as she looked along the length of the street past the cathedral towards the Christ Church campus. Matt would be in his digs there, probably still asleep. She glanced back down at the busker who'd finished her song to a small round of applause. Georgina joined in and smiled at the girl when she looked up at her and gave a theatrical curtsy.

I've seen you before, Georgina thought, but she couldn't remember from where, and the notion vanished as she turned from the window. The small suitcase on her bed was open, it was almost packed, and she walked through to the bathroom to retrieve her clean underwear from the clothes horse. As she dropped them into the case, she heard the latchkey turn in the door and felt a stab of regret, not for the first time, at giving a spare key to Declan.

'Going somewhere?' He frowned at her in that way that made him look his age.

'I told you, yesterday. I'm visiting my parents.'

He ambled across and lifted her hair at the nape of her

neck where he placed a gentle kiss. 'But I'm free this weekend. Anne and the kids are in Brighton. I thought you changed your mind.'

'No, I never said that. I don't know why you thought that.' She locked the case and slipped away from him.

'So what am I supposed to do?' He let out a dramatic huff.

'I don't know, Declan.' She looked at him and saw that look in his eyes—the look of a hurt, sulking man-child that was so unattractive—and found it hard to believe how handsome and sophisticated she once found him. Maybe Matt was right: maybe every relationship began to die from the moment it started.

'You must have some grading to do, this time of year.' She turned to the window and closed it.

'What time's your train?'

'Twelve-twenty.'

'Well . . . ' Declan sidled himself behind her again and put his arms around her waist. 'We still have an hour, at least.'

'No, I've got things to do.' Georgina noticed the frostiness in her own voice.

'Come on, just a quick one, and I'll give you a lift to the station.'

'No, Declan.' She tried to pull away and felt his grip tighten. 'Let me go.'

'But you've got me all hot now, darling.'

Georgina felt the warmness of his breath in her ear and the bulge of his cock in the cleft of her bottom as he pushed her against the window sill. 'You got yourself hot. Now stop it, I have to get ready.'

'I think you're playing hard to get.' His right hand loosened its grip and slipped from Georgina's waist to her hip where she felt it tug her mini-skirt above her thighs.

'Declan, I said no!' She grabbed the back of his right hand with her own as the window spun away from her, and she felt herself thrown face first onto the bed, the air pushed from her lungs as Declan fell with her onto her back. She struggled

15

to breathe beneath his weight as grey specks wriggled at the edge of her vision. His body shifted enough for her to gulp in a lungful of air before she heard his fly unzipping. Her brief panic transformed to anger, and she turned her face to one side as her underwear was yanked downwards with a rip. 'What are you going to do, you dirty bastard? Rape me?'

The word was like a knife and she felt Declan's whole body stiffen. A moment later he was off her and across the room, tucking himself back into his trousers. 'Of course not,' he said, his voice barely audible. 'I wouldn't do that. It wasn't like that.'

'Really?' Georgina pulled off her useless, torn briefs and threw them at the waste-basket by her dresser. She stood to face him as she straightened her skirt, aware of the tremble in her hands. 'I think you'd better go.'

'Look, I'm sorry.' He took a step forward, his palms held out, his face a deep shade of crimson. 'Let me give you a lift to the station.' A sheepish smile twitched at the corner of his mouth. 'Tell you what, forget the train, I'll drive you all the way to your parents' place.'

'Forget it. It's over. I don't want to see you again.'

'Come on, this is silly.'

'Just go.'

The smile vanished, but the redness in Declan's face remained. He shrugged his shoulders and turned for the door.

'I want my key back,' Georgina said, glad that she remembered it before he left.

He opened the door and paused to look over his shoulder. 'Actually, I think I'll keep it,' he said in a flat, soul-less voice she'd never heard him use before. 'You never know when I might want to drop in. Somebody has to keep an eye on you, make sure you don't hurt yourself.'

Georgina's cheeks flushed as her sense of anger ripened into hatred, not only at this man she'd let into her life and her bed, but also at herself for being fooled. 'Okay,' she said.

'You keep the key. You can explain to Anne and the dean why you have it. I'm sure they'll be interested to know you've been screwing one of your students for the last three months.'

'You wouldn't tell them.'

There was panic in his voice, and Georgina was glad of that. She held out her hand. 'Give me the fucking key, Declan. And then fuck off.'

Once he was gone she locked the door and sat on the edge of her bath, staring at the razor blade held between her fingers. After a while, when she could resist the urge no longer, she lifted the sleeve of her blouse and scratched a short, shallow line down the back of her arm. A long, deep sigh escaped her lips. She'd almost forgotten how good it felt.

The dining room, like the food on the plate before her, was as drab as Georgina remembered. The afternoon sunrays that fought their way through the thick net curtains were barely enough to shed light on the patterned wallpaper whose aged, white background was now just a shade less grey than the repetitive paisley print. She lifted her knife and fork and paused at the sound of her father's tut before replacing them on either side of her plate.

'It seems you've forgotten a few things since going to university,' he said, spitting the last word out as if it were a particular kind of filth.

'Sorry.' She glanced left at her mother, whose head was already bowed, and copied her pose.

'Don't worry, I'll make it short.' Her dad pushed the little round spectacles he wore up the bridge of his nose and lowered his head. 'We thank you, Father, for the food we are about to receive, and pray that you forgive us our sins—' he glanced at Georgina. '—that are plentiful in both our deeds and thoughts. Amen.'

Georgina mumbled her own *amen* along with her mother and began the task of eating the tasteless boiled mince and cabbage. The only sound besides the clink of cutlery on china was the tick of the carriage clock on the sideboard. Georgina found herself wanting to get away, the way she always did, and wished she'd never come at all. It was her mother that broke the silence at last.

'How's Matthew? Do you see much of him?'

'Yes. He's fine.'

'I saw Mr. Ward the other day,' her father said. 'He's suffered much bringing two boys up alone, sinful as he is with the alcohol. He told me Matthew never visits.'

'He's busy. He studies hard.'

'A good son would visit his father. Matthew's brother is a very good son. Mr. Ward is very proud of Simon.'

'Because he's in the army?' Georgina forced the anger down in her voice. 'Perhaps he'd be prouder of Matthew if he trained to kill foreigners as well.'

A thin smile cut across her father's sharp features. 'Despite your education, I still see the disrespectful little girl inside.' He sighed. 'But maybe that's my fault. Maybe we didn't cast out all your demons after all.'

'I'm not a little girl anymore. I'm a woman, and there are no such things as demons.' She looked once again at her mother who averted her eyes.

Her father smirked, and Georgina cursed herself for falling into the trap despite her efforts to avoid his games. 'Those vain enough to believe themselves safe from sin have no belief in God. Have you fallen that far, Georgina? Have you renounced Him?'

She closed her eyes. 'No. No, I haven't.'

'Eat your dinner, dear,' her mother said after five ticks of the clock. 'I cooked it especially for you. It's your favourite.'

Georgina opened her eyes. 'Thanks,' she said, and smiled at her mother, before forcing what she would later describe to Matt as a plateful of shit and puke down her throat.

18

The Green Man was closed until the evening session, which was just as well. She needed a drink, but knew just one wasn't enough. And besides, it would only get back to her father, whose disgust would be tangible. *A young woman, drinking alcohol in a pub on her own?* She huffed. The village wasn't quite ready for that sort of progress yet, and Georgina wondered if it ever would be.

She crossed to the green and strolled beside the pond to the old bench on its bank. A single horizontal plank formed the backrest, and she crouched behind to examine it. The once dark wood was a weather-worn and sun-bleached silver, and as she traced her fingertips over the carved signatures there she felt the years recede, as if it had been nine days, not nine years, since the four of them had scratched their names on the bench with Vinnie's penknife.

Vinnie. Georgina. Matt. Jack.

A smile twitched at the corner of her mouth. They had been eleven, then, and indestructible. Time had seemed to stand still in awe of their youth as the long summer days merged to one endless scene of friendship, fun and laughter in her mind's eye. An image came to her, as fresh as if it were yesterday, of Vinnie plunging into the pond when the branch holding their rope-swing had snapped. He'd panicked, of course, though the water was only chest high, and Matt had waded in after him. Jack was no use at all—he could hardly stand for laughing—and by the time Matt had Vinnie back on the bank the four of them were unable to talk from the hysterics they'd caught from Jack. But that was before the fire.

This is going to hurt.

Georgina snatched her hand from the wood. It was a voice she didn't recognise, but it had asserted itself like a memory. 'Mad bitch,' she muttered.

She was about to turn away when she saw another signature down on the right-hand corner. It had never been there before, Georgina was sure, and judging by the darkness of the wood on the inside ridge of the seven letters, she could tell it had been freshly etched.

Frankie.

A shiver crawled down her spine as she backed away. It had to be a different Frankie. Some young lad living in the village now. But the smiley face carved on the right of the name—the same little picture their Frankie always drew next to his signature—was too much of a coincidence. It had to be Frankie's handiwork, and it was fresh.

If not for the fact that he'd been dead for almost ten years, she might have laughed.

3

Matt pulled the finished sheet from the typewriter, scanned the last paragraph, and placed it on the pile by its side. He rolled another sheet in and began to tap at the keys without a pause.

'Here, drink this.'

Matt glanced up and took the mug of coffee. 'Thanks.'

Tom lifted the top sheet from the pile on the communal kitchen table. '*A Consequence of Life*,' he read out loud from the header. 'How's it going?'

Matt took a sip from the mug and grimaced. 'Not bad. Nearly through the first draft.' He pushed his reading glasses up the bridge of his nose.

'Don't think I'm interfering, but shouldn't you be working on your thesis?'

'It's done. Finished it on Thursday.' Matt tried the coffee again. 'Have you sugared this?'

Tom took the mug back over to the worktop and scooped two spoonfuls from the bowl. 'You told me you hadn't even started on it.'

'That was Saturday.' He flashed a smile and ran a hand through his thick, dark hair. 'I began it on Monday.'

'Oh, I see.' Tom laughed. 'Matthew the amazing wordsmith writes his last-year thesis in four days.'

'I worked nights, as well.' He returned his attention to the typewriter. 'You can get a lot done during the week if you stay away from the student bar.'

'Ouch.' Tom placed the mug on the table and picked up the card he'd spotted tucked under the ashtray. 'A party, eh? Who's Vincent?'

'An old friend. I haven't seen him in a while.'

'A good friend?'

'A childhood friend.' Matt worked his fingers across the keyboard as he spoke. 'You'll get to meet him. I can bring a guest.'

'Really? I thought you might take one of your mini-skirted groupies. You know, keep up the front.'

Matt stopped typing and glanced up. He was well aware of how attractive he was—he'd been propositioned enough in his three years at Canterbury—and he couldn't deny he enjoyed the attention. 'Vinnie's okay.'

'You mean he knows.'

'Yeah, he knows.' Matt removed his glasses. 'Look, Tom. You've got to wise up. We're living in a bubble here on campus. Some of the guys here don't give a fuck about our relationship, and some of them pretend they don't, because they think it makes them cool to have us as friends. The real bigots are in the minority here, but out in the real world they've got the upper hand.'

'That's a bit cynical, Matt. It is 1974 for Christ's sake. Attitudes are changing.'

'I'm just careful. You should be too.'

Tom leaned forward and kissed him slow on the lips. 'Well, I suppose it's nice to know that you care, you handsome bastard.'

'I mean it. There are some vicious lunatics out there.'

'Drink your coffee.' Tom tapped the tip of Matt's nose with his finger. 'I'm going for a walk.'

Matt switched on the little transistor radio by his typewriter and returned to his manuscript, glad to be alone, as much as he liked Tom's company. They were close, as lovers are, though Matt didn't feel the same affinity he had shared with Georgina and suffered a low level of guilt at the fact that what he felt for Tom fell short of that. His feelings for Tom were strong, though, and Matt guessed it was a just a matter of time before his emotions caught up with the physical aspect of their relationship.

The radio provided a background distraction as he worked, its dial tuned to the comforting voices of radio 4, and he was halfway down his third page of the day when a newscast stopped him like a brick wall. *'A soldier has been injured by gunfire in Belfast early this morning, his name, age, and regiment have not yet been released, though it is believed he is in a serious but stable condition.'* The reporter sounded so bored, like it was hardly news anymore. It had become so commonplace that the public had lost its taste for the tales of brutality, especially since the bombing campaigns had crossed the short stretch of Irish Sea to mainland Britain.

The usual panic revealed itself in the form of queasiness deep inside his stomach. Though he knew the odds of it being Simon weren't high—there were hundreds of soldiers over there—he knew he had to get to a phone. If it was Simon that had been shot, his dad would know by now.

The thump of the sound system grew as Matt neared the university bar. The Saturday night dance would be in full swing. He always made sure of that by coming late—he hated the hanging around and pontificating that everyone seemed to engage in before the effect of the beer took hold.

The smoke-filled room was dark, lit only by the multi-coloured bulbs flashing in time with the music.

'Oy, you old fucker. What time d'you call this?'

'Hello, Ben.' Matt glanced at the dance floor where a mass

of students bopped up and down to the driving guitar twang of "Tiger Feet". 'Thought you'd be out there.'

'What, dancing to this corny old bollocks? I'm a soul man, Matthew, I thought you knew that.'

'Fuck the music.' Matt nodded at the revellers. 'Look at the birds you're missing out on.'

'I'm all right, mate.' Ben grinned. 'I've just got to stay close to you. There'll be a gaggle of them hanging around you later, and when they realise you're not interested, that's when I'll strike.'

'You old smoothie.' Matt scanned the room for Tom, and spotted him among the bobbing heads, a cigarette hanging from the corner of his mouth, his blonde fringe stuck to his brow by a sheen of sweat.

'Where's Georgie girl tonight?'

'Gone to her parents for the weekend.' Matt ordered a pint of bitter, took a long swig, and winced. 'I'm sure they water down the stuff in here.'

'Is she still having it off with her lecturer?'

Matt shrugged his shoulders. 'Far as I know.'

'He's a prick. A dangerous prick. She should watch out.'

'Georgina can look out for herself.'

Ben leaned in close. 'I've seen his wife around town a few times. Mostly she looks fine. Once or twice though, she looked like she'd walked face-first into a lamp-post.'

Matt felt his face redden. He'd heard the stories about Declan Moore's relationship with his wife and had almost fallen out with Georgina over it. Maybe they were just rumours, as Georgie had insisted, and maybe his wife was just a bit clumsy, but if he ever saw a mark on Georgina's face, Declan would be sorry.

'Hey, hey, we're in,' Ben said.

Matt looked at the floor where half a dozen girls he recognised from the year below were dancing in a circle and beckoning him over. 'I thought you didn't dance to this shit,' he said.

'Come on.' Ben grabbed his elbow and led him towards the girls. 'You might not be interested in tits and fanny, but I'm fascinated by it.'

Before they even made it halfway, the room went dark and the music slowed to a stop. Everyone groaned. 'Oh, for fuck sake,' Ben said. 'Not another power cut.'

A few torches were lit by the bar staff as the task of emptying the building began. The nationwide energy strikes had been going on for months, and though the university's policy of evacuating the bar was based on safety, it didn't sit well with the majority of students. 'Well, that's Saturday night ruined,' Matt said as they shuffled towards the door.

'Sod that. I'm going to invite those beauties to a candle-lit party back at my room.' Ben stood on tiptoes. 'If I can find them.'

'Well, good luck with that.' Matt looked forward at the torch-lit double doors where he caught a glimpse of Tom as he passed through the beams of yellow light. 'Tom!' He saw him turn his head, though it was obvious Tom couldn't see him among the other dark faces in the plodding crowd. 'Wait outside!'

The whole area had lost power; the night lit only by brief glimpses of the moon through fast moving clouds. Matt moved among the chattering students and was about to give up the search when he felt a hand on his shoulder. 'You're nicked, sonny,' he heard Tom say in a deep voice.

'Oh, yeah?' He turned and smiled. 'What for?'

'Loitering in the dark.'

'Come on, we might as well go back to my digs.'

'You don't realise how dark it can be,' Tom said as they began walking under the intermittent moonlight.

'Frightened?'

'No. Not with big Matt Ward by my side.'

A Ford Cortina crammed with too many students inside crawled by, its headlights casting a yellow glow over the road ahead. 'Come on,' a girl called from the open passenger window, 'follow us.' Matt and Tom fell in with the scattered group walking behind the car as it lit the way and Matt felt Tom's shoulder press against his. 'How are you, now?'

'I'm fine.' He glanced at Tom. Though his face was no more than a shadow, he knew it would be full of concern. This morning wasn't the first time Matt had panicked over the news of a dead soldier, and he guessed it wouldn't be the last, though the feeling of emptiness in his stomach in the two hours it had taken him to confirm that his brother was all right was a sensation he'd never get used to. 'Thanks for asking.'

'No problem.' Tom sighed. 'When are these bloody power strikes going to end?'

'Don't worry about it. You'll look back on these days and reminisce with tears in your eyes.'

'I don't think so.'

Movement in a shop doorway to Matt's left caught his attention, and he squinted at the recess where a dark bundle shifted. 'Poor sod,' he mumbled. He took another two steps, stopped, and turned back. 'Wait here,' he told Tom. As he approached the shop-front he felt inside the hip pocket of his jeans.

'Throwing money at them doesn't help,' he heard Tom call, not for the first time. Maybe Tom was right, but the broken kids he saw living on the streets—and they usually were just teenagers—depressed him, and if the price of a hot drink helped one of them get through the night then he didn't see the harm.

He crouched beside the figure, whose head seemed to be buried in a blanket. 'Hello,' Matt said. The figure shifted and Matt had the impression that the blanket had dropped back from his head, though the moon was in hiding. 'Here . . . ' He pulled some change from his pocket. 'I know it's not much.' He held his palm out, and as he did so, the moonlight found a gap in the clouds, revealing the man's features. Matt gasped and snatched his arm back, but he was too slow. He glanced at the filthy hand holding tight to his wrist, its fingernails black and broken, yet familiar, and a name from long ago surfaced in his mind.

Bald Eagle!

'Fuck you, queer,' the man snarled. Matt looked back at him. His head was shaven, its sheen broken by the occasional scab, his nose bent and hooked to one side. Clouds scudded beneath the moon, obscuring the man's features as Matt yanked his arm away and clenched his fist, ready to strike.

'What did you say?'

Moonlight filtered through once more and Matt was aware of Tom's presence behind as the man, who was not a man at all but a boy of no more than sixteen with a bush of curled dark hair, looked warily back at him. 'I said *thank you, sir.*'

Matt relaxed, though his heart was pounding, and dropped the coins into the boy's upturned palm. 'Come on,' he said to Tom as he stood. Matt hadn't thought of Bald Eagle in years, and only realised now what a job his psyche had done in erasing him from his memory. Or had it been the fire?

But that wasn't Bald Eagle, that was just a poor young homeless kid, and Matt shuddered at how close he'd come to punching him. At how just remembering the bald bastard reduced him to the stark fear he'd experienced in the summer of 1965.

4

'They're in very good condition.' Vinnie watched the punter turn one of the brass candlesticks in his hand. 'Victorian. I've had it confirmed.'

The man glanced up over his spectacles. 'I can see what they are, young man, but you won't get thirty pounds for them.'

Vinnie grinned. He knew the man wanted them, and that he was probably a dealer himself. 'It's not a bad price. They're quite popular right now.'

'Hm.' The man sniffed and placed the candlestick back with its counterpart among the other glass, brass, and silver pieces on Vinnie's stall. 'I'll give you fifteen.'

'Fifteen? What're you trying to do, starve me? Tell you what. I turned down twenty-four quid for those this morning. If you give me twenty five now they're yours.'

The man pulled a wallet from his inside pocket and counted out some notes. 'Twenty pounds.' He thrust them at Vinnie. 'Take it or leave it.'

Vinnie folded his arms and leaned back on the stall. 'Come on, I have to make a profit.'

'Don't we all?' The man smirked as he turned away.

'Hang on.' Vinnie sighed and rolled the candlesticks in newspaper. 'There you go.' He placed the money in the pouch at his hip and watched the man walk away. 'Upper class ponce,' he muttered.

It was a fair price—he'd paid just ten pounds for a small house clearance lot that had included the candlesticks—but Vinnie hated the feeling of having been outwitted. He'd had his pitch in the Portobello Road for eighteen months and considered himself to be doing well. He always had a figure in mind for each item, and bumped it up if he thought he'd get away with it. In the first few weeks, Vinnie found he could read his punters within seconds—an old girl with a cockney accent would never spend a fortune on an old teapot, so he'd add a pound or two on, then knock it off, whereas a Knightsbridge girl kitting out the flat that Daddy was paying for could easily be tapped for twice the price.

The afternoon sky was a pure white blanket of low cloud, and Vinnie blew on his hands to warm them as a light sleet filled the air. The market had begun to empty and a few of the traders had packed away their wares for the day, but Vinnie would be the last, as usual. He'd gotten into the habit of spending as much time away from the flat as he could in recent weeks. With the market job during the day and his persuading either Jan or Sue to stay most nights he'd engineered a situation whereby he was hardly ever on his own at home. *Yeah, I'm doing pretty well, my own little business, a flat off the King's Road, and two willing birds on the go.* He shivered. *And too fucking terrified to sleep alone.*

Everything had gone well. The meal was good—Vinnie had found cooking both an easy and satisfying pastime since coming to London—and the sex with Jan was great. She was adventurous, and though she could never match Sue's natural beauty, she was attractive enough, and Vinnie much preferred her warm, humorous disposition to Sue's self-absorbed conversations. Yes, it had been a great evening up until the moment Jan returned from the bathroom, a small piece of material clutched in her hand. 'Who do these belong to?' she'd asked, her voice quite calm.

Vinnie sat up in bed and looked at her, naked in the doorway. The pale complexion of her face had lost any colour it had possessed, and in that moment, as Vinnie saw the pain in her eyes, he knew that he had lost her.

'I asked you a question.' She threw the underwear onto his lap. 'And don't tell me that I left them here. I know my own knickers.'

He closed his mouth, ashamed that she'd predicted exactly what he was about to say. 'Sorry,' he whispered at last, sick of having to say that word yet again to somebody he cared about.

'Who is she?'

'Just a girl.'

'Well, I didn't think they belonged to a fucking boy, you creep!' She stared at him for a moment before retrieving her discarded clothes draped across the dressing table mirror. As she put them on, her shoulders began to tremble.

'Please, don't go.'

'Are you joking?' She shook her head. 'I thought we were okay. I thought *you* were okay.' Her voice cracked. 'Why wasn't I enough for you, Vinnie?'

'You're lovely, Jan. Please, stay with me. I'd drop her in an instant.' He stood from the bed. 'Don't go.'

'Too late, Vinnie.' She slipped her coat on and wrapped her scarf around the collar. 'You know your trouble? You don't know what you want, so you grab everything.'

He heard the click of the latch on the front door as she left and instantly felt the silence, like a creeping force, swell through the little apartment. 'Shit,' he muttered. It was going to be a long night.

'You don't look very well.'

Vinnie glanced up from his pint glass. 'Thanks.'

'I mean, you look tired.'

'I'm fine. Just working hard and playing hard. Here.' He swallowed the last of his beer and passed her the glass. 'Put another one in there, Jo.'

She pulled on the pump and filled his glass. From behind he heard a cheer and turned on his barstool to the small group of men and women—all around his age—gathered by a dart board. Their accents and general manner gave them away in an instant; they were rich kids, living in a bubble where everything was so easy, exuding the kind of confidence carried only by those who know they cannot fail.

'Seventeen pence please, tiger.'

'Thanks.' Vinnie pulled a fifty pence piece from his pocket. 'Have one yourself.'

'Cheers, Vinnie.' She leaned across the bar and lowered her voice. 'It's more than I get off any of that lot. I'm lucky if I get a *please* or *thank you* off them tight sods.'

He took a long sip. 'They're real money. We're invisible to people like them.'

'Well, you ain't doing so bad for yourself.'

He knew Jo was right. At the age of twenty he had more money than any of his friends, but that wasn't making him happy right now. Jan had been gone for five days and he missed her more than he thought possible. If Sue had been around it wouldn't have been so bad, but her sudden departure two days before to visit her dying Gran in Devon had worsened his situation. He'd fucked up and was now paying the price with lonely, sleepless nights.

'Two pints of bitter, two gin and tonics, and a lemonade, please.'

Vinnie looked sideways at the young man who'd broken away from the group to buy a round. He was tall and skinny, his cheeks ruddy, and his chin sprouting fine tufts of soft hair. He glanced at Vinnie down the length of his nose for a moment—his face expressionless as if he were regarding an insect—before turning back to the barmaid. 'Oh, and a packet of nuts.'

The juke box kicked in with the opening bars of "Devil Gate Drive" to a squeal from the girls, and Vinnie saw Jo raise her eyebrows at him from across the beer pumps as a sweet scent of expensive perfume wafted under his nose. One of the girls—a redhead he'd already noticed as the looker of the group—sidled up to the young man. 'Peter, buy some cigarettes.'

'You don't smoke.'

'Sometimes I do.'

'Take those.' He nodded at the spirits on the counter as he grabbed the two pints and walked away.

The redhead lifted the drinks and turned from the bar. 'Oh, hello.'

Vinnie turned to face her. Her eyes were green, almost a perfect match for the dress that clung to the curves of her petite frame. She smiled, revealing two dimples that Vinnie found more than cute, and cocked her head to one side.

'Hello,' he said, and frowned. 'I'm sorry, do I—'

'I bought a mirror from you. Down the Portobello Road, a couple of weeks ago.'

'Oh, right.' Vinnie thought back, remembered selling a mirror, art deco, to a girl recently, but didn't recognise her.

'It looks fabulous in my hallway, just like you said it would.' She placed one of the glasses on the bar and held out her hand. 'Hannah.'

He stood from the barstool and gave her fingers a gentle shake, holding on for just a second more than was necessary. 'Vincent.'

'Drinking alone?'

'Just a couple before bedtime.'

'Well, you can join us if you like. They're a friendly lot.'

Vinnie looked over at her group, who were all busy in conversation except for the one named Peter who was staring at him. 'Thanks, but I should go home after this one. Early start tomorrow.'

She pouted. 'Oh, shame.'

They looked at each other for a moment, long enough for Vinnie to know. 'Maybe we could have a drink some other time,' he said in a lowered voice, in case Peter was the jealous type.

'I'd love to.' She grinned. 'And you don't have to talk like that,' she half whispered. 'Peter isn't my boyfriend.' She wrote her phone number on the back of a beer mat in red lipstick. 'I'm free this Friday.'

Vinnie put the number in his coat pocket and watched her walk across to her friends. Peter continued to stare, so he smiled and raised his glass to him.

'Cocky sod ain't ya,' Jo said.

'Well, I'm not going to be glared at by a long streak of piss who hasn't even started shaving yet.' Vinnie drained what was left of his beer. 'See you later, Jo.'

'Yeah, see ya.'

He left the pub happy, the familiar frisson of excitement running through his mind at what may be with a new girl.

Hannah. Beautiful, green-eyed Hannah. It was only as he reached for his door keys outside his block that he remembered he would be alone, and sighed. The brief joy he felt slipped away below waves of fear.

He took the stairwell on heavy legs to the second floor, where he paused and placed his ear to the green painted door to his flat. All was quiet, but what else had he expected of an empty apartment? He exhaled, unaware until that moment that he'd been holding his breath, and imagined how he would look to one of his neighbours if they'd happened along at that moment. *Like a fucking nutcase.* Maybe that was it; maybe he was losing his marbles and all that he'd seen and heard recently were no more than the hallucinations of a madman.

He unlocked the door and turned the hallway light on before stepping inside. The lampshade cast frilled shapes on the plain painted walls of the narrow passageway, which was empty but for a few pairs of shoes he kept lined against the right hand wall. He closed the front door and headed for the living room at the far end, and was halfway there when he heard the click of the light switch behind him. The hallway disappeared into complete darkness.

'Shit!' He rushed forward, hands out like a child playing blind man's bluff, felt his foot tread on a discarded shoe that slipped away under his weight, and slammed face first onto the wooden floor. Pain flared outward from the bridge of his nose and a quick feel with the back of his hand confirmed that he was bleeding. 'Fucking bollocks!'

He pushed himself up onto all fours and caught his breath. From behind, where the light switch had been flicked off, he heard the approach of slow, steady footsteps on the hard floor. Vinnie was on his feet in an instant, the fingertips of his left hand tracing the wall as he stumbled toward the living room. The footsteps pursued him at their rhythmic pace as he felt for the doorframe and turned into the room, the palm of his right hand sliding over the roughness of the embossed wallpaper in search of the switch. The footfalls came to a stop behind him as he groped in the darkness, and he heard short shallow gasps that were not his own, accompanied by a pungent scent of putrid breath.

He swept his hand in wide arcs over the wall, found the switch, and yelped at the ice cold touch of small fingers on the back of his hand a moment before he turned on the light. The room was illuminated in a warm glow, the ceiling lightbulb diffused orange by the coloured paper shade. Vinnie turned from the wall and scanned the room, his heart thudding as he struggled to stifle the scream he'd felt rising inside, but nobody was there.

Later—in bed with the lights on—he considered his own sanity, but, no matter how he turned it in his mind, he knew that the frozen touch he'd felt in the dark was no feat of his imagination. A single name formed itself in his mind.

Frankie.

He pushed the thought away, same as he'd pushed all memory of his brief childhood friendship with the boy from his consciousness in hopes that time and distance could cleanse his soul. Vinnie felt his face redden as his body suffered a sudden hotness—the heat of shame and guilt at the prospect of being found out by his past.

'I'm sorry, Frankie,' he whispered, but the silent walls gave no forgiveness.

5

Jack opened his eyes and squinted against the white sunlight that filled the room. He was not in his digs. The walls were painted a pale blue, not the dull chocolate-brown hessian wallpaper that he and Maurice had attempted to cover with movie posters from Woolworths.

'Where am I?' His throat burned.

'Hospital. There's been an accident.'

He turned his head to one side. 'Mum? I'm thirsty.'

He felt her hand slip under his head and gently lift it from the pillow. She tipped a glass of water to his lips. He took three gulps and laid his head back, the scent of his mother's perfume familiar and comforting. *Something's wrong.* He looked at his mother, who smiled down at him. 'You look young,' he croaked.

'Thank you.' She wiped a tear that ran free from her left eye and smiled. 'My poor little soldier.'

Little soldier? 'Mum, I'm twenty.'

She laughed, though the expression on her face was one of worry. 'You're eleven, Jack.'

'What are you—' He suddenly heard the pitch of his own voice, high and pre-pubescent. He lifted a hand and looked at its small, pale, fingers. *I* am *eleven.* He looked back at his mother, then around the small ward and the three empty beds that shared his space. *Fire and smoke.* Yes, there had been an accident, but his memory skirted around its edges, unable to grasp the moveable details of its reality.

A door swung open in the wall beyond his mother and in walked a man wearing a white coat. The clipboard he was reading obscured his face from Jack's prone viewpoint in the bed. The man stood behind his mother.

'Hm. Do you want to live, Jack?'

The man's voice, cold and detached, and somehow recognisable, sent an arrow of fear into Jack's heart. He glanced at his mother, who seemed oblivious to the strangeness of the man's question. 'Answer the doctor, Jack,' she said.

He looked at the doctor, who continued to hold the clipboard at an angle that hid his features. 'Yes. I want to live.'

'Are you sure?'

'Yes.'

The man sighed. 'Well, don't say I didn't warn you. *Again.* This is going to hurt.'

The man lowered the board and grinned, revealing the few rotted, black teeth that resided in his mouth. His nose was long and crooked, his head bald and scabbed, and Jack had just enough time to think *Bald Eagle* in the moment it took for the man to draw a scalpel from his coat pocket, grab a handful of his mother's hair, and run the blade across her throat, so deep that her head pivoted back under his grip. A wave of crimson flooded from the gaping wound.

'No!' Jack thrust himself forward as the man dropped his mother's body to the floor like a discarded piece of trash. He walked backward, his scalpel, dripping red, pointed at Jack.

'It was your choice, Jack,' he said, and exited the room.

Jack looked at the body on the floor, the head tilted back as blood pumped from the opened throat. For a moment, her features changed to that of Jack's teacher, Miss Simpkins. The white brightness of the morning sunlight intensified in the little ward until it encompassed everything. Jack screamed and screamed and—

Jack

—thrashed in the sheets—

Jack

—that tangled around his legs, and he felt something, hands on his face, and a familiar voice that he knew he loved.

'Jack!'

The whiteness vanished and he was staring at a face hovering just above his own, the most beautiful face in the world.

'Kate.' He glanced around at the familiar surroundings of his little digs, then back up into her gorgeous, dark eyes.

'You were dreaming.' She rubbed her thumbs on his temples while cupping his face in her hands. 'It's okay, you were just dreaming.'

He pulled her close and held her naked body against his as if it were an anchor that would keep him safe. *There are no monsters. There are no monsters.* It was a mantra from deep inside and long ago. One that Georgina had taught him when they were kids to help him through the night.

Sometimes it worked.

The door swung open to the thumping sound of T-Rex and a flat full of babbling voices. Vinnie held his arms out and grinned. 'Fuck me, it's Jesus Christ Superstar! When was the last time you had your hair cut?'

Jack laughed and thrust a bottle of vodka at his pal. 'Hello, Vinnie. Happy birthday, you old bastard.'

'Thank you, that's a very touching sentiment.'

Jack reached for Kate's hand. 'Kate, this is my so-called friend Vinnie. Be careful what you say yes to, or you'll be going home with a shitty old vase and an empty purse.'

'Don't listen to him. I'm a respectable trader in the best antiques.' Vinnie kissed her cheek. 'Hello, Kate. Come through and meet everybody.'

'Thanks.' She led Jack past him. 'Nice place.'

Jack felt Vinnie's breath in his ear as they followed Kate through to the living room. 'She's a bit tasty. You've done all right for yourself there, mate.'

'Thanks. I think.' He felt Vinnie's hand squeeze his shoulder.

'It's really good to see you, Jack.'

It was an odd moment of sentimentality from his old friend, and Jack sensed something within its tones, a sadness bordering on fear that Jack thought he saw reflected in Vinnie's eyes. *He wants to tell me something.*

'It's good to see you, too.' He smiled, and when Vinnie reciprocated, Jack noticed the worried expression dissipate from his features.

They followed Kate into the smoke-filled atmosphere of the living room, the sweet scent of marijuana noticeable beneath the stronger odour of cigarette fumes. Bodies packed the room, their faces and clothes tinted orange by the paper ceiling shade and bulb, their voices shouting to be heard over each other as the music blasted from the stereogram. The T-Rex single faded and there was a pause as the next vinyl dropped onto the deck and the automatic arm swung across and dropped its needle onto the turntable. The opening bars of "Waterloo Sunset" began to play to a few whoops of delight.

'You still like the old ones, then,' Jack said.

'You can't beat them, my old son.'

Jack laughed at Vinnie's new-found cockney accent which held hardly a trace of his small-town Kentish drawl.

'And as the birthday boy, I'm claiming this dance.' Vince grabbed Kate's hand and held the vodka bottle aloft in his other as he began to bob up and down. 'Come on! Let's party!'

Kate raised her eyebrows at Jack as she began to dance. 'Don't worry,' he yelled over the music. 'He won't hurt you, despite the rumours.'

'That's right. I'm used to handling beautiful, delicate objects.'

Kate mimed a gag reflex and the three of them laughed.

'Give me that, knob-head.' Jack took the vodka from Vinnie. 'I'll pour us some drinks.' He squeezed between the revellers, greeting some that he'd met before. The open door of the kitchen appeared ahead, and as he stepped into its slightly emptier space he felt as if he had escaped from a tumble dryer. The worktop was covered by bottles of alcohol and used glasses, and he rinsed a couple under the tap before filling them with vodka.

As he turned to fight his way back through to Kate, he stopped and stared at two figures deep in conversation with each other in the far corner. Georgina and Matt. He'd seen neither of them in over a year, and felt his heart quicken. *We're all here, in this apartment. Me, Vinnie, Georgina and Matt.*

Matt looked over, as if he'd heard his name called, and nudged Georgina with his elbow. The two of them stared, then smiled with such warmth that Jack felt a lump form in his throat as he walked across to his old chums. Georgina squealed his name and almost jumped at him, her arms pulling Jack close as she planted a series of kisses on his mouth.

'Hi, George,' he managed between the smack of her lips on his. When at last she released him it was Matt who embraced him in his big, powerful arms. 'Hi, mate,' Jack said.

Matt held him by the shoulders at arm's length for a moment. 'You're looking well,' he said, before releasing him. 'Here on your own?'

'No, I brought a girl.' It didn't seem enough; she was more than a girl, she was the woman he adored. 'Her name's Kate.' He nodded over his shoulder. 'Vinnie's grabbed her already.'

'God!' Georgina rolled her eyes. 'Hasn't he got enough of his own?'

Matt took a sip from the beer bottle in his hand. 'I hear he's a one-woman man, now.'

Jack and Georgina exchanged an incredulous glance.

'No, really,' Matt said. 'Her name's Hannah. She's around here somewhere. I was talking with Vinnie earlier, and he couldn't stop gushing about her.'

'Well, I wouldn't take too much notice,' Georgina said. 'He's as high as a kite.'

'What about you two?' Jack asked.

'We're a pair of sad loners.' Georgina put her arm around Matt's waist. 'I've just dumped the arsehole I've been seeing for the last three months, and his boyfriend's up in Yorkshire.'

Jack looked at Matt. 'Everything okay?'

'Yeah. Me and Tom are fine; this weekend just clashed with his sister's wedding.'

The feeling that they'd seen each other only a handful of times in recent years faded in Jack's mind as the three of them chatted about Matt's writing and Jack's art and Georgina's ambition to become a social worker. Jack had almost forgotten about the vodkas in his hands when Kate called from the doorway. 'Jack! Are you going to come and save me?'

Matt laughed. 'Come on you two. Let's get in there and go fucking mental.'

They danced and drank and laughed, and Jack sensed during one moment, as Kate boogied with her head tipped back and her fingers laced around his neck, that he would never forget this night: the low-cut red dress that she wore, the way her lush, black hair flicked under the orange light, her cute dimples and dark-as-coal eyes.

A while later, as he was holding her close and shuffling in a circle to Barry White's deep velvet croon, he felt a hand on his shoulder. 'Vinnie wants to talk. Just the four of us,' Georgina said close to his ear. Somehow, it was no surprise. He kissed Kate's brow. 'Get us a drink. I'll be back in a few minutes.'

He followed Georgina through to Vinnie's bedroom and the small balcony within that overlooked King's Road. Vinnie and Matt were waiting, and Vinnie shut the sliding glass doors behind them.

'Wow,' Jack said, as he looked onto the empty street. He checked his watch, which showed three-thirty, though it took a moment for his eyes to focus as the cool air made his head sway. 'It's been a good night, Vinnie. Happy birthday.'

Georgina and Matt repeated his sentiment.

'Thanks.' Vinnie looked at each of them. 'I can't remember the last time we were all together. I'm glad you came.'

'Wouldn't miss it.' Matt held his beer bottle up in salutation.

The four of them regarded each other in near silence, broken only by the muffled sound of Vinnie's stereo. It was Vinnie who spoke at last. 'We should talk.'

Jack caught Matt's gaze and heard Georgina sigh. 'Is everything okay, Vinnie?' she asked.

'Okay?' Vinnie gave a little laugh. 'I don't know. Is

everything okay with you three?' He let the question hang. After a few seconds, when none of them had responded, he shook his head. 'We should talk about what happened. We never spoke with each other about it back then, right after it happened, and we haven't spoken about it since. That isn't normal. It's not right.'

Georgina lowered her head. 'There's nothing to say.'

'Frankie died, Georgina. We left him, and he died. It was our fault.'

'Fuck that,' Matt said. 'We were kids. Accidents happen.'

'You think it was an accident?'

Jack felt a sudden heightened state of awareness as the adrenalin in his body seemed to overcome the effects of the vodka. 'What are you saying, Vinnie?'

'I'm saying that I can't even remember exactly what happened. And I don't think any of you can either. There was a fire and . . . that's it. Don't tell me that's fucking normal.'

'We all suffered smoke inhalation,' Matt said. 'It can do that.'

'Maybe that's true,' Vinnie said. Jack noticed the tremble in his voice. 'But if it was just an accident, why do I feel so fucking guilty?'

'It's in the past,' Georgina said. She rubbed her palm on Vinnie's upper arm. 'Leave it there.'

'You don't understand, do you?' A smile, as if he possessed a great truth that they were not yet party to, quivered on his lips. 'There's no such thing as the past.'

'Stop it.' Georgina withdrew her hand from him and hugged her elbows. 'You're upsetting yourself. What happened in Doom is over.' She slid the glass door on its runners and stepped back inside.

Vinnie looked at Matt, then at Jack. 'It isn't over. I'm telling you as a friend. Believe me.' He stalked back into the flat.

Jack pulled a cigarette from his pocket and lit it. 'He's just a little emotional,' he said. 'Drink and weed.'

'Yeah.' Matt rubbed at the stubble on his chin. 'I'd better

go and see if George is all right.' He stepped into the bedroom and stopped. 'Jack,' he said, over his shoulder. 'Do you remember anything about a guy, a real ugly bastard? We might have called him Bald Eagle?'

Jack felt his temperature drop as if he'd been dunked in an ice bath. 'No,' he lied, to Matt's back.

'Okay,' Matt said.

Jack managed to hold the vomit he felt rising until Matt had passed through the bedroom, before letting it go over the balcony with a splatter onto the pavement below.

6

Two weeks. It's too long. Georgina re-read the phone number on the scrap of paper for the umpteenth time. *So what? What can he say?* She slipped it back inside her pocket and returned her attention to the open book on the table before her.

But he seems like a nice guy. She smirked. They all seem like nice guys at first. Even Declan. 'Fucking arsehole,' she muttered, noticing the librarian shoot a severe glance her way from behind his counter. She furrowed her brow in feigned concentration and moved her lips as if she were reading quietly to herself. *Come on, concentrate.*

She read the first paragraph again, but the words were almost meaningless. With a sigh, she leaned back and looked at the wall clock above the librarian. Twenty minutes until her lecture. If she left now she could stop by the phone box and call him.

But it's been two weeks. So what? It was him who'd given her his number at Vinnie's party. He was the one who wanted to take her out. It was times like this that she hated herself for being so indecisive and needy and being so concerned about other people's opinions of her actions.

'Fuck them,' she whispered, and heard a huff from the

librarian as he marched from behind his desk, his heels clicking on the parquet floor. He placed his palms on her table.

'If you cannot keep quiet,' he said, 'I shall have to ask you to leave.'

Georgina felt the eyes of the other half a dozen or so students in the room on her and blushed. 'Sorry.' She closed the book and stood, her mind made up.

'So, you called him then?'

'Yes. I'm meeting him up in London on Saturday. Jack's letting me crash at his place for the night.' Georgina looked into Matt's dark, always so serious eyes, as they walked hand in hand through the grounds of the cathedral. It was a habit formed years ago, probably around the time they had their one night stand experiment. The sex had been fine, if a little mechanical, but their reasons for doing it were wrong, leaving each of them with a sense of guilt. Georgina felt she had pressured him into the act, and Matt believed he led her on. It had taken weeks and more than a few drunken discussions into the early hours to afford themselves forgiveness. Now they were as close as friends could be, and felt lucky to have that much, though Georgina still wondered 'what if' in her darker moments.

'Good. He seems like a nice bloke.'

'He does, doesn't he?' The last word had a raised inflection, as if she were not sure.

'Well, he couldn't be any worse than Declan.'

Georgina shuddered. 'Don't even mention his name.'

'Have you seen anything of him?'

'Only at his lectures. I sit at the back and avoid eye contact. I've only got one more lecture with him, thank God. I just wish I'd listened to you earlier.'

Matt squeezed her hand. 'Well, it's over now.'

They followed the path to the cathedral's front and passed

through the main entrance to the nave. The air was cooler inside, and shafts of diagonal sunlight from the high windows cast bright patches onto the flagstone floor. Georgina had lost count of the times she'd wandered through the ancient building, and still the gothic beauty of the enormous internal arches caught her by surprise.

'Your dad would like this place.'

Georgina recalled the year before, when her parents had come to visit. Her father was less than impressed with Canterbury. He considered it a hotbed of sin, full with student girls in mini-skirts and boys with dirty ideas. That a cathedral should be surrounded by such immorality just compounded his odium. 'He's been here. He hated it.'

Matt raised his eyebrows in surprise.

'He isn't easily pleased,' Georgina murmured.

'How was your visit the other week?'

'Oh, you know, the usual. I'm a sinner and a bad daughter, blah, blah, blah.' She glanced up at Matt. 'And he doesn't think much of you, either.'

Matt stifled a laugh.

'No, this isn't Dad's kind of church.' Georgina's mind flashed to the Bible readings performed in the back room of her parent's house when she was a child. *A child who must have her demons cast out.* She blinked and pushed the memories back down into that place where she kept them locked away.

Their shoes clicked on the smooth grey stones as they walked the length of the room. 'I don't know why you bother going back at all.'

Georgina had wondered that herself—every time she visited she couldn't wait to get away. 'Well, you know what they say. There's no place like home.'

'I suppose so. I should get back and see Dad. I haven't set foot in the village for ten months.'

'You should. Your dad must miss you. Especially with Simon over in Ireland.' She paused and looked up at the ornate ceiling. 'Plus, I want you to see something.'

'Yeah? What's that?'

'I'm not sure. It might be nothing. But if you go, take a look at the old bench on the green.'

Matt frowned. 'I'm intrigued, Miss Smith.' He pulled her hand. 'Come on, let's go and have something to eat.'

Georgina let him lead her from the nave and wondered if she'd done the right thing by mentioning the bench; she'd worried over it since Vinnie's attempt at dragging up the past at his party. But Matt was rational—more so than anyone she knew—and she was certain he'd find a reasonable explanation for the signature that shouldn't be there.

She'd been nervous, more than was normal for something as trivial as a date, but when she saw Michael's smile as he spotted her from the sidewalk opposite the Soho restaurant, her insecurities vanished. He skipped across the road with an unexpected lightness.

'Hi,' he said, in his New England accent.

Georgina smiled. 'Hello, Michael.'

He looked up at the restaurant's signage. 'Have you eaten here before?'

'Only once. The food's good.' She studied Michael's muscular frame. 'The portions aren't very big, though,' she said, almost as an apology.

Michael laughed. 'Hey, don't worry. If I'm not full we can stop by a good old fashioned English fish and chip shop on our way home.'

To her relief, the food was excellent and the portions not as small as she'd remembered. Michael was polite, attentive, and funny, and the conversation between them flowed easily. *And he's handsome*, she thought, as they were drinking their coffees.

'So, how come you left studying until now?' She noticed a slight frown form on his brow. 'If you don't mind me asking,' she added.

'Look that old, do I?'

'No, no, not at all. I—'

'It's okay.' He smiled. 'I'm just yanking your chain. For the record, I'm twenty-six. And the reason I've only just started university is Vietnam.'

'Oh.' Georgina remembered the news reports she'd seen. The place looked like hell on earth. 'That must have been frightening.'

'Kinda.'

'Do you mind talking about it?'

Michael shifted in his seat. 'It isn't usually a topic for discussion. We didn't exactly receive a hero's welcome.'

'That's awful.' She reached across and placed her palm on the back of his large hand. 'I expect you lost some friends.'

He sipped his coffee and dropped his eyes to Georgina's hand. 'I did. Some of the best buddies I ever had.'

'I'm so sorry. The world's gone bloody mad.'

He shrugged. 'The whole thing's screwed. What with Vietnam and Watergate and Nixon about to resign, it feels like America has become the world's biggest laughing stock.'

'And what do you think of England?'

'Warm beer, the lights always going out, IRA bombs going off—what's not to like?'

Georgina laughed. 'I suppose both our countries are going through strange times.'

'I guess. It's people that count though, and there's one thing I've learned. There are some nasty, crazy sons of bitches around—no matter where they come from—but for every one of those there are a thousand decent people. Trouble is, it seems to me like it's the sons of bitches that get to run the show.'

Georgina felt him turn his hand beneath hers and enfold her fingers in his palm. She cocked her head to one side. 'Do you fancy a drink? There are a few late-night bars around here.'

'That sounds great.' He signalled for the bill, and didn't insult Georgina by insisting to pay for the whole thing when she offered to split it. They paid and were making their way between the tables to the exit when Georgina heard a comment that turned her cold. She stopped and looked down at the man who spoke—one of four sitting at a table with too many empty beer bottles on it. 'What did you say?'

The man, middle-aged and wearing an expensive suit with his tie askew, grinned up at her. 'You must be hearing things, darling.'

'Is there a problem?' She heard Michael ask in his deep tone from over her shoulder. She glared at the man who continued to grin, and turned her attention on each of his three cronies who averted their gaze.

'No,' the man said. He looked at Michael. 'There's no problem here, pal.'

'Come on,' she said. 'Let's go.' She took Michael's hand and led him from the table. As they passed out into the warm night air she felt herself begin to tremble with rage. She hadn't been hearing things.

Nigger lover.

That's what she'd heard, and her stomach turned at the vileness of it. 'Wait here,' she said to Michael. 'I forgot something.'

She marched back through the restaurant and stopped in front of the man. As he looked at her, she noticed he'd lost some of the cockiness in his demeanour. *Probably thinks I'm crazy.* She leaned forward and spoke low. 'That man I'm with is worth ten of you, you disgusting little pig. Think yourself lucky he didn't hear what you said.'

'Sorry.' He frowned. Then a subtle change came over his features, as if he'd come upon a revelation. And when he spoke next his voice was quite different, venomous yet familiar. 'I wouldn't like to see him lose his head.'

Georgina felt a sickness at his comment form in her stomach—a feeling that somehow the words held an important piece of information she should dissect and scrutinize. A twisted grin formed on the man's lips that she couldn't bear, and as she turned away, Georgina hoped that Michael was right about the nasty arseholes of the world being so few and far between.

7

Matt sat up and winced.

'Hang on.' Tom turned the pillow upward between Matt's back and the metal frame of the hospital bed. "How's that?"

'Fine. Thanks.'

'Want anything to drink?'

'I want to go home.'

'You can, tomorrow. They just want to keep an eye on you, in case of concussion.'

Matt rested his head back and smiled, though it pulled at the stitches on his top lip where his teeth had pierced through. 'I'm glad you're here, Tom.' He noticed a film form in his lover's eyes.

'Somebody has to look after you.'

A thought, sudden and disturbing, came to Matt. 'You haven't called my dad, have you?'

'No. I thought I'd ask you first.'

'Thank Christ. He's got enough to worry about with Simon. He doesn't need this shit as well.'

'I just called Georgina. I hope you don't mind.'

Matt shook his head. 'No, I don't mind.' Georgina would know not to phone his dad. It was just a shame he had to put this downer on her—he couldn't remember the last time he'd seen her as happy as in the past three weeks since she'd been dating Michael.

'I hope the police catch the bastards.'

'Well, I wouldn't hold your breath,' Matt said.

'Why not? This is serious, Matt. They could have killed you.'

'Tom, I'm just another queer-bashing statistic. Do you

really think the police are going to go out of their way to find who did it?'

'They fucking well better!'

'All I'm saying is, they didn't seem that interested.'

Tom huffed. 'Well, I think it's outrageous.'

Matt smiled. He found Tom's naivety and sense of injustice quite touching. He suspected it was down to Tom's upbringing, where his homosexuality had been accepted without a blink by his family, despite them living in the tough kind of northern mining town where you'd have expected him to be made an outcast. So much for stereotypes. 'Don't let it get to you, Tom.'

'If we don't let that kind of shit get to us, things will never change.'

'That's true. But it takes time.' Matt ran a tentative finger over his swollen cheek and closed his bruised and heavy eyelids, a sudden tiredness upon him. 'It takes time,' he murmured, as the comfort of darkness took all pain away.

This is going to hurt.

'Eh?' Matt opened his eyes and focused on the woman's face beside his. 'Hello, Georgina.'

'Oh, Matt.'

'I've looked better, eh?' He turned his head. 'Where's Tom? He was just here.'

'That was this afternoon. You've been sleeping. I told him to go and have something to eat.'

Matt propped himself up and looked around at the other patients in the ward. It was visiting time, and most of them were being fussed over by concerned relatives. 'Close the curtains,' he said.

Georgina stood and pulled the screens around the bed-space before sitting and taking his hand. 'What is it?'

'I visited the old town on Sunday. Took a look at the bench while I was there.'

'And?'

'I saw the signature. And the smiley face.'

Georgina chewed on her bottom lip. 'What does it mean?'

'I don't know. But I can't believe it was put there by Frankie. I *won't* believe it. He's been dead for ten years, for Christ's sake.'

'So who else would do it?'

Matt shrugged. 'I don't know. Someone with a sick sense of humour.' He saw an expression of relief in Georgina's eyes.

'You must be right,' she said. 'It just spooked me out.'

'Try not to worry about it.'

'I won't.'

She smiled, but Matt could see it was forced. 'So, how's it going with Michael?' he asked, in an effort to lighten the mood.

'Great. I like him a lot.'

'He's an interesting guy.' Matt and Tom had double dated with Georgina and her new lover on two occasions since she'd been going out with him. Matt—always the writer—had found the anecdotes of his upbringing on the east coast of the States fascinating, tucking mental notes away for future literary use. More important than that though, Matt had the feeling he was in the presence of one of life's genuine nice guys. There were no pretensions or bullshit about the big American's manner, and he possessed a sensitiveness of spirit unexpected in one who'd seen such recent horrors. Michael hadn't spoken of his experiences in Vietnam when they met, though Matt had been made aware by Georgina of his involvement. 'Any plans on taking him to meet your parents?'

'What do you think?'

Matt considered it. 'Well, I know your dad's odd, but I've never heard him spouting any racist shit.'

'Neither have I, but he finds the idea of me having any boyfriend immoral. And I'm pretty sure the God he worships is very white and very English.'

'I'd like to say you can't live your life for your dad, but I'm hardly an example.'

Georgina began to giggle. 'Maybe we should both go back

to Doom with Tom and Michael. We could have a drink in the Green Man.'

'Fucking hell.' Matt grinned and raised his hand to his split lip with a frown. 'I don't think they've ever had a black man or a poof step foot in there.'

'I wouldn't say that—you've been in there enough times.'

'Yeah, but I was undercover. They'd choke on their beer if I entered hand-in-hand with Tom.'

Georgina leaned closer. 'So, what happened?'

'Didn't Tom tell you?'

'He said you were beaten up by four skinheads.'

'Well, that's about it. They chased me from outside the Wimpey. I got trapped in Woolworth's doorway.'

She looked down at his hands resting on the bed sheet. 'I see you fought back.'

'Yeah.' Matt raised his left fist and examined the sewn knuckles. 'I knocked a couple of teeth out of one of the wankers.'

'Good for you.' She kissed his brow. 'I'm just glad you're alive. Please, Matt, promise me you'll be careful.'

She held his gaze, and Matt thought, *she knows. She knows I didn't run at all, that I stood there on the pavement and gave them a fight.* That was all she had intuited, though, and Matt had already decided that he wouldn't tell her about the ringleader, who he seemed to recognise from a long time ago. Georgina had been shaken by Vinnie's talk of Frankie and by the carved signature on the bench, and Matt didn't want to remind her of an ugly fucker they once called Bald Eagle, who was really . . . *what?* It almost came to him, and his head began to ache with the strain of trying to remember.

'I promise,' he said. 'I'll be careful.'

He began to drift then, and some time later—in the middle of the night—he woke covered in a sheen of sweat to a silent, dimly lit ward.

This is going to hurt.

The bastard had said that just before Matt had taken his

kicking, and it wasn't the first time he heard him use the phrase.

A doctor. He's a doctor.

No, that wasn't quite right. Bald Eagle liked to cut. Bald Eagle was a surgeon.

8

'Bit early for that, isn't it?' Jack said as he passed his neighbour's doorway. The girl, a music student named Anne, was sitting on her bed with the door open. Her little radio was emitting a Radio 3 Christmas concert though it was only the second week of December.

Her eyes widened and she turned it off. 'Oh, Jack, sorry,' she stuttered.

Jack laughed. 'It's okay, don't turn it off. I like it.' He watched her, but she just sat and stared back, like a trapped animal. She'd never been one for conversation, but Jack had never seen her act as strange as this. 'See ya,' he said, after an awkward few moments, and walked on. He let himself into his room which was, as usual, filled with cigarette fumes.

'Anne's acting a bit weird,' he said as he undid his scarf and hung his coat on the handle of the wardrobe. He glanced at Maurice, who stubbed his cigarette out and stood from his bed, his expression drawn and serious. 'Fucking hell, not you as well. Has everyone been struck dumb in this house?'

Maurice took a slow step forward, then rushed across the room and pulled Jack tight into an embrace.

'What the . . .' Jack felt the onset of panic, deep in his stomach.

'I'm sorry,' Maurice said. He pulled away, but kept Jack's shoulders in a tight grip at arm's length, and Jack saw that his friend was crying.

'Maurice?'

'There's been an accident.' He paused. 'It's Kate, Jack. She's dead.'

1965—HISTORY

1

'WHAT IS IT? Is it a bear?'

Jack glanced up from his sketch paper on the kitchen table at Mary. 'It's called a badger.'

'It *looks* like a bear,' his little sister said, her six-year-old voice taking on a knowledgeable tone that made Jack smile. He returned his attention to the drawing and flicked the end of his pencil across the paper to create light shadows on the animal's snout.

'Have you seen one?' Mary interrupted again.

'No.'

'Well, how do you know what one looks like?'

Jack sighed. If there was one thing he had learned about little sisters, it was that they seemed incapable of not talking. Or maybe that was just Mary. 'I saw a picture in a book in school today.'

'Oh.' Mary leaned her elbows on the table and cupped her face in her hands, her mouth open as she watched her brother. 'How big are they?'

'I'm not sure. About as big as a dog, I expect.'

Mary giggled. 'A dog with teeny-weeny little legs.'

'I suppose so.'

'A dog with teeny-weeny little legs,' she said between her laughter, 'that looks like a bear. That's a silly animal.'

Jack tried not to grin. 'Shh,' he said. 'You're putting me off.'

She clamped her mouth shut but not for long. 'Well I

think it's a *good* picture,' she said, as if Jack's skill had been in doubt.

'Thanks. That means a lot.'

'Can I put it on my wall?'

'Yes. When I've finished.' The knocker on the front door rapped three times in a rhythm that both Jack and his sister recognised.

'Vinnie's here!' Mary said.

Jack heard his mother open the door and welcome him in. 'Go through,' he heard her say. 'You're just in time to save him from his sister.'

Vinnie entered the kitchen from behind Jack and slapped him on the back as he passed. 'Hello, Van Gogh.'

'Hello, Vinnie.' Jack began to gather his pencils.

'Watcha, Vinnie!' Mary shouted.

'Watcha, Shorty.'

'I'm not.' Mary slid off her chair and stood as straight as she could against Vinnie's arm. 'Look. I'm getting bigger.'

'You're getting louder,' Jack said.

Mary ignored him. 'Look. Jack's drawn me a picture of a banjo. It's good innit?'

Vinnie laughed. 'Yeah,' he said. 'It's cool.'

Cool was Vinnie's latest word, picked up from rock 'n' roll lyrics and American films. Jack had used it once or twice himself, but had stopped when he told his grandma her new radio was cool and she asked, 'What's the temperature got to do with it?'

'It's a badger, not a banjo. Here.' Jack handed the sketch to his sister, who ran from the room with a whoop of delight, the sheet flapping in her hand.

'Blimey, she's happy,' Vinnie said. He nudged Jack. 'She doesn't take after you. You're a right miserable sod.'

'Shh.' Jack looked at the doorway. Sod wasn't the worst swearword he'd heard Vinnie use, but he knew his mum wouldn't be pleased to hear it.

'What?' Vinnie raised his eyebrows and followed Jack's

gaze. He looked back with a sly glint in his eye. 'Sod ain't swearing.'

'Don't, she'll hear you,' Jack whispered, though he wanted to laugh.

Vinnie raised his voice a tone. 'I only said sod, you silly fucker.'

'Stop!' The pair of them began to laugh so much that Jack couldn't catch his breath. The click of his mum's approaching heels echoed from the hallway. 'What's so funny?' she asked—a quizzical smile on her lips—as she entered the kitchen with a cup and saucer in her hand. She proceeded to wash the dishes in the sink.

Jack felt his cheeks flush. 'Nothing,' he said, glad that his mum had her back to him. 'Can I go out for a little while?'

'Yes,' she said over her shoulder. 'Be back by five for dinner.'

'Yes, Mum.' He pushed Vinnie down the hall and out through the front door ahead of him. 'Blinking idiot. You're going to get me in trouble.'

'I don't think so,' Vinnie said. 'Billy Drinkwater got Lizzy Ferndale in trouble and now she's got a little bastard.'

'You're bloody mad.' They passed down the bush-lined alley between the houses on the opposite side of the road.

'Look at this.' Vinnie pulled a three-inch black oblong-shaped object from the back pocket of his trousers.

'What is it?'

'A penknife.' Vinnie unfolded the metal blade, which had brown spots of rust on it.

'Where did you get it?'

'From a toolbox in my shed. I think it must have belonged to my dad, so he ain't going to miss it.'

They stepped from the alley onto Approach Road and turned left. Vinnie blew a raspberry at their school as they passed by its front gates, chained shut for the weekend. Jack glanced at the windows of his unlit, empty classroom, and felt a slight ache at the fact that he wouldn't be seeing Miss Simpkins until Monday morning.

They came to the small three-way junction that opened

onto the village green and crossed over to it. Georgina and Matt were sitting huddled on the middle of the bench, reading a Dandy comic.

'Do you think they love each other?' Vinnie murmured as they walked toward them.

Jack shrugged. He often wondered the same thing himself. The four of them had been friends since they'd started in the same class six years ago at the age of five, but Georgina and Matt had shared a particular closeness.

The two of them looked up from the comic book. 'Watcha,' they said in unison.

'Hello,' Jack said. He sat by Matt and looked at the comic. 'Is it a new one?'

Matt nodded. 'Yeah.'

Vinnie walked around the bench and crouched behind them.

'What are you doing?' Georgina asked.

'Carving my name.'

The three of them looked at each other before jumping from the bench and crouching behind Vinnie.

'You'll get in trouble,' Jack said.

'*You'll get in trouble*,' Vinnie mimicked in a little girl's voice. 'Who's going to notice it?'

Jack watched as Vinnie's name appeared in the dark wood. Georgina took the knife when he finished, carved her own name, and passed it to Matt who did the same.

'Here.' Matt offered the blade to Jack. 'You don't have to, though, just because we have.'

Jack looked around the field to see if anyone was watching.

'Come on, you fucking sissy,' Vinnie said.

Jack took the penknife and etched his name into the back of the soft wooden plank. When he was done, he leaned back to admire their joint handiwork.

Vinnie. Georgina. Matt. Jack.

'Cool,' Vinnie said. 'Cool, baby.'

A warm glow filled the kitchen, filtered through the net curtains that hung over the big westward facing window. There were no houses beyond the back garden, just a field that stretched to the line of trees that bordered the woods toward which the sun, big and orange, had begun its descent. It was Jack's favourite room in the house, and favourite time of day, sitting with Mary and his parents as they ate.

'This is lovely, Debs.'

'Thank you.'

Jack watched his mum and dad share a smile and thought, not for the first time, how lucky he was. He couldn't imagine how it was for Vinnie, living in a house with just his older sister and his mum, his dad gone so long ago that Vinnie couldn't even remember what he looked like.

'Have you heard the news about Hope House?'

'No, Charles.'

His dad sipped at the glass of water by his plate. 'Somebody's moving in.'

'It's been empty for years. They'll have their work cut out.'

'Well, I expect they can afford to have it fixed up. You'd need money to buy a place like that.'

Hope House, big and old and built from slabs of grey stone, occupied the centre of the six acres of land that belonged to it on the other side of the woods. Its turreted top secured its resemblance to a small castle, and Jack had spent many hours with his friends running around its perimeter, playing Robin Hood and his Merry Men or King Arthur and his knights. It had been empty and boarded up for as long as he could remember.

'I'd love to see the inside of that place,' his mum said. 'It's a beautiful building.'

'It's as nice inside.'

'You've been in there, Charles?'

'Yes. I used to help with the horses there when I was a boy.'

'I didn't know that.'

'Well . . . ' He winked at Jack. 'I like to keep an air of mystery about myself.'

Jack smiled. His dad had been born in Doom and had spent most of his life there, though he commuted to London for his job, which Jack understood had something to do with banking. His mother was from Brighton, only residing in Doom since their marriage twelve years before.

'Have you any plans for Sunday, Jack?'

'No, I don't think so.'

'Good. I thought maybe we'd go fishing, now that the weather's warming up.'

'Yeah, that'd be great, Dad.'

Mary sat straight. 'Can I go, can I go?'

'Of course you can. We'll take a picnic.'

Jack leaned back and looked through the window as his sister chattered and his parents talked and laughed. He felt blessed. He felt warm and happy and loved and hoped it could stay that way forever.

After helping his dad wash and dry the dishes from dinner, Jack went up to his bedroom and pulled his stack of sketch pads from the built-in wardrobe. His parents liked his drawings and gave him nothing but encouragement, and he enjoyed the praise they extolled for each new picture he produced. He finished one the night before, though he would never show them, despite the fact he considered it to be the best sketch he'd ever completed. He pulled the pad from the bottom of the pile and opened it to a portrait two pages from the end. Pencil lines, controlled yet with a sense of urgency, formed an excellent resemblance to his teacher, Miss Simpkins, her head tilted to the left so that her eyes were focused somewhere beyond the viewer's shoulder. She was beautiful, her short dark hair swept along her jaw line in a curl to frame her pale, elfin features.

Jack closed his eyes for a moment and imagined the scent of her perfume, her smile, her voice, and wondered if this was what it felt like to be in love.

2

He that hath an ear, let him hear what the Spirit saith . . .

Georgina tried to concentrate on the words in the Bible, held open in her hands, as her father read them out loud to the small gathering, but she felt her attention begin to drift. She wasn't scared of being caught—she had a technique, mastered over the course of the countless Friday night readings her father held in the little back room of their house. Her eyes, though not reading a single word of text, moved from left to right, and she turned her page on cue from the others sitting around the dining table. In this way her mind could wander, away from the drab room and the ancient stories she'd heard and read so many times before.

. . . and his name that sat on him was death, and Hell followed with him . . .

The reading was from Revelations, which Georgina guessed to be her father's favourite of the New Testament books—he returned to this one with a regularity unmatched by any of the other scriptures. Georgina found its apocalyptic prophesies dark and frightening. It was not a text from which she could draw any comfort.

Her eyes moved in their automatic motion as she thought of being on the bench with Matt. He'd brought a comic—an object of blasphemy she would never be allowed to bring into her parents' house—and as he opened it across their laps, it was the ideal excuse for her to shuffle close so that she could feel the warmth of his arm on hers. They had often sat that way; it felt natural. One time last summer, the day after her father had made her scrub herself clean in a freezing bathtub, Matt had put a comforting arm around her shoulder in his back garden. Her crime, according to her father, had been to ask her mother how babies were made, and her sobs were bottomless as she pushed her face into Matt's neck. He pulled her close with a tenderness that she had never experienced before. 'It won't last forever,' he'd said, 'and I'll always be here for you.' Any physical contact received from her parents had only ever revealed itself as a form of punishment.

'. . . *her sins have reached unto heaven, and God hath remembered her iniquities . . .*'

She sensed her father's attention upon her and furrowed her brow in fake concentration as his monotonous voice filled the room. A few seconds later, when she was sure he was focused on his book by the rising intensity of his tone, she allowed herself to glance up. Her mother, wearing a dated hairnet and clothes as grey and drab as the room in which they sat, moved her lips in silence as she read along. Georgina imagined how wonderful it must be to have a mum like Jack's—kind and beautiful, her hair pulled up into a fashionable beehive. The other three regular worshippers— Mr. Hargreaves and his wife from next door and Mr. Poole the butcher—were all intent on the Bibles before them. Georgina looked back down and thought of Matt again, of how his thick, dark fringe ended in a straight cut above his serious eyes, and of how it might feel if he kissed her. *It would feel fantastic.* Yes, she knew that it would.

In the background, far away from her warm thoughts, her father was reaching his frenzied climax, speaking of great plagues and earthquakes, and Georgina felt relief that the session was almost over. She looked at her father, balding and pale, his eyes like tiny buttons behind his round spectacles. She hated him, and felt shame at those feelings. What kind of person hated their own father?

A round of *amens* uttered from the table to which Georgina added her own. The usual ritual of tea would now take place, and Georgina knew she would be excused from the table and the adults' gossip of local affairs.

Georgina's bedroom was cold. The large window opposite her

bed rattled from the wind and allowed a chill in from around its warped and loose-fitting edges. She flicked the light switch on and the bare walls, a shade of ochre that were once white, were illuminated by the light bulb that hung un-shaded from the ceiling. Her slippers tapped on the bare floorboards as she crossed the room and lay on her bed. An itch irritated her left forearm, and she rolled up the sleeve of her sweater to examine the scratch there. A thin scab traced a line from above her wrist to the inside of her elbow. She scrapped a fingernail under its edge and saw that it was almost ready to come off. She daren't cut herself again until it did—one scratch could be explained.

She pulled her cuff down and rolled over to the far side of the bed where she leaned over its edge, her palms on the floor, and listened. A moment later, satisfied that she wouldn't be disturbed, she prised at the foot-long piece of floorboard and pulled out the folded sheet of paper hidden there. She sat back and opened it, pulling the pencil wrapped within its crease. Its surface was covered in sentences: *I hate this house. Matt is beautiful. It feels good when I bleed*, and random, mostly obscene words. She had no idea why she did it, other than it felt good in the way that it did when she scored the broken piece of glass into the flesh of her arms. She supported the paper on her bent knees and began to write. It was only a short sentence, and when she finished it she sat back and smiled. It was the best one yet.

3

Matt read the left hook coming before his sparring partner's fist had moved an inch and ducked it with ease before planting two jabs of his own on Ronnie Peter's face.

'Good work, Matt, good work.'

He saw Ronnie take two steps back for a breather and moved away himself, letting his gloves drop to his sides.

'No, Matt. Now is when you finish it!'

Matt glanced at the coach, Mr. Nesmith, on the other side of the ropes and raised his fists. He stepped towards Ronnie, who gave him a small nod of readiness and, Matt thought, thanks for giving him a few seconds. Ronnie was a year older and more experienced in the ring—he'd had two bouts already—but was no match for Matt who had only ever sparred, though he was eligible to compete since he turned eleven. Matt threw a couple of quick, light taps at his opponent's head, skipping around him with a speed that Ronnie couldn't match, then moved in. The other boy raised his gloves in defence of his face, and Matt pummelled them, forcing Ronnie onto the ropes. Matt saw gaps, could have made contact with cheekbone and nose instead of the raised forearms that he hit, but there was no point. The contest was all but over, and he had no desire to hurt Ronnie who had been equally as fair with Matt when he'd first started at the club.

'Okay, okay, that's enough.'

The two boys tapped gloves and stepped through the ropes, their identical white vests sticking to the sweat on their pale, skinny bodies. Mr. Nesmith passed them each a cup of water, which they balanced between their gloves, and Matt sipped his as he glanced around the small hall at the other half a dozen boys who were skipping rope or thumping on punch bags.

'You're improving, Matthew, but you have to know when to finish a fight,' his coach said in his cockney accent. 'When you're ready to compete, you won't be able to mess about with any monkey business like that.' He cocked a thumb at the ring. 'You'll end up flat on your back with a nose like mine.'

Matt looked at Mr. Nesmith's lumpy face and deformed, wide nose. Despite its gruesomeness, it was not an unkind face, but Matt had no intention of ruining his own in a similar nature, either now or at any time in the future. He didn't hate boxing; there were in fact moments when he was swept away by the thrill of it, but he didn't love it enough to risk disfigurement. He would much rather spend his Friday evenings reading—his current favourites were Ian Fleming's Bond novels—or writing his own fiction.

Matt suspected his dad had introduced him to the sport for that very reason. His dad's world was a masculine one of beer, cigarettes, and football, and Matt had found him less than encouraging over any academic achievements, thinking them somehow girlish. He'd never seen his dad so proud as when Simon, on his eighteenth birthday the month before, declared his intention to enlist with the army.

'You mustn't worry about hurting your opponent.' Mr. Nesmith unlaced Matt's leather gloves.

'Yes, Coach.'

'Do that and you're dead on your feet.' He nodded at the double doors. 'Your dad's here. Better get changed.'

Matt walked to the long bench by the wall where his clothes were stacked and began to get dressed. He watched the coach walk over to his father and engage him in conversation. Every now and then, as they spoke, one or the other would glance in his direction. When he was ready he rolled his plimsolls inside his vest and shorts and walked over to them.

'See you next week, George,' his dad said to the coach as they left the hall. They crossed the road to the van his dad used for work. 'George says you're doing all right.'

Matt opened his window an inch as his dad lit a cigar and started the engine. 'Did he?'

'You sound disappointed.'

'No. Course I'm not,' Matt said. He was though, and realised that on some deep level he was hoping for a bad report from the coach. *He hasn't got what it takes*, he said in Matt's fantasy. *He may as well give it up.*

Matt looked at the shop windows as they drove along the high street of Durling, which was five miles from Doom and three times as big. At the end of the street they pulled over to the kerb outside the fish and chip shop which had a small queue of waiting customers stretching out through the doorway. This was the part Matt enjoyed most about the Friday evening ritual. His mouth watered at the aroma drifting through his window and at the thought of his treat—sausage in batter and chips wrapped in a newspaper—which his dad allowed him to devour during the drive home.

The lights of Durling faded behind them as they entered the long country lane that wound like an umbilical cord between the neighbouring towns. As he ate, Matt wondered how his dad might take it if he were to tell him he didn't want to box anymore. He wasn't frightened of him. Despite his gruff, macho nature, he'd never hit Matt, and was in fact the less strict of any of his friends' parents. The thing that most scared Matt was disappointing him, and since his mum had died two years before, Matt felt the pressure to please his father all the more. He'd been close to his mum, as Simon was to his dad, and Matt had found himself anchorless since she'd gone.

At the house, Matt jumped down from the van and held his hand out. His dad locked the vehicle, walked around its nose, and dropped the keys into his son's upturned palm, as he did every Friday.

'I'm just popping over to the Green Man for a couple of pints.'

'Okay, Dad.'

Matt let himself in and walked to the kitchen. He opened the fridge and took three big gulps of milk straight from the bottle. The house was quiet, the way Matt liked it. He wasn't one for hustle and bustle and noise, and relished the thought of having the place to himself for a couple of hours until the pub stopped serving. Simon, still enamoured with the idea of being able to buy a drink legally, would also be there with his friends until closing time.

Matt made his way up the stairs to his bedroom to

retrieve his paperback copy of *Thunderball*, which he only had twenty pages or so left to read. Despite his dad's lack of enthusiasm for Matt's love of reading, he never refused his son any book he asked for, and Matt was grateful for that.

As he left his room with the book clutched in his hand, he stopped on the landing outside Simon's bedroom. The door was ajar. Matt pushed it opened and entered. He liked Simon's room; Vinnie would have described it as cool. It was decorated in bright green and orange circled paper, hung by his dad, and punctuated here and there by Technicolor posters. He dropped his book onto Simon's bed and crossed to the nearest poster, an army recruitment advert with an illustration of a camouflaged soldier charging over a spiral of barbed wire. Beside that was a photograph of Marilyn Monroe pouting at the camera, her bosom swelling at her dress as she leaned forward. He passed that one by with hardly a glance and stopped in front of the next, a movie poster of *Rebel Without a Cause*, and stared into the eyes of James Dean. The biker glared back over the upturned collar of his red jacket.

He knew then, as he had for some time, that he could never find Marilyn as beautiful.

4

The tune that played itself in Vinnie's head wouldn't go away, and he hummed it to himself as he walked along the village's main street. He didn't know where it had come from; he was sure he hadn't heard it before, and though there were no lyrics with the tune, he had a feeling that there should be—*something about Waterloo Bridge*—but couldn't quite grasp them. The descending sun, half hidden by the church steeple, bounced sharp diamond-white reflections off the few shop windows in the short row.

'Good afternoon, Vincent.'

Vinnie looked up and waved at Mr. Pettigrew, the grocer, who was busy taking in the baskets of vegetables from the trestle tables outside his shop on the opposite kerb. 'Hello,' he replied.

'Here.' The greengrocer held an apple aloft and lobbed it in a high arc across the road. Vinnie cupped his hands and caught it like a cricketer. 'Now don't eat it 'til after dinner or your mum will tell us both off.'

'Thanks, Mr. Pettigrew.' Vinnie passed by the post office and stopped outside the tea shop next door to it. He looked through the window and saw his sister Ellie collecting the tablecloths. The only customer was a boy he didn't recognise, sitting at the small corner table with a book opened in front of him. Vinnie glanced back down the road at the bench on the green and wondered if Jack was right; maybe carving their names into the wood was a foolish thing to do. He put his hand in his pocket and pushed the penknife down as far as it would go before walking into his mum's shop.

'All right, Vinnie?'

'Yeah.' He sat at the table his sister was clearing. The sound of rattling cutlery came from the kitchen where he knew his mum would be putting everything in its place for the next day. 'Been busy?'

'Not really.' Ellie whipped the tablecloth from under his elbows. 'Saturday tomorrow, though.'

Vinnie looked across at the boy in the corner as his sister moved on to the next table. His brown hair was short with sun-kissed highlights, his face tanned and freckled, and he appeared to be about the same age as Vinnie. He glanced up and smiled. 'Hello,' he said.

Vinnie nodded. 'Watcha.'

The boy returned his attention to the book he'd been reading, and Vinnie wondered why a boy of eleven would be sitting by himself in a tearoom. It wasn't the kind of thing Vinnie could imagine himself or any of his friends doing.

Ellie cleared the table adjacent to the boy and pulled her

little book and pencil out of her pinafore. 'We're closing in five minutes, love,' she said as she wrote out his bill. 'Did you enjoy your sandwich?'

The boy looked up. 'It was lovely, thank you.'

Ellie tore the sheet from her pad and put it on his table before walking through to the kitchen. Vinnie watched amazed as the boy pulled a wallet from the satchel that hung from his chair back—he'd only ever seen wallets in the possession of grown men. The boy placed some coins on the table and pulled a pen from his breast pocket which he used to write something on the bill before standing to leave. 'Bye,' he said as he passed Vinnie on his way out.

'Yeah. See ya.' He turned in his chair and watched the boy through the window until he was four doors down, then got up and rushed across to where he had been sitting. On the bill, the boy had written *Thanks* and drawn a smiley face. Vinnie examined the money on the table and saw that the kid had left two sixpence pieces as a tip.

'Bloody hell,' he muttered, and glanced at the kitchen doorway, where he could hear his mum and sister talking. Without a thought, Vinnie slipped one of the sixpences into his pocket. A moment later, his sister walked back into the room. 'That kid just left you a sixpence tip,' he said to her.

'Blimey, he must be rich.'

'Yeah, he must be.' Vinnie thought of the air of confidence the boy had, his leather wallet and shilling tip, and looked again at the picture the boy had drawn on the bill. He admired the boy's style. Whoever the kid was, he was cool.

'I see the Bible bashers are out and about.'

Vinnie glanced up at his mum who was looking out through the living room window, and knew she was talking about the regular Friday night visitors to Georgina's house opposite.

'They make me laugh,' she continued, 'bleeding hypocrites.'

'What's that mean?'

'Never you mind.' She looked at her wristwatch. 'Where's your bloody sister? She's going to make us late.'

'I'm coming, I'm coming.' Ellie clomped down the stairs and across to the mirror above the fireplace where she proceeded to apply her deep red lipstick.

'Blimey, Ellie, we're only playing bingo at the social club. No need to doll yourself up like a film star.'

'I like to look nice.' Ellie dropped the lipstick into her handbag and clipped it shut.

Vinnie's mum crossed the room and planted a kiss on his brow. 'We'll be home by ten, sweetheart.' She turned to her daughter. 'Come on, Doris Day, let's go.'

With the house to himself, Vinnie turned the radio on and fiddled with the tuner until he found Radio Caroline. His mum would have disapproved; she preferred the stuffy BBC stations, but they didn't play the kind of music Vinnie liked. The Beatles were on, and Vinnie sang along as he pulled the penknife from his pocket and opened the blade, which he used to peel the apple given to him earlier.

The song finished, and Vinnie took a bite of the apple as the next one began. He recognised it at once, and hummed along to the tune that had been in his head earlier, that now reminded him of something. *Snowflakes, falling into the darkness.*

The song faded beneath the DJ's voice. 'That was the great sound of The Kinks and "Waterloo Sunset", one of the biggest hits of 1967,' he said, before the station was lost in a crackle of interference. Vinnie frowned. *What the hell was the DJ talking about?*

'It's 1965, you idiot,' he said to the radio. He tried to laugh at the announcer's mistake, but was unnerved by the goose bumps that had broken out on his arms. The vision of the snowflakes floating down into the darkness came back to him, and Vinnie had the feeling that something unstoppable had begun.

5

'Why can't I come with you?'

'Because you're six,' Jack said. He stopped at the kerb and held his sister's hand tight before crossing the road from his school.

'Oh, please let me come.'

'It isn't up to me. Mum won't let you.'

'It's not fair.'

They turned into the alley that led them out between the houses opposite their own. At the front gate, Jack let Mary's hand go and she ran up the path to the front door. Because she could not yet reach the knocker, she pushed the letterbox inwards and let it swing back under the force of its springs to create a loud tinny crack.

'Jack said I can't go with him up to the big house,' Mary said the moment her mother opened the door.

'That's because you're too young to go out and play.' Her mother bent and kissed her cheek. 'And besides, I'm baking cakes, so I'll need your help.'

'Cakes, whoopee!' Mary ran to the kitchen, her ambition to go out with Jack forgotten. Jack followed her into the hallway and put his school books on the table.

'You're going to Hope House?'

'Yes. I'm meeting Vinnie, George, and Matt. We want to see who moved in.'

His mum laughed. 'You nosey little so-and-sos. Haven't you any homework?'

'Only a page of sums. I'll do them after dinner.'

'Well, don't be late.'

Jack walked through the kitchen past his sister who was scooping a finger-full of cake mix from the large bowl on the table. 'You're supposed to bake it first,' he said to her as he walked through the open back door into the garden. He strode across the lawn to the loose board on the back fence, which he swung up like a pendulum on the single nail that held it in place before squeezing his body sideways through the gap.

The grass in the field was sun-dried yellow and whipped at his knees as he made his way to the woods opposite. He watched his feet as he walked. Vinnie once told him he'd seen an adder there, and though Jack was almost certain it was a lie to frighten him, he had no intention of taking any chances. He entered the cool shade of the woods and began to jog. It would take only a couple of minutes to reach the other side where his friends would be waiting; they'd taken the short cut straight from school whilst he'd escorted Mary home.

School had been a drag, worse than usual for a Monday. Miss Simpkins had not been there and Jack's class had been taken by Mr. Granger, the deputy head, whose dry, formidable nature managed to squeeze any pleasure from learning that a pupil might have. He was the opposite of Miss Simpkins, who exuded kindness and encouragement. *And she's beautiful.* Jack thought of the portrait he'd drawn and smiled. At least he'd be able to gaze at her image later, alone in his room when his homework was done.

The trees became sparse as he neared the edge of the little wood, and through the gaps he saw his three friends in the field on the other side. 'Have you seen anything?' he asked as he approached. The sound of hammers on timber and men's voices floated to him from the house in the distance.

'They're un-boarding the windows,' Matt said.

'Come on, let's go closer. We ain't going to see anything from here,' Vinnie said.

'Do you think we should?' Georgina looked at Jack for confirmation. 'If somebody's moving into the house, this is their land. We might be trespassing.'

'Balls to that,' Vinnie said. 'We've always played in these fields. No one's going to stop us now. Come on.'

Both Georgina and Matt glanced at Jack, who shrugged his shoulders. 'We're not doing any harm,' he said, and the three of them followed Vinnie.

'I hope Miss Simpkins is back tomorrow,' Georgina said.

'Me too,' Vinnie agreed over his shoulder. 'I thought I was going to die listening to that boring old fart all day long.'

They stopped fifty feet or so from the side of the house and watched the workmen, who were pulling off the boards and throwing them onto the back of a flat-bed truck.

'Look, somebody's coming.' Matt pointed off to the left, where a grey car was approaching via the road that linked Hope House to the village. It stopped short of the entrance on the dirt drive that had sprouts of weeds popping through its surface from years of non-use.

'Blimey,' Matt said. 'That's a Bentley. They must be millionaires.'

They watched as the driver, a chauffeur in smart uniform and cap, exited the car and opened the back door. A boy climbed out and walked towards the house.

'I've seen him,' Vinnie said. 'He was in my mum's cafe on Friday.'

As if he had heard the comment, the boy stopped and looked their way. Despite the distance, Jack was sure the boy was staring directly at him. Studying him.

'He looks a bit posh,' Georgina said.

The boy's serious face broke into a grin, and he gave them a quick wave of his hand before walking across to them. 'Hello,' he said, and shook each of their hands in turn, though Jack noticed that the boy gripped his a little longer than he did the others. 'My name's Frankie.' They introduced themselves one after the other. He looked at Vinnie. 'We've met already, I believe.'

'That's right.' Vinnie nodded at the building. 'Is this your house then?'

'It's my aunt's. She's inside.'

Jack opened his mouth to ask about the boy's parents but changed his mind. 'Are you going to come to our school?' he asked.

Frankie smiled in a way that made Jack feel young and unsophisticated in comparison. 'I don't think so.' He looked at the four of them, who each seemed to have lost the power of speech in his presence. 'Well, I'm afraid I have to go. I'm sure we'll see each other again . . . soon.' He held Jack's gaze for a moment before he turned and marched away.

'Stuck up sod,' Georgina muttered when he disappeared into the house.

Jack and Matt made agreeable noises.

'No, he's all right,' Vinnie said. 'You wait and see.'

6

Something was up. Georgina sensed it as soon as she let herself into the hallway. She walked along the passage to the open living room door and peeped around the frame. Her dad was in his armchair facing away from her, the back of his balding head as still as stone, though she knew he was aware of her presence. Georgina's mother sat opposite him, her Bible clutched tight between her fingers on her lap. She turned her eyes, shark-like and devoid of all emotion, to Georgina, who backed away from the doorway and took the stairs to her bedroom. Her arm began to itch, and she gave it a rub as she crossed to the window and opened the curtains to let in the last of the summer evening sunlight. As she turned back to face the room she saw it, and felt her insides drop as if she'd stepped off a cliff.

'No, no, please, please, no,' she whispered. Her legs shook as she peered at the piece of wood on her bed, and she crept towards the revealed space in the floorboards, already knowing that it would be empty. Footfalls, slow and deliberate, ascended the staircase, and she stood, unable to move but for the tremble that had worked its way throughout the whole of her body. By the time her father appeared in the doorframe, bible in one hand and sheet of paper in the other, she could hear the click of her own teeth.

'A demon has been sent to try us,' he said in a low voice. He walked to the bed and placed the paper on it. 'What blasphemy is this?' His voice was barely audible.

Georgina lowered her gaze, her cheeks blazing in shame and fear.

'I asked you a question.'

She shook her head, unable to speak.

'Is this the work of your hand?'

Georgina nodded.

'Read it. Pick it up, and read it.'

There was something about the quiet calm of his voice that terrified Georgina. She lifted the sheet and looked at what she'd written.

'Read it to me. Every single word.'

She glanced at her father. 'Please,' she said, 'I'm sorry.'

'If you wrote it, you can read it.'

The first tear ran down her face, blurring the words before her. 'Please, I don't want—'

'Read it!'

The sudden outburst—as loud as she'd ever heard her father shout—made her jump, and she felt a warm trickle of urine down her thighs. 'I . . . I hate this house,' she managed. 'Matt is beautiful.' She felt the wetness soak into her sock and was aware of the puddle spreading onto the floorboards around her shoes. Great sobs rose up in her chest. The next four words were single obscenities that she skipped over. 'It feels good when I bleed,' she continued.

'You've missed some. Read them.' His voice was calm again and ice-cold.

Georgina went back to the words she'd hoped not to read out loud. 'Fuck,' she whispered. 'Bastard. Shit. Prick.' She glanced up and saw that he was also trembling, could almost feel the heat of rage emanating from his body, and knew in that moment that he was enjoying every second of her humiliation.

She looked back at the paper and read it through to the bottom. When she reached the last line, she looked up at her father and held his gaze as she spoke. 'The Bible is a fairy story,' she read, 'and my dad is a silly old cunt.'

7

Matt finished the last of the sums on his sheet, put his pencil down, and faced front. Mr. Granger, his fingers interlaced on his desk, stared back at him. A few of Matt's classmates were still hunched over their work, busy pencils scratching across their sheets. All those that had finished sat straight and silent, not daring to do otherwise whilst under Mr. Granger's charge.

'One minute,' the deputy head said.

Matt watched the red second hand turn its laborious circuit on the wall clock above the door, glad that he had completed the math questions, knowing that those who hadn't would not be allowed to leave the classroom for lunch.

'Those who have finished please place your sheets on my desk and leave the room in an orderly manner,' Mr. Granger said.

Matt rose and stepped into the line of pupils making their way to the front of the classroom before dropping his worksheet onto the thin pile. The moment he was through the door he broke into a run alongside the other boys and girls, racing them along the corridor and down the stairwell, all of them eager to put as much space between themselves and the stifling atmosphere of the first-floor classroom. The playground felt like freedom, and he waited a few paces from the double doors under a sky of endless blue for his two friends, who came out together a few seconds later.

'That was torture,' Vinnie said.

'Yeah.' Jack huffed. 'I hate bloody math.'

The three of them strolled around the playground with no particular direction in mind, waiting for the bell to signify that lunch was ready in the little annex that served as the dining hall.

'Did you call on Georgina this morning?' Matt asked Vinnie.

'Yeah. Her dad said she wasn't well.'

'She seemed all right yesterday,' Jack said.

'It's probably, you know, girl's stuff,' Vinnie said.

Matt and Jack fell silent in contemplation. Vinnie had told them about *girl's stuff* a few months before, and Matt still found it hard to believe. He had no idea where Vinnie had heard it from, but the details were enough to make him thankful he was a boy. The deep clang of the bell rang four times from the far corner of the playground and they ambled towards the sound as younger kids around them raced towards the dining hall.

'I don't know what they're in such a rush for,' Vinnie said. 'It'll only be mincemeat and mash, same as nearly every other day.'

After lunch, Mr. Granger set them an essay. 'The title,' he said, 'is *When I'm Grown.*' He looked over the class. 'It should be about your ambitions. What you want to do, who you want to be. It is important that you start thinking about these things now, otherwise you risk drifting into a life of mediocrity and unhappiness. Look deep inside yourself and use your imagination; you don't have to do something just because your parents did.' He walked along the aisle of desks, handing out exercise books. 'Three pages, please, at the very least.'

Matt opened his book and tapped his teeth with his pencil as he thought. *What do I want to be?* He thought of Simon, and how enlisting in the army had pleased his dad. Matt had no such hankering for a military life. But what else was there?

Working on the building sites with his dad? He almost shuddered at the thought, then realised he had mentally walked straight into the trap that Mr. Granger had warned them away from. *He's right. It is my life, not Dad's.*

Matt began to write, and the words flowed. He felt his heart race with excitement for the future. He knew who he wanted to be, realised that on some level he'd always known; Ian Fleming or J.R.R. Tolkien or C.S. Lewis. He glanced up from his work at Mr. Granger. He'd always thought of him as an old fashioned and frightening disciplinarian, but realised now that his judgement may have been wrong. Mr. Granger didn't seem so bad after all.

When school was out, Matt took a detour and walked with Vinnie instead of heading in the opposite direction with Jack to their homes on the north side of Doom. 'I want to knock for Georgina, see if she's okay,' he explained. He noticed the look exchanged between his two friends, knew that they wondered if there was more to his relationship with Georgina than simple friendship.

Maybe there is, he thought. She was a girl, though, and he knew he could never be attracted to her in that way. He also knew that he cared about her more than he did any of his other friends. She'd been there for him when his mother had died, and he for her throughout the shitty times she'd had at home with her fanatical parents. Maybe it was love he felt for her.

'Do you want me to come with you?' Vinnie asked when they reached the front gate of his house.

'No, it's okay. See you tomorrow.'

Vinnie was already half way up his garden path. 'See ya, wouldn't want to be ya,' he called over his shoulder.

A vague sense of unease rippled through Matt as he crossed over to Georgina's house. It had taken seed earlier, when Vinnie told him that her dad had said that she wasn't well. Georgina's dad was usually at work by that time, so what was he doing at home? There were many reasonable explanations why he could have been there, of course, but Matt still felt a dryness in his mouth as he knocked on the door.

Footsteps approached from the other side and a moment later the door opened a few inches. The sharp features of Georgina's mother appeared in the gap. The expression on her face upon seeing Matt was of someone who had discovered a rotten odour.

'Hello,' Matt said, after five awkward seconds of silence. The woman made no reply. 'Is Georgina there?'

'She's unwell.'

'Oh. Will she be at school tomorrow?'

'No.'

The door closed and Matt stood there looking at the peeling paint. He knew then that he'd been right to be unnerved. Something was going on in Georgina's house, and that could only mean bad news for his friend.

8

The good weather had changed. The hot, clear skies of the previous two weeks had been replaced by a blanket of low grey clouds, and as Vinnie walked along the high street on his way to school the paving slabs were suddenly dotted with dark spots as fat raindrops began to fall. He pulled the collar up on his jacket and increased his pace as a flash lit the underside of the clouds, followed by a deep rumble. The rain fell with more force, and Vinnie ran into the newsagents for shelter, the little bell above the door emitting a ding.

Mr. Palin, the proprietor, glanced over his shoulder from behind the counter where he was stacking the rows of shelves with sweet jars. 'Morning, Vincent,' he said.

'Hello, Mr. Palin.' Vinnie blew a raindrop off the end of his nose and walked over to the comic rack.

'What can I do for you?'

'Oh, I don't want to buy anything. It just started pouring.' He pointed at the window which was being buffeted by the rain.

'On your way to school?'

'Yes. I'll have to make a run for it in a minute.' Vinnie plucked a copy of The Beano from the rack and flipped it open. Outside, another sharp crack accompanied a lightning flash, and in the same moment the door opened. The boy from Hope House who'd introduced himself as Frankie entered in a casual manner, as if he were impervious to the storm. He spotted Vinnie and tipped his head.

'Watcha,' Vinnie said in reply.

Mr. Palin turned to him. 'Hello, young man. Can I help you with anything?'

'Yes. I'd like twenty Woodbines, please.'

'Your dad sent you out in this weather for his fags has he?'

'Oh, no,' Frankie said. 'They're for me. You can't beat a smoke after breakfast.'

Mr. Palin looked at Frankie for a moment before letting out a laugh. 'Did you hear that, Vinnie? We've got a right joker on our hands here.' He crossed to the cigarettes and in the brief moment that he turned his attention away from the boys to reach for a pack, Frankie pulled two Milky Bars from the counter and pocketed them.

'There you go.' Mr. Palin passed the cigarettes over. 'That'll be three shillings and sixpence, please.'

Frankie pulled the money from his wallet. 'Thank you.' He winked at Vinnie, a slight smile on his lips, as he brushed by him on the way out.

'I'd better get going,' Vinnie said to the shopkeeper. 'See ya.' He replaced the comic book, rushed outside and stood in the narrow shelter of the doorway. Frankie was halfway across the road, walking diagonally towards the church, where he pushed open the iron gate and headed for the entrance. He looked both ways before shoving the big double doors and disappearing inside. Vinnie hesitated and looked along the street in the direction of his school, then back at the church.

Sod it. It won't hurt if I'm five minutes late. He sprinted across the road and into the churchyard, the fast forming puddles splashing under his feet. The church door creaked on its hinges as he let himself inside.

'Hello, Vinnie. Shouldn't you be at school?'

It took a moment for Vinnie's eyes to adjust to the dim interior. When they did he saw Frankie, halfway down the pews on the left-hand side with his feet on the chair-back in front. The tip of his cigarette glowed red as he sucked on it. Vinnie walked along the aisle. 'What are you doing? You can't smoke in church!'

'Really? Who says so?'

Vinnie stood at the end of the pew. 'Why did you nick the chocolate bars from Mr. Palin? You've got plenty of money.'

'Because I wanted them, and I had the opportunity. Because it was exciting. Because, because, because.' He blew a smoke ring. 'Sometimes, Vinnie, you just have to act.'

Vinnie watched him, spellbound. 'How come you don't go to school?'

Frankie laughed. 'What are you, a policeman?' He pulled the packet of Woodbines from his pocket and held it out. 'Do you want one?'

Vinnie looked at the doorway, wishing he wasn't there but excited that he was. 'I have to go to school.'

The rain rattled on the stained-glass windows that surrounded them. Frankie stood, dropped his butt on the floor and twisted the sole of his shoe over it. 'You don't *have* to do anything.'

'Of course I do.' Vinnie stepped aside to let Frankie pass. 'I'll get in trouble if I don't turn up.'

'So you miss one day at school. Big fucking deal. What will they do, send you to the gallows?'

For the second time in as many minutes Vinnie experienced a sense of shock at Frankie's behaviour inside a church, and glanced at the painted plaster cast of Christ on his crucifix behind the alter. Frankie followed his gaze and shook his head.

'You have a lot to learn, Vinnie.'

A sudden anger reddened Vinnie's face. Vinnie appreciated being a bit of a rebel himself, but who did this kid think he was, smoking and swearing in church and talking as if he were an adult? 'Yeah? Well maybe I'll tell Mr. Palin that you stole his chocolate. You won't be such a clever dick then.'

Frankie walked towards the door. 'I didn't steal anything, actually,' he said over his shoulder. 'You were the one who walked out of the shop with the chocolate.'

Vinnie slipped his hand inside his left jacket pocket, remembering the way Frankie had brushed by him in the shop, and felt the unmistakeable shape of two chocolate bars. He considered taking them back to Mr. Palin for no more than a second before dismissing the idea. He looked at Frankie who had stopped in the doorway.

'I'd prefer it if you weren't angry with me, Vinnie. I'd like us to be friends. I'll see you later.'

Vinnie examined the Milky Bars. They were his favourite, and he would have bought one if he had the money. He was sure that Frankie had somehow known that. So Frankie had simply taken them—and it had been easy.

I could do that. I could have what I want.

Vinnie felt as if the narrow road of his mind had opened into the biggest of freeways before him.

'Something funny's going on in Georgina's house. I think she might be in some kind of trouble.'

Vinnie looked from Matt to Jack and back again. 'Why do you say that?'

Matt looked around to make sure nobody else was listening to their conversation in the dining hall. 'When I knocked for her last night her mum wouldn't let me see her. She just shut the door in my face.'

'That doesn't mean anything—they've always been a bit weird,' Jack said.

'I know, but it was the way her mum looked at me, as if she hated me.' He frowned. 'But it's more than that. I've just got a feeling. A bad one.'

Vinnie swallowed the lump of mashed potato in his mouth. 'I told you before—it's probably just girl's stuff. She'll be back at school in a few days.' He put his cutlery down and leaned across the table. 'Have you two finished your lunch? I've got us a treat.'

'What is it?' Jack asked.

'I'll show you.'

The boys put their hands in the air to signify they had finished eating and were excused from the hall by Mrs. Spencer, the dinner lady. Once outside, Vinnie led his friends through the alley between the main school and the annex to the out of bounds bike shelter.

'Hurry up,' he said, 'we've only got ten minutes 'til break's over.' They stepped under the corrugated roof that protected a couple of teacher's bikes and a stack of work tools stacked in one corner by the caretaker. 'Here.' He pulled the chocolate bars from his pocket and passed one to Jack. 'You and Matt can share that one.'

'Thanks. Where did you get the money?'

'I bumped into Frankie.'

Jack frowned.

'You know, the kid from Hope House. Anyway, he's loaded, and he bought them for me.' He concentrated on unwrapping his own bar as he spoke, hoping they wouldn't spot that he was lying. He thought Matt might not be above eating a nicked Milky Bar, but he *knew* Jack would get all high and mighty and refuse it. Also, for reasons he hadn't really thought about, he wanted to make Frankie look good.

'But he hardly knows you,' Matt said as he took his half from Jack.

'Yeah,' Jack said. 'It's a little bit weird.'

'I expect he's just trying to make friends.' Vinnie took a big bite from his bar. 'It must be horrible moving to a new town where you don't know anybody.'

'I suppose so.'

'Shh!' Matt grabbed Vinnie's shoulder. 'Someone's coming,' he whispered.

They huddled in a shadowed corner behind an old wheelbarrow stacked with plant pots and heard the approaching voices of two teachers.

'. . . *last night. The landlady let them in. She wasn't there, though.*'

'*Maybe she's gone back home to Dorset.*'

'*Well, that's the thing. Her parents have had no contact from her, and no clothes or toiletries seemed to have been taken—she even left her purse.*'

'*It doesn't sound good. Beth's not the type to disappear on a jaunt.*'

'*No. Well, the police are involved now. She's officially a missing person . . .* '

The voices faded and the three boys crept from the shadows. 'Come on,' Vinnie said. 'We'd better get back to the playground before the bell.' He glanced behind as he led the way and saw the expression on Jack's face, as if he were about to vomit. 'What's up?'

Jack looked at him and swallowed. 'They were talking about Miss Simpkins. Her first name's Beth. Something's happened to her.'

Vinnie felt goosebumps tickle their way up his arms. There was something about the moment, something familiar about Miss Simpkins disappearing and Georgina being in trouble and the three of them eating the chocolate bars stolen by Frankie. And beneath it all, like a soundtrack, the song that kept playing in his mind that brought with it the image of snowflakes falling into a dark and inescapable abyss.

9

'I'm going to take it off, now, but if you scream I shall put it straight back on. Are you going to scream?'

Georgina looked up at her father through weary eyes and shook her head.

'Good.' He glanced over his shoulder at his wife and Mr. Poole, the butcher, who were standing by the bedroom door. 'The demon is near defeat. You are no match for the word of God,' he said to Georgina, returning his attention to her. He reached out and pulled the strip of brown parcel tape from her mouth.

'Ow,' she murmured, though the sudden pain of the tape ripped from her lips made her want to scream. Her father's face blurred as tears filled her eyes. She looked beyond him at her mother. 'Please untie me, Mum,' she pleaded, though she saw no sympathy in her eyes.

'Be quiet, devil.'

Georgina began to sob.

'Do you renounce evil?' her father asked, for the hundredth time in two days.

She nodded. 'Yes.'

'Do you embrace God, and ask for his forgiveness?'

'Yes.' She turned her head and looked at the glass of water on the windowsill. 'I'm thirsty.'

Her father sighed. 'It always comes down to your own physical needs. I want, I want, I want.'

'Selfish girl,' Mr. Poole said from the doorway.

'Perhaps you aren't quite ready yet.' Her father pulled the coil of packing tape from his cardigan pocket.

'No, Daddy, please!'

He tore a six-inch strip from the roll and secured it over her mouth despite her attempts to turn her face from him. She screamed into her gag and pulled on the ropes securing her sore wrists and ankles to the four corners of her bed. 'You are an evil child, with evil notions,' her father said, 'and your demons must be expelled.'

He turned and left the room, followed by his wife. Mr. Poole lingered in the doorway. When Georgina's parents were halfway down the stairs the butcher looked at her. 'What a pair of fruitcakes,' he said, in a low voice. 'I'm like you—I think the Bible's a load of tosh.'

Georgina stopped thrashing and looked at him, confused. He'd been attending her father's Friday night gatherings for more than a year. A faint hope rose inside her. Maybe he was an ally—a neighbour caught up in her parent's fanaticism who'd had enough.

'Please, let me go,' she said, but only managed to utter an unintelligible noise into her gag.

Mr. Poole raised a finger to his lips. 'Shh,' he whispered. His mouth stretched itself into a grin, though no mirth showed in his eyes. 'This is good, though. The thought of you here, helpless, and me just a street away with my butcher's knives.' He winked at her. 'See you soon.'

Georgina watched him leave and began to tremble. Somehow, hard as it was to believe, her situation had just gotten worse.

PART II

1984—MATT

 1

'TICKETS, PLEASE.'

Matt glanced up from his notepad at the uniformed inspector and pulled the stub from his breast pocket. 'Thank you,' he said, when the man had clipped and returned it. Matt removed his glasses and rubbed his sore eyes—it had been a long journey and he had spent most of it reading and making notes. Multiple shades of green rolled past the train carriage window as it sped through the Yorkshire countryside under the burnt orange of the early evening sun. He sensed the gaze of the young girl opposite who had boarded at the previous station and glanced her way. She was in her late teens, chewing open-mouthed on a Spearmint. Matt smiled and nodded.

'From London, are ya?'

'Yes,' Matt said. It wasn't strictly true, but he'd lived in the city for seven years now. Plus, he didn't enjoy telling people he was from a village called Doom.

'Thought so. What you doing up here then?'

'Just visiting a friend.'

She eyed his notepad. 'Are you a reporter?'

'No. I write books.'

'Oh. I thought you might have been up here for the coalmine strikes. Just as well you're not—my dad says the reporters are all lying bastards working for Thatcher.'

'No, not me.'

The train traversed a steep bank that dropped down on

Matt's side to a wide patch of allotments. Matt watched the gardeners digging and planting and he enjoyed a false sense of nostalgia. He'd never been a gardener, though he did envy their skill and patience. His particular creativity was altogether different; the seeds of cultivation that he planted and nurtured were from within his own mind. The allotments gave way to a housing estate, the back gardens pushing up to the railway track's boundary fence, and then they were gone again, replaced by an expanse of farmland.

Matt put his glasses back on and looked again at his notes. They were to form part of a memoir, the idea suggested to him by his publisher. He'd balked at the idea at first—he could think of nothing more tiresome to write about than himself—but had found a compromise that Karen Fisher, his editor, seemed keen on. He would write a semi-fictional memoir, a coming of age story of a young boy's awakening to his sexuality in a small rural town. The premise was close enough to his personal experience for his growing fan base to recognise and would give him the freedom to let his imagination roam free without the restriction of sticking to the facts. His first two novels had done well enough for his publisher to offer him a half decent advance, and Karen had been his biggest supporter, so he felt an obligation to meet her at least half way on this one.

He'd been working on background notes of Doom's history with information he'd gathered from research in the Durling town hall and library. It had all been pretty boring stuff, not much that he could use, apart from one fact that he'd never heard about before—probably because it was from way back during World War One. He read the passage he had bookmarked from his copy of *Villages of Kent*:

> *Doom, like every village and town of Great Britain, played its part in the Great War. Of the seventy-three villagers that served in the trenches— some of them barely more than boys—forty-two lost*

*their lives, and those few that did return were sure
to have suffered either physical or emotional injury.*

*Whilst the men of Doom were engaged in combat
on the continent, the women were not idle. Hope
House, under the ownership of generations of the
Higton family, was loaned to the government for the
purpose of use as a hospital, and many local wives
and daughters gave their services tending the
injured. It is estimated that over six hundred men
had passed through there by the war's end.*

Hope House. His memories of the place were vague now.
He'd been inside only a couple of times with Georgina, Jack,
and Vinnie when they first became friends with Frankie, but
Matt recalled enough to know that he hated the place.

I didn't hate it. I feared it.

He'd seen something there, and he wasn't the only one.

There are no monsters.

He remembered Georgina saying that, trying to convince
herself and the others to disbelieve the evidence of their own
eyes.

We were chased through the house.

It was a memory that had returned only recently,
instigated, Matt guessed, by his research, and still only half-
formed and dream-like as if seen through a net curtain. But
he had been eleven, it was nineteen years ago, and he
wondered if it might be a false memory.

*No, it was real. We were chased by a monster. We saw
his work, and he chased us, his rotten teeth bared in a
maniacal grin, his bloodstained doctor's coat flapping
behind as a scalpel slashed the air back and forth.*

They had all seen him, his bald head and hooked nose
reminding them of a bird of prey. Matt looked at the final
paragraph:

The last of the Higton family moved from Hope

House in the mid nineteen-fifties, and it remained unoccupied for a decade until 1965 when a new tenant moved in. It was a short-lived occupancy, however, as part of the house burned down in a tragic accident that claimed the life of a young boy later that same year.

Something had happened in Doom, but like a shadow, Matt couldn't quite catch the memory no matter how he tried. Unlike Frankie, he'd survived the fire, but the smoke inhalation that knocked him unconscious along with his three friends had erased their memories.

Really? All three of us?

A coldness worked its way through Matt's body. Maybe it wasn't the smoke that had caused them to forget. Maybe they were just too terrified to remember.

2

'Hello, Matt. It's good to see you. It's been a while.' Reg Jackson grabbed Matt's hand and gave it a firm shake.

'Too long,' Matt said. He noticed the lines fanning out from the corners of Reg's eyes, and the grey hair at his temples that had not been there before. 'It's good to see you too.'

'Come inside. They're all waiting to see you.' He led Matt through the hallway. 'I enjoyed your last book—we all did.'

'Thanks.' Matt smiled. He had always gotten on well with Tom's dad. He was an honest man and principled, his soft-spoken voice and thick Yorkshire accent carrying the kind of weight that made other men listen.

They entered the kitchen where Tom's mum, Helen, hugged him close. 'Oh, Matt, we've missed you. Tom's been so looking forward to seeing you.'

Tom's sister, Lisa, was next, pulling him close to her full body. 'Hello, sexy,' she said.

'Hi, Lisa.' Matt looked at them, gathered around and smiling as if he were one of their family. At one time, it felt as though he was. He felt his cheeks flush with a sense of guilt at the fact that he'd been away for so long since his last visit. He'd gotten to know them well when he and Tom were partners. 'Where's Tom?'

'He's in what used to be the dining room,' Reg said. 'We've converted it into a little bed-sitter. The stairs were getting a bit too much for him, what with the toilet and bathroom being on this level.'

Helen grabbed his hand. 'Come on, love, I'll take you through.'

Matt noticed her exchange a look with her husband.

'Listen, Matt,' Reg said, his voice lowered. 'We've seen the change in him, bloody quick as it's been. We've had a little time to get used to it, though.'

'He's having a good day today, Reg,' Helen said.

'He is. I'm just saying that Matt should prepare himself.'

Matt met Reg's serious gaze and gave him a small nod before allowing Helen to lead him to the living room, which was cosy and sweet smelling, just as Matt remembered it. They stopped at the closed door opposite the big front window. 'It's me, dear,' Helen said. She gave a light rap of her knuckles on the frame.

There was a pause. 'Is that Matt I heard?'

'Yes.'

'Well don't just stand there, bring him in.'

Helen rolled her eyes. 'He tells me off if I go in without knocking. I can't win.' She opened the door for Matt. 'Just call when you want a cup of tea.'

'I will. Thanks.' Matt walked into the room, well aired by the half open bay window, the net curtains fluttering in the evening breeze. He spotted Tom in an armchair at the far corner next to his bed. A lamp on the table at his side cast a dim yellow light over him.

Matt stopped in the middle of the room and caught his

breath. If it hadn't been Tom he was expecting to see he would never have recognised him. A blue tracksuit hung loose on his thin body, his bony wrists and hands protruding from the sleeves like brittle twigs. Tom's face was the shape of an underfed old man's, the skin stretched tight across his protruding cheekbones, his eyes set deep in their hollows. The lush, blonde hair that Matt remembered was thin and cut short over his ears.

'Hello, handsome,' Tom said, his voice suffering from a slight rasp. 'I'm afraid I've gotten myself into a bit of a pickle.' He smiled then, and Matt saw the old Tom in the glint of his blue eyes.

'Oh, Tom.' Matt's voice cracked. A moment later he was across the room and on his knees, his big arms wrapped gently around Tom's body, his head nestled in the crook of his skinny neck. Quiet sobs escaped him and he felt Tom's palm on the back of his head.

'I was expecting you to cheer me up.' Tom took several painful breaths. 'But you're not doing a very good job.'

Matt looked up and forced a smile. 'I know. I'm sorry.' He cuffed his eyes and cleared his throat. 'It's just...'

'A shock,' Tom said. 'I know. Sometimes, I look in the mirror, and I hardly recognise myself.'

'If I'd known how bad it was, I would have come earlier, I wouldn't have left it so long. I'm sorry, Tom.'

'Stop apologising—you've nothing to be sorry for.' He nodded over Matt's shoulder. 'Fetch a chair before you get a cramp.'

Matt stood and dragged an armchair across the carpet from the opposite corner so that they could sit almost knee to knee. He looked around the room. The walls were painted a crisp shade of mint green, the furnishings modern, bright and complimentary. A unit along one wall held a television, video recorder, and stereo system. 'Your dad's kitted the room out well.'

'Yes. I just have to click my fingers—' He rubbed his digits

together in a feeble, silent attempt to accentuate his point '—
And I can have whatever I want. I'm the king of Yorkshire.'
His chest rattled as he breathed. 'Mum and Dad have been
fantastic, actually. I worry about them. It'll all be over for me
soon, I expect.' He pulled a tissue from the box on his side
table and coughed into it several times. 'I won't be in pain
anymore. But for them, it's going to hurt. For a long time.'

'It will, more than anything, but I'm sure they're
preparing themselves. You mustn't worry about other people,
Tom. They wouldn't want you to.'

'To love is to hurt.' He gave a quick laugh. 'I'm the dying
proof.' A fit of coughs overtook him for a minute or so, and
Matt was about to call for Helen when they subsided. 'If one
good thing comes of this, it'll be that you write about me.'

Matt smiled and shook his head. There would be no point
denying it—Tom knew him so well. It was true. Even now,
though all he could feel was despair, Matt knew that at some
time down the line this meeting, these feelings, would surface
through his writing.

'It's okay,' Tom said. 'I want you to write about it. Maybe
you can make some people understand.'

'Some people don't want to. This disease just gives them
some kind of twisted justification for their hatred of queers.'

'That'll change, Matt. It has to.'

Matt sighed. He didn't want to argue. He wanted Tom to
be right, but the fact that some daily papers still referred to
Tom's terrible condition as "The Gay Plague" left him feeling
more than just a little pessimistic.

'They sacked me from my job, you know. When I first got
ill.'

Matt felt his face flush with anger. 'What happened? I
mean, how did they know?'

'I told them. I knew it would become obvious soon
enough. Better tell them first than have them accuse me of
putting my pupils at risk.'

'And they sacked you? Can they do that?'

'It was convenient for them.' Tom swallowed and winced. 'I'd already had a warning last year.'

'What for?'

'I stepped outside the lines of official guidance.' Tom leaned to one side and used both hands to lift a plastic beaker from his side table. He raised it to his lips and took two long, slow swallows from the spout. 'Only heterosexual sex is supposed be taught in schools as part of sex education.'

'And you did otherwise.'

'No, not exactly. But teenagers ask questions—they're naturally curious. I felt it my moral obligation to answer their queries truthfully.'

'Of course.'

'Anyway. None of that matters now.' He smiled. 'I'm glad you came.'

Matt smiled back at him. 'Me too.'

'We need to talk, Matt. There's too much been left unsaid.'

Matt was about to protest, about to tell Tom that any conversations could wait, but bit down on the words. Every chance to talk now might be their last. 'Okay,' he said.

Tom cleared his throat and rested his head back. 'I want you to know what happened. What I did.' He blinked slowly. 'So stupid.'

'Don't beat yourself up, Tom.'

'I only cheated on you once.'

'Tom, that doesn't matter now. I did my share of sleeping around, you know that.'

'But you kept yourself safe.'

Matt reached across for Tom's hand. 'You were unlucky.'

'But if I hadn't been so stupid we might still be together and I'd still have a future.' A single tear traced its way down his prematurely lined face. 'I'm sorry, Matt.'

'Hey, no apology needed. I'm the shit here. I'm the one who walked away when you got ill. I'm the one with no backbone.' He swallowed against the lump forming in his throat.

Matt felt Tom's hand turn in his and give it the weakest of squeezes. 'Well, it was good while it lasted,' Tom said. His cracked lips stretched in what looked to Matt like the most painful of smiles. 'And we'll always have Canterbury.'

3

'Here. You look like you need this.'

'Cheers, Reg.' Matt took the pint of bitter and drank it halfway down in one go. He glanced around the old low-ceilinged pub and saw that there were only two other drinkers playing dominoes at a round table. They raised their glasses to Reg.

'All right, lads,' he said to them.

'How do, Reg,' the players said in unison before returning their attention to the game.

'Business doesn't look so good,' Matt said.

'Everybody's skint. None of us knows how long the strikes will last or whether we'll have jobs to go back to.' Reg sipped his drink. 'The papers make us look like a load of trouble-making hooligans, but we're fighting for our lives.' He lifted his chin toward the window. 'If that pit gets shut down, this place will become a ghost town, and it's the same for every other coal-mining town in Britain.'

'Things are changing.'

'Aye, and not always for the better.'

They finished the beers and Matt called for two more. Reg was right, he did need a drink. He'd prepared himself for the worse before seeing Tom, and it still wasn't anywhere near enough. He'd at least expected to see a physical approximation of the young man he knew so well, not the wreck of agonised flesh and bones he'd found clinging to Tom's spirit that was still so strong. And Helen had said he was having a good day. He noticed Reg watching him, as if he were reading his thoughts.

'I don't think he has much longer, Matt.'

'I know. I'm sorry. It must be hell for you and Helen.'

'The worst kind. He's a good boy—always has been. Never brought any trouble to our door.' He shook his head and gazed into his drink. 'He doesn't deserve this.'

They drank enough to blunt the pain, and sometime after last orders Matt stumbled his way to the bed and breakfast he'd booked. In his room, he collapsed in his clothes onto the bed, and his mind meandered through a dark universe of dreams.

He woke late, with tears on his face.

4

Matt removed his sweater and tied it around his waist as he walked along the approach road to the coalmine. A scattered crowd of villagers ambled along beside him toward the host of bodies blocking the road ahead. The air was hot, and Matt felt an electric sense of anticipation in the atmosphere. He'd arranged to meet Reg at noon, and peered at the faces of the men and women around him.

'You'll see what's really going on,' Reg had said in the pub the night before. 'Not what they want you to read in the papers.' Some of the protestors carried placards, many with the slogan *Coal Not Dole*. The crowd slowed as it approached the bodies blocking the road.

'Matt, over here!'

He looked to his right and saw Reg, his hand held aloft. Matt waved in response and made his way to the kerb. 'Is it like this every day?' he asked when he reached him.

'There's always a picket duty, but not usually this many. Word's gotten around—two men were escorted into work by the police this morning.'

'Fucking scabs,' a man spat who'd heard Reg's explanation.

'What'll happen now, then?' Matt asked.

'Trouble, I expect. Come and look at this.'

He followed Reg along the buildings that edged the pavement until they could see to the front. Over a hundred miners, three rows deep, sat in lines across the road fifty feet from the colliery entrance. Facing them from outside the big metal gates to the mine was a line of police with riot shields, the front line of their presence. Their formation reminded Matt of a Roman army. Behind them, on either flank was a handful of mounted police.

'It's a sit-in,' Reg said. 'They may have got in to work, but it isn't going to be easy getting out.' As he spoke, four black police vans inside the site started their engines and crawled toward the gates. Matt noticed a signal pass between the officers as they raised their shields.

'This is a peaceful protest!' one of the seated men shouted at the police line.

No verbal response came, but the force's action was sudden. The front line, riot shields thrust forward and batons raised, ran at the strikers. Some tried to stand and flee, some to fight, whilst a few remained seated. The police were upon them in seconds, though, and the protestors stumbled and fell against each other in panic. Matt felt his collar pulled. 'Come on,' Reg said. 'This is going to get ugly, we better go.'

The street filled with shouts and screams, and as Matt turned to follow Reg, he saw that the police had overwhelmed the front line of strikers and seemed to be running amok, their truncheons lashing at anyone within their reach. A young man by his side, retreating the same way, stumbled to the floor and Matt saw a policeman stamp his boot on the back of the man's head as he charged past.

'You fucker,' Matt uttered, and noticed for the first time that the police were wearing boiler suits with no ID numbers. He crouched by the injured man who was unconscious, his face spattered in blood from his shattered nose. All around him the screams rose in intensity. Matt heard the clip-clop of galloping hooves over the commotion, and he grabbed the man on the floor under his arms, attempting to drag him to safety. He glanced back for Reg, hoping he was okay, but had lost him in the chaos. Some men were fighting back; he saw one with a baton, wielding it like a crazed swordsman, and others throwing stones.

Matt looked back down at the young man and guessed he was forty pounds lighter than himself as he hauled him by his armpits. Ahead, on the left, Matt noticed a grocer's shop doorway and headed for it. If he could make it there, away from the violence, he could get the man onto his shoulder and away to safety and the help he needed. He veered towards the shop, saw the man lose a shoe as his heels bumped up over the kerb, and was moments away from the entrance when a sudden, sharp pain in his right shoulder knocked the breath from his lungs. Matt dropped to his knees, stunned as the agony spread across his back, and managed to lower the man to the paving.

'Hello, Matt. It's been a long time.'

Matt turned his head and saw a pair of black boiler suited legs, a baton hanging to one side. He looked up at the policeman but couldn't see any features below the visor of the man's riot helmet. He recognised the voice, though; it was one that had spoken in his nightmares since he was a child. Matt tried to stand and saw the flash of the truncheon as it came down again on his shoulder. Worms wriggled at the edge of his vision and he felt the hard paving below his palms as he fell forward onto all fours.

'You filthy bastard, walking around as if you have a life. I'll soon change that.'

The tip of a steel-toed boot connected with an audible crunch into Matt's ribs, spinning him over and down onto his back. He gasped for breath and through blurred vision saw his assailant crouch over him. Before he could move, a knee pressed down on his chest and a powerful hand gripped his throat.

'Remember me?' The man removed his helmet and grinned, his hooked nose bent towards his rotten toothed grin, the sun glinting off the bare skin of his scabbed head. With his free hand, he pulled a scalpel from the side pocket of his boiler suit. 'I won't lie to you, Matt. This is going to hurt.'

Matt felt the sharp tip of the scalpel against his neck and grabbed the wrist above with both hands. White hot pain bit into his ribs as he strained against the downward force of the knife. Above him, the man they'd called Bald Eagle as children bared his blackened teeth and let a long drool of spittle fall onto Matt's face. 'You're not real,' Matt said. 'You can't be.' An image of an eleven-year-old Georgina flashed in his mind's eye. 'There are no monsters.'

'I'm as real as you, you cunt.'

The hand around his throat tightened its grip, and Matt gasped for air. His arms trembled and weakened and he felt the tip of the blade pierce his skin. He struggled to breathe, but could draw no air through his strangled windpipe. His head felt light, and putting all remaining strength into his shaking arms he fought against the descending blade. It was over, he knew it, but he wouldn't give up, not to this bastard.

'You fucking loser.' Bald Eagle pushed harder and Matt felt the warmth of blood trickling down his neck. 'You may as well give up, like you did with Tom.' He snickered. 'You'll both be in hell soon.'

Matt tried to shout but could only emit a low gurgle as a raging hatred for the man above him fired new strength into his arms. He strained against the scalpel and felt the pressure from its tip on his throat lessen just a fraction.

'Is that all you've got?' His assailant lowered his face and Matt caught the acrid stench from his breath. 'By the way, here's a little secret to take with you. It was me, and it was so easy. A nip from a filthy, infected needle in his thigh in a crowded nightclub was all it took. He didn't even see me— just carried on dancing like the fucking idiot he is.' He rose up so that his arm, hand and scalpel formed a straight line, and readied to put his weight above it. 'Goodbye, shithead.'

A sudden roar thundered in Matt's ears, blocking the noise of the fighting around him—*death, the sound of death*—and the rolling din was above him, filling him, and then it was gone, taking with it the pressure from his arms and chest. Air rushed into his lungs. Matt turned his head in the direction of the receding noise and saw a blur of hooves, trampling and turning the black boiler-suited body of his attacker into a tangled mess in the road.

'Matt!'

Reg's face was above him, and he felt himself pulled up. He grabbed Reg by his shoulders and raised himself onto unsteady legs.

'I thought that horse was going to kill you,' Reg said.

'No, not the horse. He didn't touch me.'

'We've got to get out of here.'

Matt looked at Bald Eagle. He was on his back, his arms and legs twisted at odd, sickening angles, his head turned away. 'Hang on,' he said to Reg. He hurried over to the prone body and bent over to study the face. *What the fuck?* Matt staggered back. *I'm losing my fucking mind.* Bile rose in his throat which burned as he swallowed it back down.

'Come on!' Reg shouted.

Matt turned away from the trampled policeman, a young man of no more than twenty with cropped ginger hair and blood-stained boyish features. *That's not the man who just tried to kill me.* It was not a comforting thought.

5

The bruises, a mass of soft-edged purple, spread from the lower ribs on the left side of his torso to his armpit. Matt winced as he buttoned his shirt over them. Every inhalation sent a stabbing pain through his sternum, confirming his belief that at least one rib was cracked. He grabbed a handful of loose change from his bedside table and left the room.

The payphone in the bed and breakfast was in the hallway on the ground floor, opposite the television room where Matt noticed an old man watching *Coronation Street* through the open door. He paused, eyeing the receiver, then let himself out through the front door into the warm evening—he'd noticed a phone box on the next street that morning and decided it would be best to keep this call private.

Reg had tried to convince him to go to the accident and emergency department that afternoon, but he'd refused. He was a stranger in town and there would be too many questions. The trampled policeman was in a bad way, and Matt didn't want to be implicated. To tell the truth of the encounter, his truth, would only lead to suspicions regarding his sanity or his honesty. They'd managed, or rather Reg had, to get the striker who'd had his head stamped on by a copper to the safety of a shop doorway. The approach of ambulance sirens could be heard by then, and Matt saw that the trampled young police constable had been surrounded by his colleagues to protect him from any further harm.

'It's a class war, Matt, waged against hard-working people by Thatcher, and she's using the police force as her own private army,' Reg had said as he'd helped Matt back to his digs. Matt was in too much pain to reply.

He opened the red door on the phone box and stepped inside. The stench of stale piss hit him as he pulled a little phone book from his pocket and flipped to the page he needed. He dialled the number and dropped a ten pence piece into the slot when his call was answered.

'Hello?'

'Hello, Vinnie. It's Matt.'

'Hey, Matt, you old dog!'

Matt heard Hannah's voice, questioning.

'It's Matt,' Vinnie said to her, his voice muffled for a moment as he turned it from the mouth piece. 'It's good you called. We're having a dinner party on Saturday, you should come over.'

Matt felt his shoulders—which he hadn't realised he was tensing—relax at the sound of Vinnie's voice. He hadn't seen him in six months, maybe longer. 'That sounds good, but I'll have to give it a miss. I'm in Yorkshire, visiting Tom.'

'Bring him down. I haven't seen him in years.'

Matt leaned forward and rested his forehead on one of the glass panes. He could tell by the speed of Vinnie's voice, the edge of excitement in it, that he was on something, and pictured him in the wide, white spaces of his ultra-modern docklands apartment looking down upon the twinkling lights of London through the glass of his wall-length window. It was a universe away from the lives of those he'd met in this small northern town.

'I can't bring Tom.' He paused. 'He's sick.'

Five seconds of silence passed as Vinnie processed the simple statement. 'Christ,' he said at last. 'How far—I mean...' His voice trailed off. 'Is it HIV, or . . . '

'It's moved on. He has AIDS.'

'Poor Tom.' Vinnie's speech slowed. 'He's a lovely bloke. I'm really sorry.'

Matt cleared his throat. This wasn't the conversation he'd intended, though he supposed it was inevitable. 'Listen, Vinnie, I actually called about something else.' The pips sounded through his earpiece and he pushed another coin into the slot. 'I want to ask you something.'

'Go ahead.'

'Do you remember much about Hope House?'

He heard a little laugh from Vinnie. 'I tried to talk to you about Hope House years ago,' he said. 'You didn't want to know—none of you did.'

'I know, Vinnie, I'm sorry. I was scared to talk about it, and I suppose it was the same for Georgina and Jack.'

'Wait a moment.' Vinnie's voice became muted as he put his palm over the mouthpiece and spoke to his wife. 'I just got Hannah to go and make a cup of tea. She thinks I'm mental enough already without hearing any of this shit. Something's happened, hasn't it?'

'Yes.'

'You've seen him, haven't you?' There was a hint of glee in Vinnie's voice. 'You've seen Frankie.'

'Frankie?' Matt felt like he'd been hit with an uppercut when he was expecting a jab. 'No,' he said, 'not Frankie.' *How could I?* He wanted to add. *Frankie's dead.*

'Then why the sudden interest?'

Matt shoved in another ten pence piece. 'I saw somebody else. What do you remember about Bald Eagle?'

'I remember his ugly fucking face. And his scalpel. I think he chased us once. I wasn't sure if it was a dream.'

'He tried to kill me today.'

'Shit. Are you okay?'

'Yes.'

'But he was middle-aged back then. He must be an old man now.'

Matt had already considered this fact. 'He looks the same.'

'Listen, Matt.' Vinnie's voice changed, as if he'd suddenly sobered from the effects of whatever drug he was on. 'I was obsessed with that place . . . and Frankie. I used to think he was haunting me. That was ten years ago, though, and six grand worth of psychotherapy has told me what I knew, deep down, all along. I imagined him, probably from a sense of misplaced guilt. It's called survivor syndrome.' He paused. 'Somebody attacked you today, and I believe you. You've just put a face from the past in his place.'

Matt considered it. The man who'd had him pinned on the floor was at this moment in intensive care, and he was a twenty-year old police constable with ginger hair by the name of Gary Baker. He breathed a sigh of relief. Vinnie was right, of course. He'd imagined Bald Eagles features, and the scalpel. It had been a stressful, violent incident after all.

But what about the things the bastard had said about Tom?

Matt pushed the thought away.

'Thanks, Vinnie. I think I needed to hear that.'

'Good. Now forget about Hope House. How long are you staying in Yorkshire?'

'I don't know. Until the end.'

He heard Vinnie sigh. 'Give Tom my love.'

'I will. Thanks.'

Matt could guess what Reg would make of Vinnie, with his high-rise apartment and Armani suits. *It's all about city traders making themselves rich with other peoples' money—real work doesn't count anymore. It's the road to hell, Matt.*

Matt wondered how prophetic Reg's words would become.

6

It was on a grey Wednesday afternoon during the third week of Matt's stay in Yorkshire that Tom's sister, Lisa, came to his lodgings. Her bloodshot eyes revealed the unmistakable effect of not enough sleep and too many tears.

'I think it's time.'

She led him by the hand—a small comfort for them both—to her parents' house. When they arrived, Lisa took him to Tom's room, where he lay propped in his bed. His eyes were closed and his chest wheezed with every struggled inhalation. Reg and Helen sat on either side, holding his hands as if afraid to let go.

Matt had watched him deteriorate fast in the three weeks since his arrival. His skeletal features were sharp and the discoloured, bruise-like rashes that had appeared on his face made it look like he'd taken a beating. Lisa sat on the edge of his bed and bent to kiss his brow.

'He slips in and out,' Helen said. 'He was awake a minute ago. He asked for you.'

Matt moved closer and placed a gentle hand on Tom's wrist. 'I'm here, Tom.' There was no sign of recognition. 'Has the doctor been?'

'Yes, this morning.' Reg looked up at him. 'He's on morphine. It's all that can be done now.'

'When he does wake, he's confused,' Helen said. She stroked the fluff of hair on her son's head. 'My boy. My poor boy.'

'I can hear you, Mum.' Tom's eyelids opened with great effort, as if their weight were almost too much. He gazed at Matt and smiled. 'You're here. Please don't go away again.' A weak cough jerked his frame. 'I don't want to be alone.'

'I'm going nowhere.'

Tom closed his eyes, and they watched his private battle for every breath as he dozed. 'That boy's here again,' he said after a few minutes. He looked beyond his loved ones at the corner of the room. 'Fuck off. You'll have me when I'm ready.' His eyelids drooped. 'Fucking Moros,' he whispered.

He slept on for an hour, the rise and fall of his chest becoming shallower with every passing minute. Matt hoped for him to wake once more, was desperate to tell Tom that he'd done nothing wrong, but as he watched Tom's struggle he became convinced that every breath would be his last. It was with a sudden, violent gasp which startled all four of them that Tom woke for the final time. He stared, wide eyed at Matt. 'I'm frightened, Matt. I'm scared it's going to hurt.'

'We're here with you, son,' Reg said, his voice thick. 'We love you.'

Matt was aware of Lisa's sobs and glanced at Helen, whose features had become as pale as her son's. Tom looked at him and moved his lips as if in silent prayer.

'He wants to say something to you,' Reg said.

Matt leaned close and put his ear to Tom's lips. Tom breathed in, and whispered three words with his last exhalation. 'You're not real.' His ribcage sank for the last time, and it was over.

Matt turned his face and rested his forehead on Tom's. 'Goodbye,' he said. He kissed his lips and left Tom's family to have some private time with his deceased body. He could hear their sobs from the kitchen and had to sit before his trembling legs gave way. A while later they joined him, and he made them tea.

'Oh, well,' Reg said as he sat down. 'I suppose that's that, then.'

Matt had never seen a man look so broken.

7

On days when words wouldn't come, and the typewriter sat like a poisonous creature daring Matt to touch its keys, he would take the short walk from his South London town house by the park to the Kennington Library. It was a favourite building, it's four-floor Victorian splendour all the more noticeable for the newer, flat-featured structures that had been erected on either side. It was a place to think, and to create, when his own space wouldn't do.

Today, he tipped a nod to the librarian as he passed and headed for the table by the far left corner, glad that nobody was already sitting there. He hated to admit it, being a hard liner on the inanity of superstition, but that particular desk had become something of a talisman. He dropped his pad onto the old scratched surface and sat down. His editor Karen had been on the phone with him earlier, her anxiety working its way along the line to his earpiece. As sympathetic as she'd been in the weeks since Tom's death, his publisher had a schedule, and Matt couldn't afford to forego the advance if they pulled the plug.

Weeks. That's all it had been. Three weeks and two days to be exact, since he'd kissed Tom goodbye. But the sleepless nights and long days doing nothing other than watching the crap on daytime TV had made it feel more like months. He took a pen from his jacket pocket and opened his notebook. Things would get better, he knew that. Humans had always lived with bereavement, and survived. Right now, he had to work, and that too would be another step forward.

He began to write. *Sundays back then were always the same, wherever you happened to be in England. The sixties were in full swing—fuck, it felt like we invented the sixties— but the colour, the music, the noise, seemed only to have the stamina for six days.* Matt lifted his pen and tapped it on his chin. *Sundays were grey and quiet. They were the long exhalation before the sharp intake of breath—*

Fucking Moros.

Matt looked up from the page. Something had bugged him about that. Not at first, not even during the eight days between Tom's death and the funeral. He assumed it'd been delirious death-bed rambling. But since Matt returned home the word had wormed itself into his brain. He'd heard the name long before Tom had mentioned it but couldn't remember where.

Moros. It sounded ancient, and not at all British. The 'os' ending led him to think Greek. As a writer, he'd studied Greek mythology and philosophy, but the name still didn't ring any bells.

He glanced at the couple of sentences he'd managed, then put down his pen and strode between the book aisles. Less than two minutes later he was back in his seat with a heavy tome. Its binding and thickness suggested an air of seriousness about its contents. A quick study of the appendix led him to the page he needed, where he found a paragraph devoted to the name.

Moros was indeed a being from Greek mythology. A demon-god of impending doom whose decree of destiny could never be changed. He was considered omnipresent, omniscient and omnipotent, and was master of the Keres, the bringers of violent death.

'Charming,' Matt muttered. He closed the book and

leaned back in his chair. The logical conclusion was obvious; Tom knew of the myth, possibly through his studies at university, and had conjured an imaginary Moros in his doped-up mind as he was waiting for eternity to take him. Matt had heard of people on their death beds seeing ghosts, angels, and even God—it wasn't unusual. The mind does what it has to when faced with its own mortality.

But still...

An unease gripped Matt despite his dismissal of the name. Something fought to surface from the depths of Matt's memory. Something that happened before the fire. That name. Matt closed his eyes, tried to focus, as the images flashed and merged.

A smoke-filled room. Georgina, Jack, and Vinnie gasping for air. Frankie, his clothes on fire. An ache took hold of the centre of Matt's skull at the fragmented recollection, and he felt his own throat tighten. He kept his eyes shut though, willing the whole memory to reveal itself, knowing that otherwise it might be lost again, possibly forever. His chest heaved, and one final image that lasted no more than a second hit him a moment before he opened his eyes and took a sharp breath.

Matt refused to believe it was a real memory, so strong had his disbelief in the supernatural always been. But the image of an upturned wine glass, moving freely in a never-ending figure of eight on a wooden Ouija board, seemed as real as memories of his mother.

1989—VINNIE

 1

'I WANT A BABY.'

Vinnie half closed his eyes and leaned back in his chair. It always came around to this. 'I know' he said, struggling to keep the weariness from his voice.

'We need to do something.'

'We are. We have been.'

Hannah stared at him across the flickering candle on the table. 'For how many years, Vince?'

Vinnie glanced around the restaurant. 'Come on, we're supposed to be on holiday. This isn't the time.'

'It never is with you.'

He reached across and placed his hand on hers. 'You could be pregnant right now. I wouldn't be surprised if you are—we haven't stopped doing it this week.'

She shook her head, and Vinnie noticed the glisten emerge in her green eyes that he still found as beautiful as he had the day they'd met, despite the lines that now fanned out from their corners. 'It isn't going to happen for us, Vince.'

'You don't know that.'

'I want to adopt.'

Vinnie frowned. It wasn't an option he'd considered before, and he knew in an instant that he hated the idea. 'Give it a little more time.'

'I want a baby now!'

'Shh.' Vinnie saw a couple of heads in the little Venetian restaurant turn their way. 'Not so loud.'

Hannah leaned nearer and lowered her voice. 'Think about it. We have a lovely house, in a nice area, and more money than we know how to spend. We're an adoption agency's wet dream, Vince. We'd go straight to the top of the list.'

'I don't think it's quite that simple.'

Hannah slipped her hand from his. 'I sometimes wonder if you want a baby at all.'

Vinnie ignored the statement and waved at a waiter for the bill. Hannah was right, though he would never admit it. He didn't want a child. He had at first, when the idea was fresh. But unlike everything else in Vinnie's life that he'd grabbed, the fact that he couldn't have a child didn't make him want one all the more. That rule only seemed to count with women, money, and cars.

'Just say you'll think about it. Please.'

'Okay. I'll think about it. There are things we need to consider, though.'

'Like what?'

He nodded at the empty wine bottle. 'The adoption agencies take more than just material things into consideration. We've finished off four of those tonight. And you did three of them.' He saw the pain in Hannah's eyes at that, and felt an equal measure of gladness and shame.

'You bastard,' Hannah barely whispered. Her bottom lip trembled. 'I may be a drunk, but without me you'd be nothing. You were a fucking barrow boy flogging shitty vases when we met. And you're not so innocent yourself—at least alcohol is legal.'

Vinnie felt his face redden. It was true, of course. If he hadn't met Hannah, he would never have landed the job at the city trading firm with her father. But he was good at what he did; he'd repaid David's faith in him a thousand-fold. And so what if he did a little coke to unwind. Who didn't?

'We're both tired. Come on,' he said, 'let's go back to the hotel.'

The Italian sky was a deep plum, dotted with a thousand glistening stars. Vinnie put his arm around his wife as they passed through the narrow-cobbled walkways. Hannah rested her head on his shoulder. 'I hate it when we argue.'

'Me too. It was my fault.' He kissed the top of her head. 'Sorry. I'm an insensitive idiot.'

'I think we're both a little messed up.' Her voice had a slur to it. 'When we get back to London I'm going to quit drinking.'

Vinnie laughed.

'I mean it. We should both take a look at our lives.'

'Hmm.' Vinnie didn't like the sound of that. He had a feeling he wouldn't care too much for what he'd find if he were to scrutinize himself too closely. He'd been there and done that, and had the bills from his shrink to prove it. He didn't want to stand still and meditate, he wanted to keep moving, keep his eyes on the next goal. He'd found that to be the best formula for survival.

They crossed a courtyard with a stone fountain dribbling green lamp-lit water in its centre. A group of teenage boys and girls babbled in their excited Italian voices, flirting and laughing with each other.

'This is a lovely place,' Hannah said. She gazed at the youngsters as they passed. 'I wish I was still young and attractive.'

'You're thirty-four. That's hardly ancient.' They passed from the square into an alley with overhanging balconies that led onto a hump-backed bridge. Vinnie stopped at its mid-point and looked down into the canal, which was black and smooth as glass. 'And you're more than attractive. You're beautiful.'

Hannah kissed him on his cheek. 'Thanks. Even if you are just saying it.'

Vinnie wasn't just saying it. She was stunning, and of all the women he'd been involved with, Hannah was the only one he'd ever truly loved, even if he had lost count of the times he'd cheated on her. He moved his thoughts away from that before the self-loathing could get a grip, as it often did, and leaned his elbows on the bridge's ornate stone coping. Hannah clung to his arm as he gazed down into the deep, liquid darkness, and he shuddered at the thought of how inviting it looked.

2

'How was Venice?'

'Great.' Vinnie took the offered whisky glass from David. They were in the relative cool of the kitchen, and Vinnie looked through the window at the guests in David's garden which was the size of a field, its tended grass and flowers resembling the idea of a perfect landscape straight out of a centre-spread from *Country Life*. He returned his attention to his father-in-law and raised his glass. 'Happy anniversary.' He took a swig.

'Thanks.'

'How's the Erikson account? Any breakthroughs?'

'There's a meeting on Thursday. But let's not talk about work today.' David smiled, though Vinnie noticed a nervousness in place of its usual warmth. Vinnie had always found him to be an unassuming, likeable man—a pair of traits that made him something of an oddity in the world of high finance.

'Is everything okay, David?'

'Yes, yes, of course. I just wanted to have a little chat.'

Vinnie felt a flutter in his stomach as he tried to think of what shameful little secret David might have become aware of, but there were just too many in both his work and his private life. David was old-school, as straight as they came, and Vinnie knew that if he were to become aware of the unethical—not to mention illegal—methods that Vinnie occasionally used to gain trading information, the shit would hit the fan. As it was, he considered Vinnie a natural talent at making profit with other peoples' money. Vinnie felt no particular guilt at this. He considered himself part of a new generation of dealers, ones who knew what it took to be the best.

He looked at David with the open, honest expression of a man who had never sinned. 'What about?' he asked.

'Well, Audrey and I were wondering if you and Hannah were still trying for a baby.'

Vinnie raised his eyebrows.

'Not that it's any of our business, of course,' David quickly added. 'It's just we've noticed, well I should say Audrey has, that Hannah seems a little down lately.'

Vinnie felt a surge of anger, though not so much at David. It was Audrey who was behind this intrusion, poking her fucking stuck-up nose where it wasn't wanted. He saw David's face; the expression on it betrayed his realisation that he'd broached a sensitive subject.

'Vinnie, I'm sorry,' he said. 'I shouldn't have brought it up. Bloody stupid of me.' He patted Vinnie's shoulder. 'Come on. Let's go outside.'

'I'll be out in a minute. I need the bathroom.' He watched David leave the kitchen, and saw him through the window, shaking hands with guests as he made his way across the manicured lawn to Audrey, who was talking with a small group outside the canvas marquee with the banner HAPPY 30TH ANNIVERSARY printed in big letters above its entrance. David spoke in her ear and she glanced at the house. 'Fucking bitch,' Vinnie muttered.

Up in the bathroom he locked the door and pulled the open window on its hinge so that only an inch gap existed. He didn't need this. Hassle from Hannah for a baby he didn't seem capable of providing, Audrey getting involved for reasons of her own. He pulled a little bag of white powder from his pocket and sprinkled a line on the porcelain lid of the toilet cistern before inhaling it through a banknote with a greed that seemed insatiable of late.

113

He sat on the edge of the bath, closed his eyes and thought of David. David had never done anybody any harm. He'd worked hard for years, amassed a fortune with an honest integrity, given his wife and daughter the best of everything. And when Hannah had become serious about Vinnie he'd welcomed him into his home and business like a son.

You know your trouble? You don't know what you want, so you grab everything.

Someone had accused him of that a long time ago. Perhaps it deserved to be inscribed on his gravestone.

Vinnie felt sick at his betrayal. He constantly swore he'd change, but it never stuck. And worst of all, for the past two years, Vinnie had repaid David's kindness by screwing his wife whenever he had the chance.

3

'This is more like it!'

'Yeah,' Vinnie said. He looked at the sweating bodies jerking on the dance floor, hands held in the air. He felt out of place; most of them were in their early twenties and spaced out on ecstasy. He should never have let Giles bring him here—it was after two a.m. and he'd already had a skinful. Hannah would be tucked up and warm in bed and he had a longing to be there with her instead of inside this shithole, which was no more than the converted space under an old train arch. A creeping uneasiness had already taken over him when they'd pulled up in the taxi and he'd recognised the area; they were a couple of streets away from where Jack's girlfriend Kate had lived.

Oh, Jack. I'm sorry. The years receded to the night of the car crash, and he saw Kate's car as she pulled away from his place, unaware of the dark figure sitting behind her. But there had been someone there, and all this time Vinnie had said nothing. He felt the fear like it was yesterday. But what could he have said? How could he ever explain to Jack why Kate had been at his apartment that night, and why she had stormed off in a rage?

Giles nudged him. 'I'll be back in a minute.'

Vinnie watched the dancers under the red light that throbbed in time with the driving beat of the acid house music. He didn't get it—every tune sounded the fucking same. The throng on the dance floor moved as one hyper-fast beast to the track that was playing, apart from a fair-haired girl who seemed to be grooving slowly to her own tune. She glanced his way, saw she was being watched, and smiled. The pupils in her eyes were like two black plates. Vinnie smiled back, and she danced her way from the crowd until she stood before him.

'You're a bit overdressed for this place,' she said.

'Yeah, I feel it.' Vinnie looked down at his suit. What had started as a business lunch that afternoon had escalated into an ugly pub crawl, with himself and Giles the only survivors. The girl was young and lithe, and dressed in the faded jeans and loose t-shirt that seemed to be the uniform of the rave scene.

'What's your name?'

'Vinnie.'

She smiled. 'My name's Fran.'

'How old are you, Fran?'

'Twenty-three. Is that a problem?'

'Yes. You make me feel like a bloody dinosaur.'

'You look like a fucking bank manager to me.' She touched the tip of a long red-painted fingernail to Vinnie's temple and ran it down his jaw line to his chin. 'A very naughty bank manager.' She laughed. 'Have you done any acid?'

Vinnie shook his head. He'd dabbled with ecstasy a couple of times and did coke almost on a daily basis, but he had reservations about LSD.

115

'This is your lucky night, then.' She stepped close so that their bodies were touching and glanced around. 'Come with me.' She grabbed his hand and led him toward the fire exit. He looked around for Giles, but he was dancing like a fool and was oblivious to Vinnie as he followed Fran into a narrow corridor with black painted walls.

'This'll do,' she said. They had the walkway to themselves, and she pulled a little tin from her denim pocket. Vinnie understood at once that she was a dealer. She opened the lid and pulled out a tiny square of paper which she balanced on her fingertip. Vinnie squinted at it, and saw it was adorned with a yellow smiley face. 'This is new stuff,' she said. 'It's out of this world.'

'How much?' Vinnie asked.

She studied him. 'A tenner, usually. But I like you. This one's on me.'

Vinnie held his hand out.

'No,' she said, and moved his hand away. 'Like this.' She placed the spot of paper on the tip of her tongue, grabbed either side of Vinnie's head and pulled him towards her. Vinnie felt a warm, soft wetness in the corner of his left eyeball. She leaned back and studied him. 'Just relax and let it dissolve. Most people put it in their mouth, but it goes to your brain quicker this way.' She held his eye open with her fingers for a few seconds. 'That's it; all gone.'

'What now?'

'Now we go fucking mental.'

In what felt like the next instant, with no sense of how he got there, Vinnie was on the dance floor, punching his hands in the air and yelling along to the music. He felt a tap on his shoulder.

'Fucking hell mate,' Giles shouted over the beat, 'what the fuck are you on?' He laughed like a hyena and Vinnie joined in, lifting his face up and howling at the ceiling. He lowered his head and saw Fran, jumping up and down in front of him, the nipples of her small breasts visible through her sweat soaked t-shirt. Strobe lights turned the packed room into a black and white stop-motion movie, and Vinnie felt Fran's body against his, grinding her pelvis into his hard on.

'What the fuck?' It was quiet, the thumping music gone, though his eardrums buzzed from the thrashing they'd taken. He was sitting down, though the seat he was on had a gentle, rocking motion. He felt warmth against his right arm and saw Fran leaning on him.

'The next block's ours,' she said, and Vinnie followed her gaze forward to the man she was talking to, in the driver's seat of the taxi.

Vinnie looked out of his window and drew his breath in. The road they were travelling over was thirty feet beneath them. He could see onto the roofs of parked cars, and flinched as the top protrusion of a lamp post missed the back tire on his side by an inch.

'What the fuck?' he repeated, and remembered in a flash the little square of acid he'd taken. He was tripping, though it seemed clearer than reality itself. 'We're flying,' he said, and smiled at the wonder of it.

'I told you it was good stuff,' Fran whispered in his ear.

A breeze blew around his legs and up against his bare arse and spine. He looked down, patted his naked body as if to confirm it belonged to him. He was standing in a dim room, cool air blowing at him through the open window at his back, though he was sure it was just a moment ago that he was fully clothed in the back of the taxi-cab. A bitter taste, one that he almost recognised, filled his mouth. He heard a noise, quiet sobs, from down low in the far corner of the room. Fran was there, on a mattress, hugging her knees to her bare, white body.

Vinnie felt unnerved, and tried to remember what had occurred. 'What's wrong? Why are you crying?'

'You bit me, you fucking animal.'

He raised the back of his hand to his lips and wiped at the thick wetness there. *Blood. It's blood I can taste.*

'Shit. Sorry. It's that fucking acid you gave me—I don't know what the fuck's going on.' He took a step forward. 'Is it bad?'

Fran lowered her knees and straightened her legs to reveal a deep oval gash on the inner thigh of her left leg, a flap of shredded skin hanging from one corner of the injury. Blood oozed down onto the mattress where it began to spread like a dark rose unfolding its petals.

'Jesus, you need to go to hospital.' A wave of thoughts washed through Vinnie's mind in a millisecond, most of them concerning either Hannah or the police. 'We'll call a cab. I'll look after you; I've got money, lots of money.'

Or I could just do a runner. She doesn't know who I am. I only told her my first name.

Fran let her head drop back against the wall behind as her sobs turned to a painful laughter. 'You fucking yuppie idiot. We were having a good screw until you spoiled it.'

Vinnie glanced around for his clothes. 'We've got to get you to A and E—say a dog bit you or something.'

'I've got a better idea. Let me bite you back and we'll call it quits.'

'What?' He looked at Fran, who emitted an agonised grunt as she raised herself upright. 'Are you serious?'

'Would you rather I told the police?'

'No. But bite me back? It's mental.'

She limped forward a step. 'You did it. I want to know how it feels.'

Vinnie raised his palms. 'Look, if you want to make a deal, let's talk. I'll give you a grand, cash, in the morning.'

She shook her head and continued towards him.

'How much do you want?'

'What's your limit?'

Vinnie felt the cold wood of the windowsill against his arse and realised he'd been backing away from Fran, about whom he'd come to a major conclusion: she was a fucking nutcase. He was used to dealing with all types in his professional life and knew at once that she was not the sort to haggle with. He'd have to swallow his medicine and go in big. 'Three thousand pounds. And I ain't fucking about. It's yours if I walk out of here with no comebacks.' His eyes wandered to the bite mark he'd left, the blood dribbling down past her knee to her ankle.

'I don't need money.' She stopped a couple of paces away. 'So how about it?'

He looked into her eyes, hoping for a sign that she was having some fun at his expense.

She's just trying to scare me. Any moment now she'll laugh and ramp my offer up another couple of grand.

Fran cocked her head and licked her lips. 'I want to bite you.'

She made it sound almost sensuous and Vinnie thought, *how bad can it be? One bite and it's all over.* 'Where?' he heard himself ask, as if detached from his own voice.

She looked him up and down. 'On your cock.'

Vinnie's hands instinctively covered his genitals as Fran laughed at him. 'If you could see your face,' she snickered. 'No. Your chest will do. You have a nice chest.'

Vinnie felt his pulse throb in his ears, and noticed the walls bending in at their midpoint in time with his heartbeat. *Fucking acid. Never doing that shit again.* He looked at Fran who had stepped closer and felt a sudden twinge of arousal. *Yeah, let her bite me. Let her bite me as I thrust myself inside her.* 'One bite,' he said.

Her mouth stretched into a grin. 'This is going to hurt.'

4

'Oy, sleeping beauty. Put these on.'

White light, painful and pure, attacked Vinnie's eyeballs through the slit of his half-opened lids. The single shaft of sunshine that hit on his face cut a diagonal path from a window high in the wall at the foot of his bed. He pulled the rough blanket tight around his shivering cold body and looked at the man in the doorway, who threw a bunch of folded clothes and a pair of training shoes at him. It took only a moment to recognise the man's uniform, and the fact that he had woken in a prison cell.

'Your wife's here.' The policeman chuckled. 'She don't look too happy.'

Vinnie sat up and felt a thud in his head as if it had been hit from the inside with a knuckle-duster. 'How did I get here?' he groaned.

'In the back of one of our vans. They spotted you running down the middle of the Old Kent Road stark bollock naked.' The copper laughed again. 'I don't think your missus will be letting you out for a while.'

'Have I been charged with anything?'

'Yeah, being a plonker. Now get dressed and get out of here. I'm too busy for drunks this morning.'

Vinnie put his clothes on and followed the policeman out and along a corridor through a pair of locked doors to the front desk, where Hannah was waiting. The copper was right; she looked furious. She turned and led him from the station to her car, her lips pulled tight.

'You are something else,' she spat as she sat in the driver's seat.

'Sorry.'

'That's all I ever hear from you, Vinnie. It's getting old. *You* are getting old.' She turned her face to him at last. 'You're thirty-five, Vinnie. I did not plan on having to pick my husband up from police stations because he's been caught streaking in the early hours at this stage of my life. Lucky for you, they thought you were just pissed.'

'I was. I'd been drinking all day with Giles.'

'Really? And what else were you on? Cocaine? Ecstasy?' She started the engine and floored the accelerator with an anger that pushed Vinnie back into his seat.

'Maybe a little coke,' Vinnie murmured. *And something else.* A sudden image came to him of being on a dance floor, a girl grinding her body into his. *A little yellow smiley face, slicked onto my eyeball by the girl's tongue.*

A smiley face . . .

'I've had enough, Vinnie. You have to give it up. The drugs, the girls, everything. Or it's over.'

Vinnie looked at Hannah, the tears on her cheeks. He opened his mouth to apologise again, but stopped himself. He was sick of apologising. He was sick of being him. Neither of them uttered a single word for the rest of the journey home.

5

Vinnie read through the figures again. Something was wrong. 'Shit,' he muttered. He spun his chair and looked out of his office window at the Thames. *Eight hundred grand up the fucking Swannee.*

He had to think fast. There was a meeting in thirty minutes in Potter's office and he needed an explanation. He'd fucked up big-time, buying a load of stock on the say-so of his insider at the Future Finances Exchange. The tips he'd gotten from the man before had always paid off, but it would open one titanic can of shit if he had to explain why he'd bought a load of shares that the arse had fallen out of overnight. And Giles, who was in on it with him, would throw him to the dogs to save himself if he got wind of it.

Vinnie turned back to his desk and looked again at the sheet. By its side, in a thick black folder, sat the Erikson file. It was David's baby, though Vinnie had lent a hand. He opened it and flicked through the two hundred plus pages— a complication of shares, insurances, and bonds that David had put eight months into. He glanced back at his balance sheet. *Nobody has seen it yet. Nobody knows but me.* He tore it to pieces, dropped it in the wastebasket, and typed another without the loss.

People owe me favours. It's time to pull them in. He picked up the phone and made four phone calls. He'd have to do some paperwork later to cover his arse, but for now he was safe. His balance sheet wouldn't be questioned. The eight hundred grand loss, if it ever came to light, would be accredited to the Erikson account.

Three quick raps sounded on the oak of his office door and Giles let himself in. He was slipping his pin-striped jacket on over his red braces. 'Meeting's in five.' He frowned. 'You okay?'

Vinnie closed the cover on the Erikson file and pushed it away. 'Yeah, everything's fine.'

Giles smiled and lowered his voice. 'That was some night on Friday. What did you think of the Rave at the Cave?'

'It made me feel a little old, to tell the truth.' Vinnie stood and lifted his own jacket from the cast-iron, custom-made coat stand that cost more than the average family car and avoided eye contact with his colleague. Giles was unaware that the night had ended for Vinnie in a police cell.

'Really?' Giles laughed. 'You could have fooled me. So, did you shag that little tart you went home with?'

Vinnie stopped with one arm in the jacket's sleeve. He had no memory of anything between taking the LSD—*from Fran, her name was Fran*—and waking in the police station. The weekend had been hell, Hannah ignoring him for the most part while he racked his brain trying to remember what had happened. *I did go back to her place, and I shagged her.*

'No,' Vinnie said, 'I dropped her off and went home.'

I want to bite you.

'Oh.' An expression of disappointment crossed Giles' face. 'Are you sure you're okay? You don't look too well.'

'Yes.' Vinnie took a deep breath and felt his knees weaken at the sudden flashback of memories. 'Go on ahead. I'm right behind you.'

Giles backed out of the room, his brow creased in a frown. 'Don't be long. Old Potter hates tardiness.'

Vinnie dropped onto the soft leather of his chair when Giles had gone. 'Fuck,' he whispered. 'Shit.'

The room was dim, a mattress on the floor, and he'd bitten her, though he couldn't remember doing it, and had said she could bite him in return. The girl had her fingers laced around the nape of his neck at arm's length, and she'd opened her sweet little mouth. And it had opened, and opened, down on its hinge like an anaconda's about to swallow its prey. Moonlight from the window at his back glistened off her teeth that were sharp and long, and she'd darted her black pointed tongue out between them.

Vinnie shook his head at the images. They couldn't be true; they had to be a hallucination.

He'd screamed, and grabbed her throat as her jaws snapped shut inches from his face, and he'd swung her, thrown her, and . . .

'No, no, no,' Vinnie groaned and held his head in his hands.

The puddle had spread fast, gushing from the back of her head into her blonde hair that was fanned out around her on the floorboards like a halo, and her eyes were staring and dead, and he'd screamed again, and ran from the house, and ran and ran.

'No. No way.' Vinnie stood and straightened his tie. It had happened in his mind; a bad trip. He refused to believe he had killed the girl. He grabbed his paperwork from the table and left for the meeting, his heart thumping so hard he feared it might explode.

6

'What's that you're reading?'

'Hm?' Vinnie glanced up from his newspaper at Hannah. 'Oh.' He lifted it to show her the cover.

'The South London Press? Why are you reading that?'

'I'm looking at the property section.' It was a fiction he'd already prepared—he had learned years before that every good liar has a cover story. In the three weeks since his encounter with the girl named Fran, he'd scoured every national and local rag for a report on the discovery of her body. To his relief, he'd found nothing, and was at last willing to let himself believe that her death had been an illusion. He'd gone back to her place, sure, and he'd had sex with her. Maybe he had even bitten her, though that was not his scene at all. But he hadn't killed her; the body would have been discovered by now. He hoped.

'Oh, don't say you want to move, Vince. We've just got this place the way I like it.'

'No, I like it here too. I'm just looking at investment opportunities.'

She smiled. 'I'm glad you took today off. And I appreciate what you're doing.' She reached across the breakfast table and touched the back of his hand. Vinnie put down the newspaper and interlaced his fingers with hers. They'd booked an appointment with an IVF specialist for that afternoon. 'Life could be good now, Vince, for both of us. We just have to grow up a little.'

'I know. I'm trying.' He returned her smile. It was true— he was determined to make changes. He'd laid off the coke and sworn off other women, though he knew that might prove a little tougher. The ease with which he'd dropped the cocaine had come as a surprise. He'd had no cravings that he couldn't handle, and just thinking of that night out in south London was motivation enough to stay clean. Hannah had done her part as well; she'd poured every drop of booze in the house down the sink with Vinnie as witness and he'd done the same, retrieving his drug stash from its hiding place in the laundry room and flushing it down the toilet.

'Coffee?' Hannah stood and crossed to the worktop. The telephone chirped and Vinnie pushed his chair back. 'I'll get it,' Hannah said. She crossed to the wall phone and lifted the receiver.

'Hello? Oh, hi, Dad.' She listened. 'Yes.' She looked at Vinnie. 'He's right here. Is everything okay?' A pause. 'Good. Love you, too. Here's Vince.'

Vinnie took the phone with a sense of apprehension, the expression on his wife's face telling him that something wasn't quite right. 'Hello, David.'

'Hello, Vinnie. Can you talk?'

'Yes, certainly.' He noted a hint of panic in David's voice.

'I'm presenting the Erikson account this morning. I think I've made a terrible mistake.'

'What do you mean?'

'The figures don't add up. I've gone over them all morning, Vinnie. I've underestimated on some purchase prices—God knows how, and the account has made a loss. Eight hundred thousand.'

'Look, don't panic. It sounds like a lot, I know, but the firm's had worse days on the stock exchange.'

'I know, but it's the exact opposite of what 1 told them yesterday. It looks bad. It isn't a great deal to Erikson, I know, but it's all about confidence. If he doesn't trust us with his money and pulls out, we'll lose millions in the long term.'

'Look, calm down, David. I'll come in right now and have a look with you, see if we can sort something out.' He exchanged a look with Hannah, who gave him a nod of approval.

'Thanks, Vinnie, but there's nothing you can do. I just wanted to warn you, and let you know that I take full responsibility for this. I know you've helped me out a bit on this one but this error has nothing to do with you.' David's voice softened. 'You've been like a son to me, Vinnie. I won't drag you down with me because of my own stupid mistake.'

The line went quiet and he heard David speak to somebody in his office. 'I have to go now, Vinnie. I'll see you later.'

Vinnie replaced the receiver.

'What's wrong? Is Dad okay?'

'He's in a bit of a spot. I have to go in.' Vinnie glanced at his watch. 'The hospital appointment's at three. I'll be back here by noon, I promise.'

She kissed his cheek. 'Just go. Please, whatever's going on, help Dad sort it out.'

Vinnie opted for the Porsche 911 over his other two cars, as if its engine could get him there any quicker in the London traffic. Not that he believed there was anything he could do now, anyway. His action was no more than a gesture; he had no intention of admitting to something that would cost him his career, and maybe even his liberty.

By the time Vinnie arrived at the office, David's meeting was over, and he'd resigned to save himself and the company the embarrassment of firing him.

7

'We've been watching you for a while.'

'Really?' Vinnie looked from Potter to the other board members around the big oval table.

'Yes,' Potter said. 'And we like what we see. You know how to get results.'

Vinnie tried to suppress the relief from showing on his face. 'Thanks.'

Potter leaned back and studied him. 'Bad business with your father-in-law last week. Shame he had to go.' He let the sentence hang in the air, and Vinnie felt like a germ under a biologist's magnifying glass.

'He's a good man,' Vinnie said into the silence. 'Despite what happened, I have no doubt of his integrity.'

'Hm.' Potter shrugged his shoulders. 'Maybe. Your loyalty

is understandable, but life moves on. Business moves on.' He leaned his elbows on the walnut table. 'Are you ready to move on, Vincent?'

'Of course.'

'Good.' Potter stretched his lips in a small predatory smile. 'How would you feel about taking over David's position?'

'I'd be honoured.'

'And your family? Does David's possible reaction to this news worry you at all?'

'I'm positive of his support, as I am of my wife's.' It was true. He knew David would want him to take the job, and whatever was okay with David was always okay with Hannah. Audrey would be the one spitting blood.

'Good. We'll formalise the contract tomorrow. Congratulations.' The other board members echoed his sentiment. 'You may as well go and make yourself at home in your new office.'

Vinnie shook each director's hand and made his way to his new desk which was twice the size of his former one in a room three times as big.

It was 1989, and for men like Vinnie, everything was getting bigger.

2001—GEORGINA

1

GEORGINA SWITCHED OFF the engine and scanned the case notes one more time, though she had scrutinized every page the night before. A mother and daughter, Linda and Carly Howard. The mother, forty-five, with an alcohol problem and previous convictions for soliciting. Claimed she was "out of the game" now, though Georgina's predecessor suspected she was using her home as a private brothel. The daughter, thirteen, was a truant who'd missed as much school as she'd attended in the past year. Her teachers described her as a bright, friendly girl—when she was there.

Georgina looked through the windscreen at the high, grey concreted block of flats where they lived and wondered what whiz kid architect of the sixties had thought building rakes of them across London for council tenants was a good idea. *Probably one who'd gone to Cambridge and lived in a country house with no neighbours for a mile.*

She locked the car and noticed a group of teenage boys with their hoods pulled up over their heads watching her from a bridged walkway that joined two identical shabby buildings. She was glad that her car was so old that the notion of stealing it would be laughable to any potential car-thieves. Stereotypical, she knew, but that was how it went around here. Most of the kids were good, with aspirations for a better life, but some of them were bitter about their circumstances and took what they could grab, whether it was theirs or not.

She'd worked with scores of youngsters like that, and when she had gotten to know them she'd found that the roots of their frustrations were always similar: they lacked attention, love, and opportunity.

The lift, to Georgina's relief, was working, but as she stepped inside and pressed the button for the ninth floor she gagged at the stench of urine and saw the puddle in one corner as the doors closed her inside. Graffiti covered the walls—tags and profanities and a red spray-painted portrayal of a cock and balls, probably three feet long. The elevator creaked its way upwards and she gasped for air that was only a little fresher as it opened for her onto the ninth-floor landing. The Howards' apartment was one of four, and she pushed the button to one side of the metal safety door.

'Who is it?'

The voice was harsh, aggressive, and Georgina held the identity badge she wore around her neck up to the spy-hole. 'Georgina Smith, social services.'

She heard grumbling littered with swear words from the other side.

'Mrs. Howard? I have an appointment.'

The rattle of latches being undone echoed in the dim landing and the door opened. A woman with peroxide hair that greyed at the roots looked her up and down. Her face was thin, her eyes sunken and dark rimmed, and though she was two years younger than Georgina, she could have passed for being a decade older. The smell of alcohol emanated from her. 'Better come in then.'

Georgina followed her through the short hallway, stepping over the shoes that covered the floor in a haphazard pattern. The early afternoon sun failed to bring any brightness to the living room, every surface of which was almost hidden by the detritus of discarded cigarette packets, beer cans, and unwashed plates and mugs. The only object in the room with any colour or potential for joy was an old acoustic guitar propped in one corner, its yellow-painted surface faded in areas so that the light wood had shown through.

The woman sat in an armchair in front of the long window, lit a cigarette, and studied Georgina. *Shark eyes*, Georgina thought as she lowered herself onto the couch opposite.

'Mrs. Howard—may I call you Linda?'

The woman shrugged. 'What else you gonna call me, Cindy Crawford?'

'My name's Georgina.' She attempted a small smile. 'I'll be taking over for Robin Lange and working with you and your daughter. Is Carly here today?'

'No, course not. It's a school day, ain't it?'

Georgina had checked with Carly's school that morning— she was absent for the third day running. 'Well, that's one of the things we need to discuss.'

Linda laughed. 'Just one of the things?' She pointed at the folder on Georgina's lap. 'What we got to talk about? You know everything about us. I'm a bad mother who's always pissed and can't look after my own daughter.'

'I'm not here to judge you, Linda. I'm here to help you, if you'll let me.'

The woman tilted her head back and exhaled a long plume of smoke. 'Heard it all before, love.'

Georgina studied her. 'Okay. Tell me something I might be able to help you with. Something that will ease your situation.'

'You could nip down the offy and get me a bottle of scotch. I'm skint until my giro comes.'

'I'm not sure that's a good idea.' Georgina glanced over her shoulder through the open door of the kitchen. 'Have you enough food, until you're paid?'

'Yeah. I never let Carly go hungry, if that's what you're thinking.' She squinted through the cloud of smoke around her head. 'There is one thing. You could help me get out of this shit-hole. The council won't give me a transfer.'

'Do you think a different environment would enhance your life?'

'Yeah.'

'There's nothing in your notes about wanting a move. Empty properties are a rarity—you would need a very good reason.'

'If we moved, I could give up drinking.' She stared at Georgina and spoke for the first time in a voice that was earnest. 'I ain't joking. I know I could.'

Georgina opened the folder to a clean sheet, scribbled a few notes, and glanced up at Linda. 'And what is it about this place that makes you feel the need to drink?' It was a stupid question, she knew. Who could live in a place like this without feeling the need for some form of escape?

'It's haunted.'

Georgina blinked, and thought how comical she must look. 'Haunted?'

'Yeah, fucking haunted.' Linda sucked on her cigarette and Georgina noticed her bottom lip begin to tremble. 'There's a ghost or something. It throws things about.'

'I see. It might be hard to convince the council—'

'But that's not the worst of it,' Linda said. 'Sometimes, it gets inside Carly, like in that fucking film.' The tears came then, in deep, hiccupping sobs. 'I'm scared,' she said. 'For both of us.'

2

'Have you spoken to Michael since we last talked?'

Georgina shook her head.

Doctor Sinclair narrowed her eyes, but not in an unfriendly way. 'You told me that you would try to discuss some things with him.'

'I wanted to.' Georgina sighed and looked away from the doctor. 'It's hard. Never seems to be the right moment. I planned to, just the other night. But I couldn't.'

'Are you afraid of talking about your problems with him?'

'I'm afraid of what he'll think.'

The psychiatrist held Georgina's gaze, waiting for more. After a minute of silence between them, it was the doctor who spoke. 'But you think he is aware of the fact that you self-harm.'

'I know he is. He came home one time, a couple of years ago. I was in the bathroom. I made some excuse about an accident with scissors, but he knew. He's a paramedic, so he's pretty much seen it all.'

'And he didn't confront you, after?'

'No.' Georgina looked down at her lap. 'He dressed my wounds. Then he just put his arms around me and said he loved me. We never spoke of it again.'

'How did that make you feel?'

'Ashamed.'

3

'Oh no, not Britney.' Georgina glanced at the radio. 'Please turn it off before my ears explode.'

Michael reached for the dial. 'They don't make songs like they used to.'

'I know. Give me Marvin anytime.'

The crackle of static filled the car. 'Bad reception 'round here.'

Georgina slowed at a crossroads in the country lane and turned left. 'God, we sound like a couple of old farts.'

A man's voice broke through and welcomed his audience to Radio Kent before spinning an old sixties disc, *Those Were the Days*. 'Were they?' Michael mused.

'For some. Not so much for others.' A brief memory fluttered through Georgina's mind of a girl with a yellow guitar singing that same song as she watched her from the window of her student digs in Canterbury.

132

And Declan was there.

Georgina shuddered—she hadn't thought of that creep in years. She accelerated away from his memory along the bush-lined lane that narrowed and twisted for a couple of miles before opening again onto a wide, raised road that overlooked pastures on both sides. A thick, black plume of smoke swirled from behind a farm's outbuildings a quarter of a mile away on Michael's side. 'Jesus Christ,' he said. 'What a waste.'

Georgina sighed. It wasn't the first livestock bonfire they'd seen on their journey from London, and according to the incessant media reports it would be the same across the whole of the country. The foot and mouth epidemic had spread with cruel speed and the government had deemed a nationwide cull to be the only solution.

'Is it me,' she said, 'or is everything getting shittier and shittier?'

They crossed a roundabout, and Georgina saw the old wooden road sign that had been there for as long as she could remember, though she hadn't seen it in more than twenty years: *Doom, 5 miles.*

'It must seem strange, going back home after all this time,' Michael said.

'No. I feel nothing actually.' It was true. There was no sense of nostalgia, or trepidation. She was as numb to her homecoming as she had been to her father's death when she'd heard the news three weeks before. She hadn't attended the funeral—nor had she her mother's back in 1993. When Georgina had walked out of that house for the last time, hand in hand with Michael, she'd made her decision: her future was with the big American, who had shown her love and respect from the very start, not that pair of unfeeling bastards who were supposed to be her parents.

They took the Durling bypass, a road new to Georgina, and within minutes they entered Doom. She slowed the car as they passed the village green where two teenage boys were kicking a football back and forth, watched by a pair of girls sitting on the bench. A band of pointed reeds edged the pond and a raised bed of multi-coloured flowers faced the road in an arrangement that spelt WELCOME TO DOOM.

They drove by the Green Man and along the little row of shops, of which only the post office and the paper shop remained from her last visit. The general store was now an estate agents office and the greengrocer's and butcher's shops had been knocked through to create a mini-market.

'Everything seems so much smaller than I remember.'

They took a left at the corner and less than a minute later they were parked at her parents' house.

Only it's not their house anymore. It's mine.

She killed the engine and looked through her windscreen at the dull net curtains.

'You okay?' Michael placed a gentle hand on her knee.

'Yes. Come on.'

The house hadn't changed; it was as grey as it ever was, as if the sombreness of her parents had been absorbed into the bricks and plaster. 'Jesus,' Michael said, looking at the walls. 'Didn't they know what the hell a paintbrush is?'

'No. They were a pair of fucking idiots.' It felt empowering to swear in that shabby house, to insult her mother and father. She led Michael through the downstairs to the little back room where she'd spent countless Friday nights listening to the drivel of her father's Bible readings and wondered how she'd ever endured it. There were times, she remembered, when she'd come close to pushing the shard of glass she used just a little deeper into the flesh of her wrists. 'This was my dad's church.'

Michael whistled and raised his eyebrows. 'Boy. It sure as hell ain't no St. Paul's Cathedral.'

'I'll show you my bedroom.' They walked up the creaking staircase and crossed to the open door at the end of the landing. 'This is it.' She watched Michael's face as he examined the room, which was furnished with just a single bed and a wardrobe. The paper on the walls had peeled and turned up at the bottom edges and the floorboards were bare.

'This is where you slept?'

'Yes. It's exactly as it was.' She felt Michael's big arm slip around her shoulder, and for the first time since her homecoming, Georgina felt something—a deep, gut wrenching sadness for the little girl that had managed to survive the insanity of this shitty little two-bedroomed house.

'Oh, baby,' was all Michael could say, and Georgina heard the emotion choked back in his throat, and loved him for it.

'Things happened in this room.' She looked up into her husband's dark eyes. 'Things I haven't told you.'

'Hey, it's okay. Whatever happened, it's over now. You don't have to tell me anything if you don't want to.'

'I do. I don't want any secrets between us.' She thought of Michael's experiences in Vietnam. It hadn't been easy for him to discuss—the information had been drip fed to her bit by bit over the course of twenty-seven years, and she still wasn't sure if she'd heard it all. But she empathised with the feelings of guilt and shame, even if it was misplaced, that were just below the surface of his words on the rare occasions he did talk about it.

Georgina walked around the bed, crouched, and slipped her fingers under the loose floorboard. It came away from the joist beneath with no resistance. She sat on the old mattress and looked down into her little hiding place. 'My father thought I was possessed by a demon. He tied me spread-eagled to this bed for a week.'

'Oh, Georgina. I'm so sorry, baby.' He came and sat by her and held her hand. 'What about your mum?'

'She did all she could to help him.' She remembered her mother's face, hard and unflinching, as Georgina begged her to be set free. 'If anything, she was worse. I think my dad actually believed what he preached—he was crazy enough. But that fucking bitch could have saved me.' She wiped the cuff of her sleeve across her eyes. 'And there were others in on it too.'

Michael shook his head. 'I know the way it goes. One sick fuck's idea of the right thing to do can become a policy for his followers pretty damn quick. So how many were there?'

'Mum, Dad, Mr. and Mrs. Hargreaves from next door.' She lowered her voice. 'And Mr. Poole, the butcher.'

'Do any of these guys still live in Doom?'

Georgina shook her head. 'The Hargreaves moved away years ago. Mr. Poole dropped dead from heart failure in the eighties.' She ran a finger down the faded wood of one bedpost. 'They tied my wrists and ankles to these. They gagged me, and sat around saying prayers. Dad called it an exorcism.'

'For a week? Did they feed you?'

'Mum would prop my head and feed me soup once a day, and water. They didn't let me go to the toilet. I had to lie in my own piss and shit. They told school and my friends that I was ill. By the time they released me I really was. It took another week to recover.' She looked at Michael and saw the muscles in his jaw flex. 'Sometimes, Mr. Poole managed to hang back for a few seconds, on his own. He'd tell me he was going to return in the middle of the night and chop my feet off, or cut my tongue out. I was terrified—I'd stay awake every night. He didn't come. He just liked getting off on scaring me. I tried to tell my Dad when he removed my gag one time, but he called me an evil liar.'

'Did you tell anybody about it after?'

'No. I was ashamed.' Georgina clasped her fingers together to stop the tremble in her hands. 'What kid wants the world to know her parents are a pair of weirdos? If my teacher, Miss Simpkins, were there when I returned to school, I might have said something. But she was dead by then.'

'You told me about her before. Murdered, right?'

'Yes. And that's the worst part. Her body was found in the

woods and we heard rumours, sometime after, that her hands and feet had been removed.' Georgina's voice lowered. 'And I said nothing.'

'What could you say?'

'I could have gone to the police and told them that Mr. Poole was a psycho, and that I believed he killed Miss Simpkins. But I never did. I was a coward. And every time I saw that bastard, he smiled as if we were the best of friends. I've had to live with that ever since.'

'Hey, you can't know that it was him. You're not to blame for anything, Georgina. You were just a child. An abused child. You were the only innocent one in all that happened here. And that bastard Poole is long dead now.'

'I know he is. And I'm not a child any more. But whenever I think of him I turn back into that terrified little girl.' She swallowed and lowered her gaze. 'There was something else he said. And it haunts me.'

'What is it?'

She looked into the dark eyes of the man she loved more than she thought possible. 'He told me that I was cursed. That everybody I ever loved in my life would suffer. He said I would watch them die in agony.'

'He was a sick son of a bitch, Honey. Forget him. Forget everything he said.'

Georgina leaned her head on his shoulder. 'I'm glad I told you. I've been afraid of telling you for so long. Afraid of what you'd think.'

He kissed the top of her head. 'I'll tell you what I think. I think you're the best thing that's ever happened to me. I also think you're the kindest, warmest person I know.' He stood up. 'Come on,' he said. 'We can't sleep here tonight.'

Georgina rose early the next morning and made coffee while Michael was still asleep, the white sheets wrapped around his long legs as he snored gently. She kissed his brow and placed his mug on the little side table. The hotel room was small but comfortable, with a view onto the Durling street market that was just setting up for the day. She sat in an armchair by the big window and sipped her drink.

'Hey, what time is it? I thought we were sleeping in.' Michael rubbed a palm over his eyes.

'It's just after eight. Go back to sleep if you're tired.' They had shared a bottle of wine with dinner the night before, a rarity for them both, and it looked to Georgina that Michael was feeling rough. Neither of them drank much; the long hours and seriousness with which they each treated their careers had made that an easy decision for them years ago, and Georgina was glad of that. She'd seen too many families fall apart because of booze and drugs in her line of work.

Michael groaned, sat up, and took a gulp of coffee. 'That's good.' He looked over at his wife who was already showered and dressed. 'Bad night?'

'Just a little. Lots to think about. And I want to get out early this morning.'

'Give me thirty minutes and I'll be with you. The quicker you get that place up for sale at the estate agents, the better.'

'Actually, I've decided not to sell.' She watched for Michael's reaction, but there was none. It was one of his many attributes that she so loved; he never pressured her, never made presumptions, always made it quite clear that he trusted her decisions, however many times she changed her mind.

'Where're you going then?' he asked.

Georgina nodded at the window. 'There's a hardware vendor stall at the outdoor market. I want to get some tools, wallpaper strippers and what not. We've got a fortnight off work; I'm going to start on the inside of the house. I need to change it, beyond recognition maybe. If I can do that I think the old house might make a nice weekend getaway for us. Maybe it will help me bury some ghosts.'

Michael smiled. 'That's my girl. Remember our saying?'

'Of course.' Georgina returned his smile and the two of them spoke in unison: 'Never let the bastards grind you down.'

4

Georgina handed over the form she was required to fill in before each session that was supposed to determine her state of mind. So far, since she'd been seeing Doctor Sinclair, she found her answers to the questions on stress, anxiety and other emotions to be unchanging, and wondered when there might be some measurable improvement. She sat opposite her psychiatrist and sipped from a glass of iced water before placing it on the table beside her. The blinds were half-drawn against the afternoon sun, throwing shadows around the edge of the office. She looked across at Doctor Sinclair. 'I spoke to Michael.'

'That's good, Georgina. What did you tell him?'

'I told him what my parents did to me.'

'And how did revealing this make you feel?'

Georgina thought for a moment. 'Relieved. It was easier than I thought it would be.'

'That's good, isn't it?'

'Yes. I suppose.' Georgina shifted in her seat. 'But I couldn't talk about the other stuff.'

'You mean cutting yourself?'

'Yes. But at least he might understand why I do it . . . when I do tell him.'

'Hm.' The doctor crossed one leg over the other. 'So you see this as a step towards that.'

'Yes.' Georgina took a quick swig from her glass of water and changed the subject. 'We visited my parents' house. I've inherited it. I thought I'd hate the place, but I've decided to keep it.'

'For any particular reason?'

Georgina thought for a minute. 'Because I want to destroy what they'd made there. I want to turn it into something good, something beautiful. I don't want a single trace of my mother or father to remain.'

'And what does Michael think about this?'

'He thinks it's a good idea. That's what he says, at least. I don't think he's ever disagreed with me since we've been married. Not over anything major. We've been saving for a few years for a big tour across the USA, but he said we can use that money to fix the place up instead.'

'He seems to afford you a lot of freedom within your relationship.'

Georgina frowned. 'What do you mean?'

'Well, he ignores the fact that you self-harm. And now he's giving up what I presume is his dream trip across America.'

Georgina felt her face redden. It was true; she did get her own way in their marriage. She loved Michael, more than she'd ever loved anybody, but hearing the effects of her control over him spoken out loud made her feel like the biggest bitch on earth. 'He loves me.'

'Is that what love is?'

'You mean letting me do what I want even if it hurts him?' Georgina felt a tear trickle from the corner of one eye. 'No. That's not love.'

5

'You're back then. I thought you'd given up on us like all the rest.'

Georgina followed Linda Howard into her flat. 'I had a couple of weeks off.' It was her fourth visit to the tower block since their first encounter. They sat in the living room which was in its usual state of decrepitude. Georgina had arranged a meeting with her head of department after the first visit—

she'd been deeply worried about Linda's psychological state after her claims, and even more worried about her daughter, Carly. Georgina knew too well the way things could go if her mother believed the girl was possessed. Her manager had suggested it was a ploy, some playacting on Linda's part in her attempt to get a house move. Either way it was bad news. Georgina had met with Carly twice and found her to be an articulate, thoughtful girl, and had made it quite clear to her and her mother that if Carly's absence from school continued there could be charges brought against Linda. It seemed to have worked, Carly's attendance had improved. Georgina had so far seen no evidence in the girl of her mother's supernatural claims. If it was a ploy, Carly was either unaware or unwilling to play along.

'Have they put me on the list for a new house?'

'It's being looked into, Linda. But I have to tell you, my recommendations have more to do with your mental well-being than your claim that the flat is haunted. You can't expect the council to take that seriously as a reason for a transfer.'

'No, I don't suppose they would. They don't have to live here though. *You* don't have to fucking live here.'

Georgina glanced around the room. She had noticed from her notes before coming that it was Carly's fourteenth birthday. There were no cards, or any other sign in the living room that it was a special day.

'Carly's school attendance has improved lately. That's progress. She's a bright girl and getting qualifications is very important. The next few years will shape the rest of her life.'

'Yeah. We don't want her ending up a loser like me.'

'Everybody should want their children to better themselves, Linda.'

'Well she didn't go in today.'

Georgina sighed and rubbed a palm over her face. 'Oh, Linda. You're going to mess things up. If she slips back into her old ways, it'll cause trouble for both of you.'

'She ain't well. It's not my fucking fault if she's sick!' She glanced at the hallway and Georgina noticed an expression, both sly and smug, cross the woman's face. 'She's in her room. You'll see.'

'This isn't good, Linda. This doesn't help your case.' She walked into the hallway and tapped on the bedroom door. 'Carly? It's Georgina.' She glanced into the living room at Linda who was watching her, her arms folded across her breasts. 'May I come in?'

'Yes.'

Georgina opened the door and entered. She'd never been in Carly's room before, and took a deep breath at the sight. It had one window, one bed, one wardrobe on the cusp of collapse, and nothing else. A lump formed in her throat as she looked at Carly, who was lying in the bed with the threadbare cover pulled up to her chin. It was a mirror of her childhood bedroom in Doom, the only difference being the feel of uncarpeted, cold concrete beneath her shoes rather than wooden floorboards. She looked at Carly, and struggled to keep her voice level. 'Are you okay?'

'I don't feel well.'

'What's wrong?' Georgina closed the door, crossed the room and sat on the edge of the bed. She touched the back of her hand to the girl's forehead. 'You're a little hot. Do you have a headache? Sore throat?'

Carly shook her head, and Georgina saw an expression of deep sadness in her eyes. She glanced at the door, wondering if Linda had her ear pushed to the other side, and pulled an envelope from her satchel. 'Here,' she said in a low voice. 'Happy birthday.'

The girl made eye contact with her for the first time. 'For me?'

'Yes.'

Carly pulled herself into a sitting position, took the envelope, and pulled the card from inside. 'It's pretty.' A single teardrop fell onto the picture of a bunch of tulips. She opened it. 'Happy birthday, with love from Georgina,' she read. She glanced up. 'Thank you. It's my first ever birthday card.'

Georgina forced a smile and cleared her throat. 'Now, what's wrong? You can talk to me, Carly. I really do want to help you.'

'I've got something inside me.'

Georgina felt an anger swell as she remembered the look on Linda's face. *This is it. This is where the poor girl starts acting like she's possessed. Forced into it by her mother.* 'What do mean, inside you?'

'In here.' She placed a slender, pale hand on her stomach. 'A baby.'

Georgina closed her eyes for a second. 'Oh, Carly. Are you sure?'

'I did a test. Positive.'

Georgina placed her hand over the girl's. 'What about the father? Have you told him?' She didn't know why she'd asked—it didn't matter. The father would be just another acne-faced teenager with no intention of facing up to a lifetime of responsibility.

'He knows. He doesn't care. He's a horrible man.'

'Man?' Georgina felt her heart quicken. 'Carly, how old is he?'

She shrugged and wiped the free-flowing tears from her face. 'I don't know. Old.'

Georgina heard a tremble in her voice as she spoke. 'Where did this happen, Carly?'

'Here. He's one of Mum's.'

The door to the bedroom burst open and her mother charged in. 'See? See what the stupid little cow's gone and done? The council will have to move us now—we're gonna need another bedroom.'

It all became clear to Georgina in one lucid, horrific flash. The woman had prostituted her own daughter, sold her to some dirty old man to get her pregnant, all in the hope of getting the move she desired. She stood on unsteady legs, clenched her fists and for one moment imagined herself punching Linda Howard's face until it was a bloody mess.

'It's not my fault.' Carly's mother glanced from Georgina to Carly. 'I don't know why you're looking at me like that!'

Georgina looked over her shoulder. 'Get dressed, Carly. We need to get you somewhere that's safe.'

Carly rose from the bed. 'Can I come home with you?'

Georgina felt a knot in her stomach at the note of hope in the girl's voice. 'No, I'm not allowed. We'll find you a nice family, though.'

'Hang on! You can't do that, she's my daughter. Carly, you put those clothes down.'

The girl froze, one leg inside her tracksuit bottoms. 'Ignore her,' Georgina said. 'You don't have to do anything she tells you anymore.' She stood between the girl and her mother as she dressed, then led her by her hand from the room.

'You can't do this. This is kidnapping. I'll have you sacked,' Linda spat as Georgina shoved past her.

Georgina turned and glared at her. It was quite possible that she could be reprimanded, but she'd worry about that later. 'If I get my way, you'll never see your daughter again, you fucking heartless bitch. And as for moving, the only new place you'll be seeing is the inside of a prison cell, along with the dirty old bastard you sold your daughter to.'

She led Carly to the lift, swallowing down the anger that was in danger of exploding. 'It's okay, now,' she said when the doors slipped shut, enclosing them inside the acrid space. Carly clung to her and cried into her shoulder as Georgina stroked her head. On the inside of the elevator doors, she noticed graffiti that she was sure had not been there before. It was a circle, the size of a football, painted yellow with two black eyes and an upturned grin. Below the smiley face, in capital letters, a question: ARE THERE NO MONSTERS?

6

'There are some things I can't remember.'

Doctor Sinclair frowned. 'Such as?'

'What happened before the fire, when I was a child.' Georgina studied her therapist's eyes for a reaction. 'That's not right, is it?'

'It's unusual, but not unheard of.'

'The doctors back then said it was because of the smoke. Could that be true?' She watched Doctor Sinclair, noticed the hint of a wry smile at the corner of her mouth.

'I'd say that is unlikely,' the doctor replied.

'So why can't I remember?'

'It was a traumatic event. The mind can sometimes repress memories that are too painful, or frightening, to face.' The psychiatrist folded her fingers and rested her chin upon them. 'So what exactly do you remember?'

'Not much. Just flashes. I don't even know how much of it is real.' She closed her eyes. 'We went to visit Frankie. I think we were chased by somebody.'

'Chased?'

'Yes. A man in a white coat with a knife.' Georgina opened her eyes. 'He wanted to kill us.'

The doctor leaned forward, her brow creased. 'Why?'

'I don't know. Maybe we caught him doing . . . something. All I know is Vinnie named him Bald Eagle, afterwards. That's what he looked like. And there was a fire, which I don't remember. And we all woke in hospital . . . Except Frankie.'

'Can your friends fill in these blanks?'

'No. And nobody wants to talk about it, anyway.'

7

'Wow. This place looks amazing, Georgie.' Matt put his overnight bag on the floor and scanned the room.

'Thanks. I found a great team of builders, local guys. They ripped the place apart and put it to together again in five months. I did the decorating myself on weekends.' She squeezed Matt's hand. 'Come on. I'll show you the garden.' She led him through to the extension she'd had built in place of the little dark back-room. It was now four times the size with cream coloured walls and a high ceiling with recessed spotlights. A light oak dining table dominated the centre of the room, which was filled with natural light from the glass sliding doors that opened onto the garden.

'It's so bright—you wouldn't think this was the same house.'

'That was the plan.' She looked sideways at the profile of her oldest friend. He was as handsome as ever, though his dark cropped hair was now flecked with grey. She always had a feeling of warmth and safety in his company, and an indefinable connection with him that, even when they were apart, gave her comfort to know that he was out there somewhere in the world.

'Does it feel like the house you grew up in?'

'Not a bit.'

'Good.' They walked out onto the wooden decked patio. The long thin garden, separated from its neighbours by tall shrubberies in every shade of green, gave the back of the property a feeling of solitude. 'You've done great. It just feels so peaceful.' He smiled at her. 'Maybe I'll come and write my next book here.'

'You're always welcome.' Georgina smiled, and saw in Matt's eyes that he knew as well as she did that there would be no more books. He'd been unable to finish a novel since Tom's death seventeen years before, and it was only thanks to the success of his early work that he was financially comfortable.

'Michael would love it. He was gutted that he couldn't be here to see you today.'

'Yeah, me too. I haven't seen him since last Christmas. How's his work?'

'He loves it as much as ever. He was offered a promotion last month, but he turned it down. Said he didn't become a paramedic to sit in an office doing paperwork.'

'Good for him.'

'So, what do you want to do tonight?'

Matt turned and looked at the back of the house. 'You know what? I'd like a night in, with a home cooked dinner. It'll make a change from the micro-waved crap I live on.'

'That sounds like a great idea. We'll take a walk down to the mini-market and get some ingredients.'

They decided on chicken casserole, it was simple and not beyond the basic stock of the shop in the village. Matt stopped and looked across at the green as they left the shop with a plastic bag of goods each. 'How many hours did we spend on that bench?' he asked.

'Enough.' She linked her arm through his. 'We shared a lot of laughs over there. And tears.'

'That's what life's all about, I suppose. When it's good, it's bloody good. But it can hurt sometimes.'

'Come on.' Georgina turned her back to the village green and headed towards the house. 'Have you seen your dad lately?'

'Yeah, he's doing fine. Living with his lady friend in Herne Bay.'

'Nice. And Simon?'

'He's a granddad now. I'm heading over to his place next Sunday for dinner.'

'Is that what you do now, travel around poncing meals off your friends and family?'

Matt smiled. 'Basically.'

'How's he finding life outside the army?'

'He says it's fine, but I can tell he misses it. It must be hard to walk away from something you've devoted most of your life to.'

A buzz sounded from the hip pocket of Georgina's jeans as they turned into her road. 'I hate these bloody things.' She fumbled for her mobile phone. 'Hello, Georgina Smith,' she said as she raised it to her ear. 'Hello?' She pulled it away and looked at the display which showed no number before hanging up. 'Bother,' she muttered.

'What's up?'

'It's a work phone—they make us have them now. This is my third one this year. Somebody keeps getting my number and calling without saying anything. I'll have to get it changed again.'

'That's a bit unsettling.'

'Probably someone with a grudge. There are some that see me as the enemy rather than an ally when I knock at their door.'

Matt glanced at the house opposite as she opened the front gate. 'Does Vinnie's family still live there?'

'His sister Ellie lives there alone. We meet for coffee now and then. She hasn't seen Vinnie since their mum's funeral, three years ago.' She raised her eyebrows. 'Too big for Doom, now.'

Inside, they dropped the groceries in the kitchen and boiled a kettle. 'It's strange how things turn,' Matt said. 'I could never imagine you coming back to live here.'

'It's usually only on weekends. I just had a couple of day's holiday to spare this week.' She noticed Matt watching her. 'I thought it would be nice, just you and me, spend a little time together.'

'You haven't slept here overnight on your own yet, have you?'

Georgina shook her head and felt a little foolish. 'No. I'm not scared, exactly. Just not ready for that yet. Silly, I know.'

'Of course it isn't. And I'm happy to stay.'

The kettle boiled and Georgina reached for it as the familiar buzz of her phone sounded. She exchanged a glance with Matt as she answered. 'Hello?' Silence. She hit the red button. 'Trouble is,' she said to Matt, 'I have to answer it in case it's an emergency with one of my cases.' The phone sounded again and she snapped it to her ear. 'Hello!'

'Honey? You okay?'

'Oh, Michael. Hi. Yes, I'm fine.'

'Have you seen the news?'

'No.'

'Switch on the TV, any channel.'

Georgina felt her insides churn at the tone of Michael's voice. 'Why? What's happened?'

'Hang on.' She heard the muffled voice of his ambulance partner before Michael returned his attention to her. *'Hey, I've got to go, Honey. Go switch the TV on, we'll talk later.'*

'Everything okay?' Matt asked.

'I don't know.' She led Matt through to the living room and switched the TV on. It took a few seconds for the image to appear, and when it did there was a scene that could have come straight from a Hollywood disaster movie. Black smoke billowed from two white skyscrapers into a marine blue sky, and Georgina stared at the BBC Newsflash logo at the bottom of the screen to convince herself it was really happening.

'What the hell?' Matt mumbled. 'That's the World Trade Center.'

Georgina turned the volume up.

'. . . into the North Tower at 8.46 am local time. Another passenger jet, reported to be American Airlines Flight 175, crashed into the South Tower shortly after at 9.03. That was forty-five minutes ago, since then another apparent attack on the Pentagon . . .'

The camera zoomed into one of the towers, where occasional specks were falling from the building. 'Oh, my God.' Georgina raised her hand to her mouth. 'Those are people.' She heard her own voice waver. 'They're jumping from the windows.' A sudden, unstoppable tremble shook her knees and she felt Matt's big arms around her. 'What kind of monsters would do a thing like that?'

Matt's voice was low and solemn. 'The worst kind of all. Human beings.'

The television showed everything—the Twin Towers' collapse, the cloud over New York, the re-run footage of the jetliners smashing into the buildings—and as the afternoon passed Georgina felt a little piece of her humanity die with every dreadful, passing moment.

8

Georgina sat opposite Carly at the kitchen table. 'How are you doing?'

'Fine.'

'Are you getting along with Mr. and Mrs. Finnegan?'

'Yes, they're really nice.' Carly looked around the room. 'I like it here.'

It had been six months since the night Georgina had rescued Carly from her mother, and she wondered how a girl so young had coped with all that life had spewed at her. She'd had an abortion—there had been meetings and advice from other health and social workers—but the decision had ultimately been Carly's, and Georgina was relieved at the choice she had made.

'How's school?'

'It's good. I've a bit of catching up to do, but I don't mind.'

Georgina smiled, and felt her heart rise at the slight curl of lip returned by Carly. It was the first sign of anything that resembled happiness that she'd seen from the girl. 'You know your mother's trial starts on Monday.'

'Yes.'

'And it's been explained to you by Miss Forbes that you can give evidence remotely. You won't have to see your mother.'

'I never want to see her again.'

'You'll never have to, Carly.'

'What about the man?'

Georgina swallowed. Carly had never been able to give a full description of him, other than the fact he was old. It was understandable—trauma victims often shut the horrendous details of their experiences from their conscious minds. 'I'm afraid the police still haven't been able to trace him. But you don't have to be afraid, he can never find you.'

'I think I've remembered something, but I'm not sure. I wanted to ask you if I should tell Miss Forbes.'

'Anything at all may help, Carly.'

'I dreamt it, last night. So I'm not sure if it's real.'

Georgina leaned forward. 'Nobody will blame you if you get anything wrong. Tell me what it is, and we'll decide, together, whether we think it's relevant.'

'It's something he said to me.' She looked down at her hands, clenched together on the table. 'Every time.' Her face reddened.

'It's okay, Carly.' Georgina reached across and touched Carly's wrist. 'Just tell me what he said.'

'He always said the same thing.' She raised her eyes to meet Georgina's gaze, and when she spoke it was almost a whisper.

'This is going to hurt.'

Georgina dropped her car keys onto the kitchen table and headed for the sink where she filled a glass from the cold tap. The traffic had been slow, with an open window the only air conditioning available in her old hatchback. She drank the water half-way down and held the glass against her brow to cool off.

A dull throb in the centre of Georgina's head had tormented her for the last ten miles of the journey home which she guessed was due to dehydration, and probably a little stress. She swallowed the remainder of her drink and checked her watch before walking back through the living room to the hallway and up to the bathroom. Michael would not be home for another hour which gave her enough time.

Is that what love is? She pushed the words of Doctor Sinclair from her mind.

Georgina stood before the mirror, kicked off her shoes and stripped to her underwear. Her body was pale and skinny, and she traced the fingertips of her left hand from her throat to her breasts and down to her stomach, which fluttered with the familiar mixture of excitement and shame.

She didn't want to do it. She wished she could just go back down stairs, make a cup of tea, and listen to the radio. But she *needed* to do it. To keep them safe. Especially after what Carly said.

This is going to hurt.

Georgina opened the wall cabinet and grabbed a packet, from which she pulled a new razor blade. Holding it between thumb and index finger she peeled off the thin protective paper and studied it.

'This is for Michael,' she said. Her days of being a cutter had transformed to this ritual—an old one by now, practiced since the threats of Mr. Poole—and she was no longer alarmed at the sound of her own voice. She placed the edge of the blade against the outside of her thigh below her hip and pressed it against the soft flesh. A crimson spot appeared and grew to a bubble before running down her leg. She moved the blade down an inch, gasped, and withdrew it.

'This is for Matt,' she whispered, and repeated the procedure a little to one side of the first cut. She would not let the people she cared about suffer, and treated her pain as a sacrifice of sorts. Her logic was twisted, and a victory to that sick bastard Poole and the worm he'd planted in her young mind, but it felt right.

'And this is for Carly.' She added another cut, deeper and longer this time.

She raised her eyes and took in her reflection. 'You stupid little girl,' she said. 'You don't deserve anybody's love. All you deserve is pain.' Without looking she flicked the blade again at her leg and yelped. She began to cry and looked down at the mess. That was enough. That would do. Her loved ones would be safe . . . for a while.

2009—JACK

1

'**H**I. **HOW'S YOUR** day been?'

Jack peered over the top of his little round spectacles, the tiny point of his paintbrush left to hover in mid-air an inch from the canvas. 'Good. Busy.'

Bev squeezed by him in the little corner of his studio-shop he used as his workstation and on through to the backroom that served as a kitchenette. 'Got you some doughnuts. Have a break.'

'Is that an order?' He swished the brush around in a jar of green tinted water and placed his multi-coloured wooden palette onto the table next to it among the tubes of acrylic paint.

'Yes. Bev knows best, so do as you're told.'

Jack smiled and looked over his shoulder at her as she poured a couple of glasses of lemonade. Her cut-down denim shorts and bikini top provided a scant interruption between the golden tanned flesh of her long legs and slim midriff, and her plum dyed hair was pulled back in a ponytail, revealing the tiny butterfly tattoo on the nape of her neck. He studied her profile, the way her lips pouted in concentration as a single loose strand of hair hung over one eye, and thought how amazing it would be to paint her before pushing the thought away.

She came through to the shop, the doughnuts and drinks balanced on a wooden tray. 'Come on. We'll lunch al fresco.'

Jack followed her outside and they sat at the two-seater

154

on the beach-front boardwalk. The heat felt good as Jack closed his eyes and tipped his face to the sun. The noise of seagulls and the crunch of beach-stones underfoot served as a backing track to the sound of voices—happy holiday voices—and Jack thought for what must have been the thousandth time in five years that the idea to move here was the best he'd ever had.

'Oh, wow. You sold *The Starfish*!'

He opened his eyes and followed Bev's gaze to the empty easel among the half dozen displayed on the boardwalk. 'Yeah. A young couple. Bought it for their first house.'

'Did they knock you down?'

'No. They offered full price. I threw in a couple of prints that caught their eye—they were very pleased.'

Bev leaned over and kissed his cheek, leaving a small dusting of doughnut sugar there.

'What's that for?'

'Being a nice man.'

Jack fought to keep the red from forming on his cheeks and thought himself ridiculous for blushing at a kiss from a lover at his age. He glanced at the easel and felt a brief sense of loss. *The Starfish* had been the longest displayed painting in his shop. He'd known when he had painted it that a four-foot square intricate study of a starfish in shallow surf would be a hard sell, and as pleased as he was that it had found a good home he realised that he was going to miss it.

'So,' he said to Bev, 'what've you been up to?'

'Coffee with Kim in the lanes.'

'How is she?'

'Fine. Still in love with you.'

Jack grinned. Bev's Aunt Kim was the wittiest, craziest, most intelligent person he'd ever met, and he loved her in return. At the age of ninety-three she was one of the popular faces among the residents of Brighton, what many of them would describe as a character. Though Bev was only five years younger than him at forty-nine, she had the face and body of a woman in her prime, whereas Jack—bald, short-sighted and a trouser size bigger than he'd like—had not aged as well. On a couple of occasions he'd even been mistaken for her father, much to Aunt Kim's delight. 'See,' she'd said to Bev. 'You should give him to me; we're more physically suited.'

The clear July sky was an endless sheet of blue that merged without fuss into the sea at the horizon, where the sunlight glinted off white sails. A constant flow of holiday makers and day trippers strolled along the wooden planked walkway that separated Jack's studio shop from the stone covered beach that dropped in a shallow curve to the surf. Some of the tourists paused to gaze at his artwork or leaf through the posters and postcards displayed on a pair of revolving metal frames. Having his work turned into affordable prints had been Bev's idea, and it now accounted for almost fifty percent of the income made in his shop. Bev was the practical one in their relationship; Jack was happy to just sit and paint, and he appreciated that it was her business acumen that enabled him to do just that.

He glanced left at the pier and held his hands at arm's length with his finger and thumb tips touching to form a square through which he peered with one eye closed. He'd painted the pier more times than he could remember from a multitude of angles and never bored of it, which was just as well as it was by far his best-selling subject. A silver haired man walked through Jack's hand-frame, obscuring the pier, and turned his face to him for just a brief moment before looking ahead again as he walked on. Jack dropped his hands and watched the man—who walked with a stick though he only appeared to be in his early sixties—as he ambled away.

'What's up?' Bev asked. 'Do you know him?'

'Yes, I think I do.'

'He didn't seem to recognise you.'

'No.' Jack looked at Bev. 'He wouldn't. I don't think we ever actually spoke. He was Georgina's lecturer when she was at Canterbury back in the seventies. She had an affair with him.'

'Isn't that a little unethical?'

'Yes. That's why I remember him. He was a right bastard, married with kids. We heard a few years after Georgina had dropped him that he'd gotten in bother with the law. Lost his job as well.'

'At it again with another pupil?'

'Oh, I've no doubt of that.' Jack sipped his lemonade. 'But that's not what he got in trouble for. He was arrested for beating his wife. Grievous bodily harm. He was a whisker away from killing her.'

'Charming creature,' Bev said.

The man, whose name Jack couldn't remember though he was sure it would come to him later, disappeared into the throng of tourists. Jack had seen many faces he'd recognised from his past since he'd had the shop; anyone who visited Brighton Beach would almost certainly pass by on the boardwalk.

'Oh,' Bev said. 'I almost forgot. I've got us a DVD to watch tonight. *The Curious Case of Benjamin Button.*'

Jack grimaced. 'Have you seen how long that film is?'

'So what? Fall asleep if you don't like it. I'll carry you to bed.'

'I might hold you to that.'

Later that afternoon, when they'd closed up shop and entered the cool shade of the apartment they rented by the marina, Bev didn't carry him to bed, she led him by the hand, and they undressed as the descending sun cast burnt orange stripes across their naked bodies through the slats of the half-closed window blinds.

'I love you, Bev,' Jack said as she moved close. He'd only ever said that to one other woman in his life, and he'd meant it then too. That had been a long time ago, though he still woke on occasion with wet cheekbones, her name on his lips, and no recollection of the dream. He wished he could remember—he'd give almost anything to see Kate again even if only within the confines of his slumbering imagination.

'I love you, too.' Bev put her lips to his and slipped her tongue inside, running it slowly over the edge of his teeth. He pulled her tanned body tight, felt the softness of her breasts against his chest and the wetness of her crotch on his. She moved her hips, grinding her lower half against him as they kissed, but as much as he wanted to, he felt nothing.

'Lie down,' she said. Jack got onto the bed and lay back, aware of the flabbiness and pallor of his own body as she positioned herself by his side. He felt the warmth of her grip as she took him in her palm. 'Come on,' she whispered. 'I want you.'

He traced his fingertips across her hardening nipples and tried to feel the moment, tried to put thoughts of Kate from his mind. He wanted to make love to Bev more than anything, wanted to satisfy her, to *show* her that he loved her. She kissed his neck, his chest, his stomach, and he felt the warmth of the inside of her mouth surround him, but the only thing that grew was his embarrassment. After a few minutes when it was plain to them both that it wasn't going to happen, Bev sat up and sighed.

'Sorry,' Jack said.

'Don't worry. It happens.' She crossed the room and grabbed her bathrobe from the back of a chair. 'Maybe you should see a doctor. Get some Viagra.'

Jack pulled the duvet across the lower half of his body. She was right; it did happen to everybody at some point. But it had been happening just a little too often of late, and always for the same ridiculous reason. Kate had been dead for thirty-five years, and he'd thought little of her since falling in love with Bev, so why now? Jack didn't know, but he'd had a feeling lately that the past was somehow getting closer, and clearer, as if his life were a running track and he was coming back round to the start.

'I'll make an appointment.'

She made no reply as she tied the belt on her gown with her back to him, and that's when the fear hit. What if Bev had given up on him? Had the thought hit her that he was no longer interested? The problem had started three months or so before and he'd done nothing about it, but maybe she had; maybe she was on the lookout for somebody younger.

'I'm sure it's just a phase, something to do with my age. You're right—some pills should sort me out.'

Bev turned to look at him. 'Maybe you just have other things on your mind.'

The statement hung in the air between them like a balloon that they were both afraid of bursting with sharp words. *She knows*, he thought when she had left the bedroom, and he wished he could explain, but he knew the right words would never come.

Later, Jack ordered a pizza as Bev poured a couple of beers and put the DVD in the player. He enjoyed the film more than he thought he would at first, but as it went on, he was overcome by an illogical sense of dread as Brad Pitt's titular character regressed through his life. There was something about it, something familiar about the unnatural passage of time that Jack couldn't pin down.

There's no such thing as the past. Vinnie had said that once, with a look in his eye that betrayed the belief that he alone was party to that certain, twisted knowledge. *The past, the present, the future, it's all the same.* Had he said that as well?

'You okay?'

'Yes.' Jack looked at Bev and smiled, but when he glanced back at the screen Benjamin Button was a preteen boy and the sight of him caused a thick nausea to rise in Jack's stomach. He turned his face away. 'I'm a little tired, to tell the truth.' He stood from the settee. 'I'll make us some coffee.'

'I'll pause the film, it's almost over.'

'It's okay,' Jack said as he left the room. 'I'll watch from the kitchen.'

He filled the kettle, placed his palms on the work top and took deep breaths to calm his illogical sense of foreboding as he waited for the film to play out before taking Bev her coffee. An hour later, in bed, he held onto her as if she were a lone buoy floating atop the surface of an endless, deep ocean, and vowed to himself that he would never paint her. He'd already made that mistake with Miss Simpkins and Kate.

2

The care worker led Jack along the corridor from the front desk. Her name was Liza, and Jack guessed she was in her early twenties. *Too young to be doing this job*, he thought. She had taken a special liking to his dad and Jack was grateful for that. It wasn't easy to like an old man who seldom knew his own name. Jack loved him, of course, but that was different. He hated what his father had become, hated the diminishing light in the eyes of what had once been the most intelligent, kindest of men as his brain moved through the gradual process of shutting itself down.

'He's in the common room with your sister,' Liza said. 'Charles has been really good today, best I've seen him in weeks.'

'Talking?'

'Yes, on and off.' She opened the door for him. 'Just call if you need anything.'

'Thanks, Liza.'

She smiled and marched off along the passageway, no doubt to perform some ritual involved with caring for the aged that Jack preferred not to think about. He looked around the large room at the dozen or so white-haired men and women sitting mostly in silence, some of them watching the low volume TV, others dozing or staring at the space in front of them. He spotted his sister Mary and his dad in the far corner and made his way over, dragging a spare chair from the middle of the room on his way.

'Hi,' he said as he sat.

'Hello, Jack.'

'How is he?'

'He recognised me when I got here, half hour ago,' Mary said. 'But now...'

Jack leaned forward. 'Hello, Dad.' He noticed a faint flicker in his father's left eye. 'It's me, Jack.' He studied the slack, lined face. The features were still recognizable as the man that had loved and nurtured him, despite the sunken cheeks, snow-white eyebrows and liver spotted bald pate.

Me in thirty years' time. Would he live that long? Would he want to, in that state of being? Jack shrugged the questions away as pointless; nobody knows how long they have.

He turned to his sister. 'How is everybody?'

'Fine.'

Jack noticed a sour note in her reply. 'Really?'

She sighed. 'Thing's aren't so great with Mark's business. I think this slump they're talking about is beginning to bite. I hate it when Mark worries.'

'Oh, Mary. If there's anything I could do . . . ' He paused and looked at her, reminding himself that she was his little sister. 'Listen, it's not much, I know, but I have a couple of grand you could have, for as long as you want.'

'Still trying to look after me?' She forced a smile. 'It's really kind of you, Jack, but a couple of grand wouldn't even scratch it. Don't worry. We'll find a way.'

'Well, I mean it. If you need it, just ask.' They sat and watched their father in silence. 'I wish he still wore his dentures,' Jack said after a minute. 'It makes him look even older without them.'

'They're not much use to him now, I suppose. He only eats soft foods.'

'He's deteriorated quick. Especially since Mum died.'

Mary pulled a tissue from her pocket and dabbed at a drop of spittle on the corner of her father's mouth. 'I sometimes wonder if that's what kicked it off. He seemed to lose the will to live after her funeral.'

'I'm sorry, Jack.' The old man's voice was clear, almost younger, and Jack saw the surprise on his sister's face, which he guessed mirrored his own. The two of them turned to their father.

'I'm sorry, Jack,' he repeated. He looked at his son with an expression of complete despair upon his face.

'There's nothing to be sorry for, Dad,' Jack said in what he hoped was a gentle voice. 'You've done nothing wrong.' The old man's bottom lip began to tremble and Jack leaned forward and placed his palm on the back of his father's cold hand. 'Try not to get upset.'

'There was nothing I could do.' He began to sob. 'I know that you loved her.'

Jack exchanged a glance with Mary, who mouthed the word *Mum*.

'Of course I loved her,' Jack said. 'We all did. It isn't your fault, Dad. People die.'

'Not like that,' he shook his head. 'Not that young.'

Mary wiped the tears off her father's face and whispered to Jack: 'He's confused.' She held her father in an embrace as his whole body shook from deep, uncontrollable sobs. When they subsided at last, he fell into an exhausted slumber in Mary's arms. 'We may as well go,' she said to Jack. 'He'll sleep for hours, now.'

Jack stood and kissed his father's brow.

Not like that. Not that young.

Jack considered his father's words and at the same time doubted his sister's explanation. Their mother had been seventy-five when she died, fading peacefully in her sleep after a severe chest infection that had developed into pneumonia.

He's talking about Kate. His father had seen how devastated Jack had been over Kate's sudden death, had been there for him through those first few tough years when Jack's disinclination to carry on with life had propelled him into a circle of drink fuelled self-destruction. If it hadn't been for his father, Jack believed that he would never have had the strength or will to reach the other side of what had been the darkest of tunnels. Kate had been twenty when her life was extinguished in a few seconds on Waterloo Bridge. She'd somehow lost control of her car and rammed it into a lamp-post on the central reservation. *That was how nobody should die. That was far too young.*

Even in his state of dementia, his father had reached across to Jack, still trying to comfort him after all these years. For all of the brain cells that were dying, Jack guessed that love somehow remained, like the last brave soldier of a defeated platoon defending his trench.

He walked Mary to her car and kissed her goodbye. He didn't mention the money anymore—he could see that her refusal had been through embarrassment—but he'd already decided to send her a cheque. He and Bev were okay; they lived a simple life, and despite her practicalities as far as money and business were concerned, Bev had never been a bread-head. *And I'm fucking it up with her, throwing it all away because thoughts of my dead girlfriend are stopping me from getting it up.*

Jack sat behind the wheel of his little hatchback, turned the engine on and looked at the sign above the facility's front entrance.

DURLING AND DOOM CARE HOME

He glanced at the clock on his dashboard which showed quarter past two. The home was set in countryside between the town and the village, just a couple of miles outside of Doom. He turned right out of the grounds and took the east road instead of the southbound.

He hadn't seen Georgina in almost three years and knew she'd be pleased to see him if she was home. He turned on the radio to a news report as he weaved along the thin country lane, and changed the station to one playing music less than a minute later. He was sick of the rising body count of young Brits losing their lives in Afghanistan, which was now higher than the tally in either Iraq or the Falklands. It seemed there was nothing but bad news every time he switched on a radio or TV—if it wasn't the war it was the global financial crisis, or kids in London stabbing each other.

He turned onto Georgina's road and spotted her pruning the lime coloured privet that separated her front garden from the pavement. 'Anywhere I can get a cup of tea around here?' he called through his open window as he pulled up alongside her. She turned and lifted her sunglasses with one hand.

'Jack!' She dropped the shears and was on him as he rose from the car, her lips smacking against his face as she hugged him. 'What are you doing here?'

'My Dad's in the care home up the road. Thought I'd drop by on my way home.'

Georgina pulled back and frowned. 'How is he?'

'Oh, you know. Good days and bad days. He seemed to recognise me for a moment today.'

'Oh, that's such a shame. He's such a kind man. I think you take after him quite a lot.'

Jack blushed and felt himself pulled back into the arms of his old friend and had a sudden urge to weep that he swallowed down. He held on tight to her. 'It's good to see you, George.'

'Hey! Get your goddamned mitts off my wife!'

Jack looked over Georgina's shoulder and saw Michael coming towards him from the open front door of the house, his teeth displayed in the biggest of grins.

'Michael!' he managed to say before he was passed from Georgina into the stronger embrace of the big American who almost lifted him from his feet.

'Man, what happened to your hair?' Michael asked when he'd released him.

Jack ran his palm over the skin of his bald pate and glanced at Georgina. 'I take after my dad, I suppose.'

164

'Don't worry about it. Shaved mine off years ago,' Michael said. He winked at Jack. 'Georgina finds it sexy.'

She smiled. 'You look like a pair of billiard balls.' She grabbed Jack's hand and led him into the house. 'Come on, I know where you can get a good cup of tea.'

The three of them sat in the big white extension that overlooked the back garden and talked about old times as the afternoon sun cast elongated tree shadows across the close-cut lawn, and about old friends that one or the other of them hadn't thought about in years.

'Do you still see Maurice?' Georgina asked of Jack's old university roommate.

'Yes, we've never lost touch. He's rolling in it now; inherited his dad's scrap metal yard. He comes down to Brighton for the weekend every now and then.' Jack sipped on his fourth cup of tea. 'Oh yeah, I just remembered. I saw somebody from Canterbury the other day, but I can't remember his name.'

'A student?'

'No, a lecturer.' Jack saw Georgina's smile falter and cursed himself for mentioning it without thinking. She'd hardly want reminding of the creep she'd had a fling with.

'Declan?'

'Yes, that's him. Sorry, I should have kept my big mouth shut.'

'Not at all, it's not your fault. It's just.. .' She glanced at her husband who gave her a nod. 'We had a bad experience, a few years back.'

Jack looked from Georgina to Michael. 'With Declan?'

'Yeah,' Michael said. 'Turns out he's a nut-job, as well as a wife beater.'

'I was getting phone calls,' Georgina said, 'silent ones at first. Went on for months. Then they got a little disturbing. I'd answer the phone, and though I could tell it was a grown man speaking, he'd talk like a child.'

Jack felt nervous. He wasn't sure he wanted to know the details.

'He'd say nasty things, like what he'd like to do to me, which consisted mostly of chopping off pieces of my body.'

'And this was Declan?'

'The police couldn't prove it, not conclusively,' Michael said. 'But some of the calls were traced to a phone he had access to at the school he was working in. They gave him a warning, scared him off.'

'And the calls stopped immediately,' Georgina said.

'Shit,' Jack muttered.

'Exactly,' Michael said. 'Little motherfucker.'

The growl in Michael's soft, deep voice was something Jack had never heard from the American before, and assured him of the fate that would have befallen Declan if Michael had gotten his hands on him.

3

Jack first noticed the man on the pier while he was bringing in his easels from the boardwalk to lock away for the night. With elbows resting on the handrail and collar turned up despite the warm evening, the figure was too far off to see any distinctive features, but Jack was sure his face was turned to him, watching Jack. When he'd finished putting away his art supplies and begun the walk to his home on the marina, Jack caught sight of the man again, idling behind at a distance, and became aware of the suspicion, as crazy as it was, that began to take form in his mind: he was being followed. *Who'd want to follow me?*

Jack detoured into the pedestrianised lanes instead of taking his usual, more direct route along the seafront and picked up his pace along the narrow alleyways where diners and drinkers spilled from the busy restaurants and bars to enjoy their evening in the open air at candle-lit tables. He turned left and right and ducked inside the open door of a pub. He saw the man through the window as he rushed past him along the busy lane and slipped back outside, twenty feet or so behind. *See how you like being followed.*

The man came to a T-junction and glanced both ways before taking the left. Jack went the same way, careful not to get too close, and spotted the back of the man's white-haired head amongst the crowd. He was suddenly sure of the man's identity.

It was Declan.

Shit. He must have seen me in my shop. But why follow me? The answer was obvious. The man was a lunatic who'd already stalked Georgina, and now he recognised Jack as an old friend of hers.

As he walked faster, Jack thought of the things Declan had said to Georgina, and felt a sudden rage rising inside like a volcano about to blow. *Who the fuck does he think he is?* Jack gained on him, dodging between the evening tourists, until he was within arm's length. He reached out with his hand, was about to grab the man's collar when an image, unbidden and terrifying, flashed through his mind of the man whipping a white hairpiece from his head to reveal a scabby pate as the scalpel in his free hand slashed at Jack's throat. His fingers gripped the collar and stopped the man, who spun on the spot and gaped at Jack, his expression one of surprise. It took Jack a moment to recognise him.

'Vinnie?'

'Fucking hell, Jack, you scared the shit out of me!'

'Scared *you*?' Jack let out an incredulous little laugh. 'I haven't seen you in three years and you start following me around like a fucking secret agent.'

Vinnie smiled and gripped Jack's elbow. 'Let's get a drink.'

Jack studied his old friend. He was immaculate as always, his clothes stinking of high-end London boutique, his face tanned, his grey close-cut hair only adding to his appearance of distinction. Vinnie raised his eyebrows and Jack felt the anger wash away. He never had been able to stay annoyed with Vinnie for long.

'Come on,' he said. He led Vinnie back to the pub where they ordered drinks and found a corner table. 'So, what's with all the sneaking around?'

Vinnie took a swig of his lager and glanced around the dimly lit bar. 'Just being cautious.'

A feeling of unease settled over Jack. 'What's going on, Vinnie?'

'I wanted to talk to you.' He looked at Jack with a sudden earnestness. 'I *need* to talk to you.'

'Okay.' Jack sipped his beer. 'Why didn't you call first?'

'Spur of the moment. There are some things I need to tell you. If I don't tell you now, I might not get the opportunity for some time.'

'Does Hannah know you're here?' Jack noticed the grimace on Vinnie's face and lowered his voice. 'Are you in trouble, Vinnie?'

'Hannah has no idea where I am—we split last December. And yes, I am in trouble.'

'Wait a minute. You and Hannah broke up?'

'Yes.' Vinnie averted his eyes. 'She found out about my affair with her mother.'

'Jesus, Vinnie.'

'It was twenty years ago. Thought I'd gotten away with it. But Hannah's dad died last year, and the old bitch thought the funeral a good time to bring it up.'

Jack shook his head. He knew Vinnie's morals were little better than an alley cat's where women were concerned, but this was something else. 'Poor Hannah.'

'I know,' Vinnie said. 'Pretty low even for me, eh?'

They finished their drinks in silence.

'So what kind of trouble are you in?' Jack asked at last.

Vinnie laughed. 'Legal. Spiritual. You name it. Come on, we can't talk in here.' He stood and walked from the bar, and for a second Jack considered just sitting there, ordering another pint, and letting Vinnie walk out of his life, but he knew that kind of desertion was beyond him. 'Bollocks,' he mumbled as he rose from his seat.

They walked back to the pier, up onto its boardwalks and along to its midpoint where they stopped and leaned side by side on the rail. The setting sun was half obscured by the horizon, sending golden dapples across the calm surface of the water. Half a dozen seagulls swooped and hovered by them, squawking for titbits, and flew on when it became apparent they had none to give.

'It's nice here. Got yourself a good little set up.' Vinnie looked sideways. 'Still with that bird?'

'Her name's Bev. Yes, we're still together.'

'Are you happy?'

Jack noticed a thickness to Vinnie's voice. 'Yes. I am.'

'Good. You deserve to be happy.' Jack felt his friend's hand grip his wrist. 'You're a good man, Jack. The very best.'

'What's going on, Vinnie?'

Vinnie let go of his arm. 'When I return to London, I expect to be arrested.'

'Bloody hell. What have you done?'

'All sorts. Insider trading and what not.' Vinnie shook his head. 'The shit's hit the fan. My solicitor said I could be looking at a couple of years inside. That's why I need to talk to you. I've done some terrible things, Jack, things I hate myself for. When they arrest me I'm going to tell them everything. It'll be a relief.' He sighed. 'Back in eighty-nine, around the time I ended the affair with Hannah's mother, I screwed her father over. I lost a load of money, illegally, and shifted it his way. He lost his job, and I stepped into his shoes.'

'I can see why you hate yourself.'

'That's not all. I was doing a lot of drugs—coke mainly—and I dropped some acid. I picked up a girl. I couldn't remember anything after, other than the image of her lying dead on the floor.'

'Fucking hell, Vinnie!' Jack looked around, worried that somebody might have heard.

'I checked the news for weeks, months, but there was no mention. I'm pretty sure it was just a bad trip. I'm going to tell the police about it when they take me in, though, just in case.'

Jack walked away, rubbed his hand across his head before returning to the handrail. 'Why are you telling me this? What's it got to do with me?'

'Nothing. Just getting it off my chest.' Vinnie turned to face him. 'The reason I've come to see you is to apologise. I did something stupid, Jack.' He dropped his gaze to his feet. 'I ruined your life.'

Jack felt his mouth go dry. 'What are you talking about?'

Vinnie shook his head, opened his mouth to talk and clamped it shut. When he spoke at last, it was just audible. 'If it wasn't for me, Kate would still be alive.'

The boards beneath Jack's feet seemed to become unstable, and he gripped the rail tight in his right hand, aware of the sudden weakness in his legs that threatened to give way under the weight of his body. He took a deep breath, tried to sort the muddled thoughts in his head. 'She died alone in her car.'

'She was driving back from my place when it happened.'

Jack felt his heart thud. It had been a point that had always bothered Jack and Kate's parents—the mystery of where Kate had been driving home from that evening. He looked at Vinnie. 'What the hell was she doing at your place?'

'I invited her over. Told her I was interested in investing in the flower business she wanted to start. It was an excuse, of course. She was beautiful. I wanted to seduce her.'

'You fucking bastard,' Jack whispered.

'That's what she called me. She sussed me out—she wasn't stupid—and told me to get lost.'

An image formed in Jack's mind of Kate, her foot pressed on the accelerator as she sped, full of rage, away from Vinnie and across Waterloo Bridge. 'You fucking bastard,' Jack repeated as he cuffed a single teardrop from his cheek.

'I don't expect you to forgive me, but I'm sorrier than you'll ever know, Jack.'

'You're sorry.' Jack stepped forward and thrust his face within inches of Vinnie's. 'It's thirty-five years too fucking late for that.' He grabbed the lapels on Vinnie's jacket, imagined gripping him by the throat until his eyes bulged before tipping him over the handrail. Vinnie gave no resistance as his back was shoved against the metal bar. 'This is what you want, isn't it? It's why you've come here. You're too much of a fucking coward to do it yourself!'

'Hey, what's going on?'

Jack glanced sideways at the young man who'd spoken. He looked scared. His wife stood a few paces behind, their baby held in her arms. Jack released his grip on Vinnie and stepped away.

'Are you okay?' the young man asked.

'Yes,' Vinnie said. 'Leave us, please.'

The man looked from Vinnie to Jack, shrugged and led his wife away by her elbow. Jack watched them until they were off the pier before returning his attention to Vinnie. 'You were supposed to be my friend, Vinnie.' He was surprised at the calmness in his own voice. He sighed. 'Don't contact me anymore. I never want to see you again.' He turned to walk away.

'Wait, Jack, there's something else.'

Jack ignored him.

'I saw something, as Kate drove away. You should know everything, Jack.'

Jack closed his eyes and stopped. If there was something else about the night that Kate died, he had to know. He looked over his shoulder.

'I went onto my balcony when she left,' Vinnie said. 'There was somebody in the back seat of her car. He waved at me as she drove off.' He paused. 'It was Frankie.'

171

Jack felt his shoulders slump. 'You are something else. Kate got killed because of you, and you try to blame it on a boy that died when we were eleven-years-old. Fuck you, Vinnie.' He strode away.

'I'm sorry, Jack,' Vinnie called after him, 'but none of this is over. The past, the present, the future, it's all the same.'

The apartment on the marina was empty when he arrived, and Jack was relieved. He had no wish for Bev to see him like this. He turned the tap in the kitchen until the water ran cold and drank a glass straight down.

I need a beer. He opened the fridge but it was empty of lager, so he filled another glass with water, walked through to the living room and sank onto the settee. An old memory, one he'd often returned to, replayed itself. They were at a party, and Kate was facing him with her head tipped back and her fingers laced around his neck as they danced, her low-cut red dress and lush, black hair tinted orange under the light. She smiled, and Jack knew as he looked into her coal black eyes that she was his, forever.

Jack sipped at his water, heard the glass tap against his teeth from his trembling hand. It was all so long ago, but seemed so fresh.

The past, the present, the future, it's all the same.

He wished that were true, that life were a book he could pick up and flip through to his favourite page.

A sharp crack sounded from his knee joints as he rose from his chair and walked through to the spare bedroom, where a rack with three horizontal shelves ran the length of one wall. Canvases with an identifying strip of masking tape on each of their edges stood on end along the three levels so that it resembled a giant's bookshelf. He retrieved a canvas covered in protective paper from the top shelf and unwrapped it. It was a portrait in oil of Kate sitting naked on the edge of a bathtub, her pale flesh backlit from a window so that a line of sunlight silhouetted her figure. Her hair and eyes, both the deepest shade of brown, stared out from the canvas.

'I shouldn't have painted you,' he whispered.

He placed it against a wall and pulled a sketch pad from the slim space on the shelf left by the removal of the portrait. *Jack Porter, aged 11* was written on the cover. He opened it to a page near the end where his untrained pencil lines formed an excellent resemblance of his murdered teacher, Miss Simpkins. It was superstitious nonsense, he knew, but sometime after Kate had died he vowed never to paint anybody he loved again. Miss Simpkins looked so young to him now—less than half his age—and Jack could see why he'd been so infatuated with her in junior school. She was pretty, her pale, elfin features framed by short dark hair that swept along her jaw line in a curl. He closed his eyes and pictured her, looking over her shoulder at the class as she chalked sums onto the blackboard. She had her reading glasses on, a detail he'd omitted from his drawing of her, though she had appeared no less beautiful to him with or without them.

They were pink framed, with spots of blood on one cracked lens.

Jack's body jerked, as if an electric current had passed through, and he dropped the pad on the floor. His insides felt like mush and an instant sweat covered his body.

What the hell was that?

The image remained of Miss Simpkins's damaged and blood stained spectacles, held in his young boy's hand, and he tried to see around the edge of it—knew there was more— but the whole memory was beyond his reach.

He put his hands over his face and began to cry. It seemed today was a day of revelations. Not only had he discovered the events leading to Kate's death, he'd also unearthed part of an older, darker memory that had somehow been repressed for more than forty years.

Jack put the sketch pad and Kate's portrait back on the shelf and left the room. He'd had enough of memories, half remembered or otherwise.

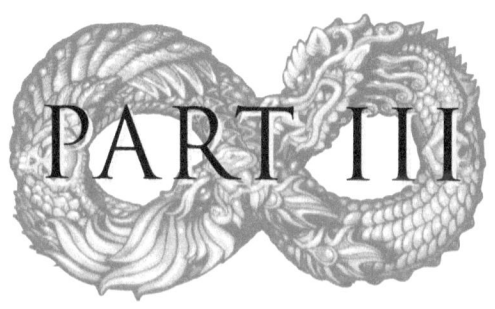

PART III

2016—FUNERAL FOR A FRIEND

 1

'THANKS FOR HELPING out.' Georgina tore a large strip of foil from the roll and placed it over the tray of sandwiches. 'This would have taken me all night.'

Carly smiled. 'No problem.' She looked at the kitchen window as she continued to spread butter on slice after slice of bread. 'I don't fancy driving home tonight anyway.'

'I'm glad you're staying over.' Georgina looked at the slow-falling fluffs of white that had begun to settle on the back lawn. 'I hope Michael gets home before it gets too thick.' She took the buttered loaf from Carly and began to fill it with sliced ham. 'How's work?'

'Good. Couple of difficult cases, but that's what it's all about. You know the score.'

Georgina watched her. A single strand of blonde hair loosened itself from Carly's hairclip and hung over one eye. She was a good looking young woman, though not quite beautiful. Her small frame gave her the appearance of a teenager though she'd just turned twenty-eight, and Georgina loved her as if she were her own daughter.

She also considered Carly to be somewhat of a miracle. In all the years Georgina had worked in social care until her recent retirement, she had never witnessed such a turnaround in someone whose life had gotten off to such a dreadful start. Carly had settled well with her foster parents after her mother's trial, excelled at school despite being so far behind, and gone on to university where she gained the grades that enabled her to secure what had become her dream job as a social worker. Georgina regarded her career choice as the highest form of flattery.

She'd kept constant contact with Carly—first as her case worker, then as her friend, and it had seemed a natural progression for Carly to move in with Georgina and Michael when she had turned eighteen. There had been more than a few tears shed by herself and Michael on the evening Carly had asked if she could call them Mum and Dad. Now she was grown, with a flat of her own in south London where she strived to help kids with circumstances as bad as hers once were, and Georgina and Michael could not have been more proud.

Carly protruded her bottom lip and blew the hair from her face. 'Is this the last batch?'

'Yes. I'll fill them and pop the lot over to Ellie.'

'How is she?'

'Pretty low. She hadn't seen much of Vinnie in recent years, but I don't suppose that softens the blow of losing her only brother like that.'

'No.' Carly helped with the sandwich fillings. 'Suicide's a terrible way to lose somebody. It's so hard to gain any kind of closure.'

'And Vinnie was her only family. Ellie never married.'

'That surprises me. She's very attractive, even now. She must have been stunning when she was young.'

Georgina pictured Ellie, serving in her mum's tea room in the village, so long ago. 'Yes, she was. I'm sure she's had her offers.'

Carly wrapped the last tray of sandwiches in tin foil. 'Shall I take them over?'

'I'll do it. You can put the kettle on. I'll ask Ellie if she wants to join us.'

The street was empty, the inch of snow that had fallen

untouched as yet by footprint or tire-track as Georgina crossed to Vinnie's childhood home, the trays stacked and balanced on her arms. Christmas was a week away, and the tree lights she spotted through windows with undrawn curtains made the old street resemble a scene from any number of Christmas films she'd seen throughout the years.

Why did you do it, Vinnie? The world can be so wonderful. Life can be so wonderful.

She approached Ellie's front door and managed to press the bell with an outstretched finger from beneath the sandwich trays. Ellie's figure approached, disjointed through the patterned glass.

'Hi, George.' She took the snacks from her. 'Thanks so much. I've made a ton of stuff myself, not that I'm expecting that many people.'

'Well, it's always best to have too much. Carly's just put the kettle on—do you want to come over?'

'No. Thanks anyway, but I've still some stuff to sort out for tomorrow.'

'Okay.' Georgina leaned forward and kissed her friend's cheek. 'I know Vinnie alienated some people, but I loved him, Ellie. I just wanted you to know.'

A sad smile flickered on Ellie's lips. 'I loved him too. There were times I just didn't like him very much.'

2

The view onto the marina was an artist's dream, and the foremost reason for Jack taking the apartment. He stepped onto the small balcony and looked down onto the various crafts moored there. The morning sky was an off-white sheet that diffused the atmosphere to a cold, pale grey. The predicted snow had not yet appeared in Brighton, though Jack had a feeling it was imminent. He pulled the collar up on his dressing gown and sipped from his steaming mug of coffee. The squeak of the sliding glass door sounded from behind and a moment later he felt Bev's arms around his midriff. She kissed the back of his ear. 'Up early,' she said.

'Yeah. Didn't sleep too well.'

'You should have woke me.' She rested her chin on his shoulder. 'Look at that sky. It's definitely going to snow.'

'Maybe I should stay home today.'

Bev moved around to his side, one arm still around his waist. Jack offered her his coffee which she took a quick swig from. 'You're not going then?' she asked.

'No.'

'It's a shame.'

He glanced at her. 'You know what Vinnie did.' A single gull glided above the boats and settled on the mast of an expensive looking yacht. 'Besides, I hadn't seen him for five years. I'd feel like a hypocrite. I didn't even reply to his letters when he got out of prison.'

'That doesn't matter now, Jack. None of that matters. He did some atrocious things that pushed you away, but I'm sure, despite all that, he knew you didn't hate him.'

'Didn't I?'

Bev placed the coffee on the balcony handrail, moved around in front of Jack and cupped his face in her hands. 'You would have had every right to hate him, but I know you didn't. *You* know you didn't. It's not in you, Jack; you're just too nice.'

'Why didn't I reply to him then? Those letters were desperate. If I'd written back, or called, maybe he wouldn't have—'

'Stop it,' Bev said. 'Vinnie ruined his own life. And there's always a choice.' Her voice softened. 'Vinnie killed himself, sweetie. It was his decision—you have nothing to feel guilty about.'

Vinnie killed himself. The words cut into Jack's heart like a scalpel as the reality took hold. *Vinnie's dead.*

Bev was right, he hadn't hated Vinnie. He'd been furious

with him, had wanted to hurt him, but Jack had found hate a difficult emotion to muster for someone who'd once been his best friend. He kissed Bev on the forehead. She could read him so well, and had always been good at showing things in the right light. And she'd stuck with him through his own bad patch, when his obsession with Kate had almost ruined their sex life and their whole relationship along with it. He'd wondered at the time if her insouciance to his impotence was a smoke screen, a cover for the fact that she might be looking for physical comfort elsewhere, but had not confronted her for fear of being branded a paranoid arsehole who couldn't bring himself to believe he was worthy of love. 'What do you think I should do?'

'You should go. If you don't, you'll regret it.'

Jack closed his eyes. When he'd learned of Vinnie's death in a phone call from Matt a fortnight before he'd told himself there was no chance he'd attend the funeral; he felt it would be disloyal to Kate. He realised now how ridiculous a notion that was. Vinnie was vain, and corrupt, willing to betray Jack by trying to sleep with the girl he loved, but Jack knew from the letters Vinnie had sent that he had never meant Kate any harm, and wished more than anything in the world that he hadn't acted with such selfishness.

He'd shown the letters to Bev. *Maybe he's changed,* she'd said. *Maybe you should see him.*

Jack had refused though, enjoying the cold revenge he knew he'd be sending Vinnie's way by not even acknowledging his existence. But he should have noticed the craziness in Vinnie's latest correspondence. Vinnie had become obsessed with Frankie again, convinced that the boy they had briefly known was haunting him.

He's fucking with me, Jack, and he's fucking with Matt and Georgina too, he'd written. *Our fates are intertwined, but something went wrong. You're the key, Jack, and he'll come for you. Me, Georgina, Matt—we're just playthings, like Katie. He'll use us to break your heart.*

He opened his eyes and pulled Bev close. 'You're right,' he said. 'I should go.'

She patted his behind. 'Go and take a shower. I'll make breakfast.'

He missed out on the morning jog that had been his routine for the past few years, and an hour later he was on the road, his windscreen wipers fighting against a thin, driving sleet as the robotic female voice of his sat-nav guided him back to his childhood home.

What am I doing? I know the route like the back of my hand. He switched it off and reflected on how lazy he'd become because of technology. There seemed to be no avoiding the trappings of the modern world even at the age of sixty.

The daylight dimmed despite the early hour as he crossed into Kent, and ten miles from Doom the sleet became snow and he slowed to keep his tires within the traffic-made ruts. 'Bloody hell,' he muttered and switched on the radio to BBC Kent, where the constant debates on Trump and Brexit were only interrupted by weather bulletins that warned listeners to only travel by car if necessary. 'Bit late to tell me that now.'

The view beyond his windscreen was a blur of white. He turned off the main carriageway onto the narrow B-road that wound its way to the village, struggling to find ruts to use as runners, and felt the tires slip away on the sharp bends as he crawled in second gear. He approached a steep drop in the road—the locals called it The Dip—and guided the little car down its fifty-foot slope. The snow was deepening, and when he hit the bottom of the hollow his bumper began to plough it. 'Oh, shit.' He knew the car would not make it up the opposite side, and managed, with a whine of revs and wheel-spinning, to park it close into the bushes on the left. Twenty feet ahead he noticed another car, stranded by its owner. He was half a mile from Georgina's and knew he had no choice; he'd have to walk the rest of the way.

3

The snow was incessant and had covered the oak lid of the coffin in less than a minute of it being lowered into the hole. Matt glanced across at Jack, Carly, and Ellie who were huddled together on the opposite side, their downcast eyes blinking against the fat snowflakes that blew against their faces. Georgina was pressed between Michael and himself, their arms linked. At the head of the grave the priest spoke in a loud, quick voice.

' . . . For I know that my Redeemer lives, and that at the last he will stand upon the earth; and after my skin has been thus destroyed . . . '

It was a piss-poor turnout, and Matt felt sad for Vinnie's sister. He wasn't sure how many mourners she'd expected, but the snowstorm hadn't helped. He'd travelled from London in his four-wheel drive Range Rover, and even that beast had struggled to traverse the final three miles of the journey. The Dip had almost stopped him and he'd noticed Jack's hatchback dumped alongside another car at the bottom as he kept a steady pressure on the throttle that just saw him up the opposite slope. Two hundred yards further on he'd picked up Jack, ruddy cheeked, breathless and very grateful.

' . . . And we indeed have been condemned justly, for we are getting what we deserve for our deeds . . . '

Matt had hoped that Hannah would be there; he knew it had ended in a real mess between her and Vinnie, but he'd thought that thirty-two years of marriage might be enough of a reason for her to attend. He closed his eyes and pictured Vinnie, not as a silver-haired sixty-two-year-old man but as a child, a pointed origami hat fashioned from newspaper on his head and a branch in his hand for a sword as the four of them played Robin Hood and his Merry Men in the woods. *We steal from the rich and give to the poor,* Vinnie yelled in his vision. It hadn't quite worked out that way for him.

Matt noticed a silence and felt a gentle tug on his elbow. He opened his eyes and looked at Georgina, whose face was pale. 'It's over,' she said. 'Come on, let's go home.'

He glanced down at the snow-covered coffin. 'Bye, Vinnie,' he muttered, before turning away. He looked over his shoulder and saw that Jack had remained by himself, crouched by the hole, his lips moving as he at last broke the five-year silence he'd imposed upon himself in regards to his oldest friend.

The inside of Ellie's house was warm and the small party of six settled in the living room, the mountain of sandwiches and snacks that would never be eaten a further reminder of the smallness of the occasion.

'Thank you for coming,' Ellie said. 'Vinnie would be glad.' She looked from Matt to Georgina and Jack. 'I know you were special to him. I just wish Hannah had come.'

'I'm sure more people would have turned up if it wasn't for the weather,' Georgina said.

'Maybe.' She forced a smile and put her palms on the arms of her chair to push herself to her feet. 'Who would like a drink?'

Carly stood. 'I'll do them, Ellie. You stay there.' She took the orders; they all chose hot drinks to thaw their insides over the plethora of alcohol on offer.

'Thank you, Carly,' Ellie called after her as she left the room to boil the kettle. She turned to Georgina. 'She's such a lovely girl.'

Matt noticed Georgina and Michael exchange an almost imperceptible smile. 'She is,' Georgina said. 'She's the very best.'

'I have something for you, from Vinnie.' Ellie reached into the handbag by her feet and pulled out a white envelope. 'Vinnie left it on his kitchen table. Here.' She passed it to Matt who was sitting closest to her. Matt saw that it was sealed and read aloud the few words written on its front. 'To Jack Porter, Georgina Smith, and Matthew Ward. To be read in private.'

'I think you three should read it later, alone,' Ellie said.

Matt tucked the envelope in his pocket with a feeling of embarrassment; he knew Vinnie had left no note of explanation for his final action to either Ellie or Hannah. 'If there's anything in there . . . ' He looked to Jack and Georgina.

'Yes, of course,' Georgina said, catching Matt's inference. 'If there's anything in the letter you should know about, Ellie, we'll tell you.'

Ellie sighed. 'If Vinnie's given any kind of explanation, it'll be the first time. Vinnie acts; he doesn't think, or explain.' Ellie looked down at her hands and cleared her throat. 'I still speak of him in the present tense. I suppose it takes some getting used to.'

'It does,' Jack said. It was the first time he'd spoken since the funeral and Matt noticed just how old and tired he looked. *We're all bloody old.*

He looked at the window, where the snow that had gathered in the corners of the panes reminded him of an illustration from a children's Christmas book. It failed to make him feel any younger.

4

Georgina stood by Jack's side at her front window as they watched Matt and Michael examine Matt's car. 'You'll have to stay over. You've no choice.'

'I know,' Jack said. 'Matt's going nowhere either.'

She saw Matt and her husband circle the Range Rover, which was buried in white to the top of its tires. The two of them spoke; Michael shook his head and patted Matt on his back as they turned towards the house.

Although she wouldn't admit it, Georgina was glad they had been snowed in. It had been a hard day, and the thought of Matt and Jack's company for the night gladdened her. They had stayed with Ellie well into the evening, long after the grey afternoon had turned a deep indigo, the reflected light off the snow not allowing the December sky its usual, total darkness. Georgina checked her wristwatch; it was just after eleven and the snowstorm showed no sign of easing. The front door opened and the sound of the two men kicking the excess snow from their boots echoed from the hallway.

'Looks like you're stuck with me,' Matt said as they entered the room.

Georgina sunk into the nook of the big L-shaped soft leather sofa that dominated the room. 'I figured that out years ago,' she said.

Matt sat beside her and Jack made himself comfortable in the armchair opposite.

'You guys look like you could do with a real drink,' Michael said.

Matt glanced up. 'I could murder a beer actually.'

'How about you, Jack?'

Jack was gazing at the orange flames of the log fire, hypnotised.

'Jack? Beer?'

He looked up. 'Oh, yes, please. Sorry, Michael, miles away.'

'Not for me, thanks,' Georgina said.

Michael went through to the kitchen and poured some beers which he returned with on a tray. He handed them out and seated himself next to his wife. 'Where's Carly?' he asked her.

'She's in her room, writing up some reports for work. I don't think we'll see her again tonight.' She watched the three men sip their beers, the comforting crackle of the fire the only sound in the room. It was Matt who broke the silence after a minute or so.

'I suppose we should take a look at this.' He pulled the envelope from his pocket.

'Not yet,' Michael said. 'It's for you guys. I'll take myself off to bed when I've drunk this.'

'I've no objections . . . ' Matt began.

'No, Michael's right,' Georgina interrupted. 'Vinnie addressed it to us. We should respect that.'

'And you three should have some time together alone,' Michael said.

Georgina watched him sip on his beer. Like Georgina, he seldom drank alcohol, and she was unsurprised when less than five minutes later he left it unfinished. He kissed her cheek and took himself upstairs. She turned to Matt. 'Do you have to call anyone?'

'No. Nobody's expecting me.'

'I already rang Bev,' Jack said.

Matt sat back, his big frame sinking into the leather. 'First time we've been together for a while,' he said. The three of them looked at each other and smiled a sad, resigned smile. He held the envelope up. 'Who wants to read it?'

'You do it,' Georgina said. 'Please.' She didn't think she could stand to read it herself, and Jack seemed quieter than usual, as if Vinnie's death had just hit him, or hit him hardest.

Matt put on his glasses, opened the envelope, and pulled the sheet of paper from inside. He read aloud.

Dear, Jack, Georgina, and Matt,

By now, you will know the decision I have taken. Please forgive me this at least, if nothing else. Jack, I am so sorry for betraying you, my oldest friend. I have no excuses. Georgina, you once held me and told me there are no monsters, a comforting lie for which I am eternally grateful. Matt, the bravest of us all. We looked to you when we were frightened, and you never let us down.

If I ever truly loved anybody, it was you three, so

I tell you this in the hope of saving you. The past was real. Hope house was real. Frankie and Bald Eagle were real. The three of you just won't talk about it, or accept it, but you'll have to if you want to survive. There are monsters, and they are coming.
I send this warning with nothing but love,
Vinnie.

Matt turned the paper in his hand, as if there might be more on the back. 'That's it,' he said.

Georgina realised she had been holding her breath and let it out in a long sigh. Somehow, she had expected this, had known that there would be mention of the demons they had each tried to bury in the dimness of the past.

'There are no monsters,' Jack said. 'You *did* say that to us, Georgina. After we saw . . .' He frowned.

'Bald Eagle,' Matt finished. 'That's what we called him.' He glanced once more at the letter. 'And Vinnie's right. We never talk about any of it.'

'Was it real?' Georgina asked. 'Or were we playing a game? A childhood fantasy?'

'I have an image of him, in my mind. He wore a long, white coat, and he had a scalpel. He was a surgeon.' Matt took a long swig of his beer. 'Real or not, he's been in here—' he tapped his head '—since my childhood. I've imagined seeing him several times since.'

'Vinnie used to say he was being haunted by Frankie,' Jack said. 'He told me he saw Frankie in the back of Kate's car on the night she died.' He rose from his chair and crossed to the window. 'Do you believe in ghosts?' he asked over his shoulder.

'No,' Georgina said. She felt a sudden anger take hold. *Ghosts?* It was a ridiculous notion. As crazy as the idea of a young girl tied to her bed for being possessed by demons.

'I did some research on Hope House back in eighty-four, when I was working on *Small Town Boy*,' Matt said. 'I discovered that Hope House had been used as a military hospital at the back end of World War One.'

Georgina huffed. 'What are you saying? That Bald Eagle was the ghost of a surgeon? Come on, Matt, you're the last person I'd expect to believe in that sort of nonsense.'

'I'm not saying I do. But the research jogged a few memories. Like when we played with the Ouija board.'

Georgina felt her body temperature drop. *The Ouija board. It belonged to Frankie's aunt.* It was another incident she'd forgotten, or blocked from her memory, and all at once, as if the recollection of that event had been a key, the doors opened in her mind to a flood of images from the past. She saw Jack's shoulders tighten. He turned to face her, and she knew from his expression that he'd experienced a similar revelation. He returned to his armchair and looked from Georgina to Matt, the flames from the fireplace reflecting orange under the black shadows of his features. 'Vinnie was right,' he said. 'We need to talk.'

1965—BLOOD STAINED GLASSES

1

THE MORNING AIR was warm and the sky a light, clear blue. Georgina took a deep inhalation as she stood on the garden path and lifted her face up to the heat of the morning sun. Even if it were cold and raining, Georgina believed she would have gotten just as much pleasure from the sensation. There had been more than one occasion in the past two weeks when she'd convinced herself she would never see the world beyond her bedroom again. She crossed the road and knocked on Vinnie's door.

'Georgie! You're better!' He grabbed his satchel and rushed outside. 'Bye, Mum,' he called over his shoulder as he closed the door. They turned left and headed towards school. Georgina noticed Vinnie sneaking a sidelong look at her. 'Are you all right now?'

'Yes.'

'You look different.'

'Do I?' A brief panic caused her pulse to quicken at the illogical thought that Vinnie could tell what she'd been through by her appearance.

'Yeah. I think you've lost weight.'

Georgina looked down at her grey school dress which she had already noticed didn't fit as snug as it had before. 'I haven't been able to eat much.'

'What was wrong, then?'

She shrugged her shoulders. *He doesn't believe me. He knows something happened.* 'Doctor said it was a virus.'

'Oh. Right.'

They strolled on to the village green and along the row of shops. As they passed the butchers on the opposite side of the road, Georgina kept Vinnie between her and the shopfront to stay from Mr. Poole's view, whose meat cleaver she heard come down on his wooden chopping board with a dull thump. 'Anything happen while I've been off?'

'Yeah. We haven't got Miss Simpkins anymore.'

'Why not?'

'She's disappeared. Just didn't turn up one morning.'

Georgina was overcome with a simultaneous feeling of hopelessness and relief: hopelessness that she would not be able to confide what had happened to the only adult she trusted; relief that the decision of whether or not to tell had been taken from her. But the thought of not seeing Miss Simpkins again gave her a weird sensation inside her stomach, as if it had become hollow. 'She isn't from around here—maybe she had to visit her family.'

'She hasn't just gone away, she's *missing*. The police are looking for her. It was in the paper.'

'Oh.' Georgina became worried then at what might have befallen her teacher.

Maybe she's tied to a bed somewhere.

They neared the school's front gates and Georgina was greeted by several classmates who asked after her health, and the more she told the lie about being hit by a virus, the more it seemed like the truth. She wondered if it were possible to recite the untruth enough times so that she could believe it herself and let the memory of being bound to her bed, half-starved and stinking of piss and shit, slip from her mind forever.

The single-storey school seemed smaller somehow, and as they crossed the playground she saw Matt and Jack, patting a tennis ball against the brick wall to one side of the entrance with their palms.

'Oy, Laurel and Hardy,' Vinnie called as they approached. 'Look who I found.'

The boys glanced around and Georgina felt something like real happiness for the first time in weeks. A warmth grew in her chest as she caught sight of the genuine smiles on their faces upon seeing her. They left the ball to bounce away and rushed over.

'How are you?' Jack asked, 'Matt's been worried sick.' His face reddened. 'I mean, we all have.'

'Thanks. I'm fine now.'

'Hello, Georgina.'

'Hello, Matt.' She looked into his gorgeous, dark eyes and wished they were alone so that he would put an arm around her, the way he had after her father had made her scrub her skin in a bathtub of freezing water to be rid of her sins. Tears welled in her eyes and she urged them away.

Matt opened his mouth to say more but was interrupted by the clang of the big brass bell being swept up and down by Mrs. Andrews. 'Time to go in,' he said, but Georgina caught a message from his expression that told her they would talk later.

They walked up the stone steps to the entrance where Mr. Browning, the deputy head, was informing all the children that passed to go straight to the little assembly hall instead of their classrooms.

'What's going on?' Georgina asked.

'I don't know. Old Browning looked even more miserable than usual, though,' Vinnie muttered.

In the hall, the children arranged themselves cross-legged on the floor facing the long window where the headmaster, Mr. Clarke, conducted the daily assemblies. Georgina was between Matt and Jack, and a low hubbub of chattering voices filled the hall for five minutes until Mr. Clarke entered from the side door and made his way to the front. The pupils fell silent as he faced them, and Georgina noticed how pale his usually ruddy complexion appeared, as if he were about to be sick on his shoes.

'Good morning, children of St. Jude's,' he said in a low voice devoid of any hint of the good humour it sometimes carried. 'This morning is a special assembly.' He paused, cleared his throat, and cast his gaze across the children as if reluctant to continue. 'I'm afraid it is my very sad and unfortunate duty to have to tell you that Miss Simpkins has passed away.' A few children gasped and Georgina felt Matt's warm palm on the back of her fingers on the floor between them. She turned her hand and gripped his tight.

'This has come as a great shock to us all,' Mr. Clarke continued. 'I know she was as popular with the pupils of St. Jude's as she was with the staff. She was first and foremost an excellent teacher, but she was also a valued friend to both her colleagues and pupils, and we shall all miss her very much.' He bowed his head. 'Please join me in the Lord's prayer.' He recited the words in a low voice and, halfway through, Georgina felt the slight jerk of Jack's shoulders against hers. She reached for him and held onto his trembling hand. It was a bad day to return to school.

The day dragged, and when they were at last released from their classroom that afternoon it was into a scorching atmosphere. Vinnie had arranged for the three boys to go over to Frankie's and watch his auntie's colour television. They each only had black and white sets at home, apart from Georgina whose parents refused to have any television in the house at all. 'You can come, Georgina,' he said. 'Frankie won't mind. He's all right when you get to know him.'

'No, I haven't told my mum. I'll have to go home.'

'Actually, I don't really feel like it now,' Jack said.

'But it's *The Flintstones*,' Vinnie said. He looked at Matt. 'Don't tell me you ain't coming.'

'I'll meet you there. I'll just walk Georgina home first.'

'All right, don't be long.' Vinnie took a few paces, turned, and came back to where they stood. 'See you tomorrow, mate,' he said to Jack, with a gentle pat on his shoulder. 'Keep your chin up.'

'Him and Frankie good mates now, are they?' Georgina asked when Vinnie had gone.

'Seems so,' Matt said. They walked with Jack to his house first, although it was in the opposite direction, before doubling back to the village green where they sat on the bench.

'Jack's really upset,' Georgina said.

'Everybody is,' Matt replied. 'I think she meant more to Jack, though. I think he loved her.'

Georgina smiled. 'Yes, I had thought that before. Jack isn't very good at hiding his feelings.'

'I called for you a few times when you were off school. Did your mum tell you?'

'No.'

Matt shuffled closer to her. 'You don't have to tell me what kind of trouble you were in, Georgina, but I want you to know that you can. I told you before, I'll always be here for you.'

Georgina wanted to tell him but stopped herself. What could Matt do? He was a kid, just like her, and her father's threats over what would happen if she spoke about her treatment made her feel cold inside. If Miss Simpkins were alive, she might have had the courage to tell her. Miss Simpkins would never have let any more harm come to her, she was sure.

She shook her head. 'I can't talk about it.'

Matt rested his arm across her shoulders. 'That's okay. I understand. But if there's anything I can do to help, I will.'

2

'Jack! Jack!' Mary ran along the narrow hallway to meet him

as he stepped through the front door. 'Mummy's making a doll's house with me. Come and help.'

She slipped her little hand in his and tried to tug him towards the kitchen. Jack glanced through the open door and saw his mum there, her sleeves rolled up amongst a pile of egg cartons and cereal boxes at the table. She saw him and rose from her seat, her face as sad as he'd ever seen it. 'Oh, Jack,' she said.

'I'll come in a minute, Mary. I need the toilet first.' He let go of his sister's hand and ran up the stairs two at a time to the bathroom, where he pulled the brass latch across to lock himself inside. He sat on the edge of the bathtub and leaned his hands on his knees, his heart racing.

A familiar image formed in his mind of his teacher, looking over her shoulder at him through her pink-framed glasses as she scraped her chalk across the blackboard, the slimness of her waist revealed by the blouse tucked tight into her skirt which rose just above the backs of her knees.

A moment later the room seemed to tilt and Jack was on his knees at the toilet bowl where he spewed until his stomach was empty, though he continued to dry heave. Three light taps sounded on the door behind him.

'Jack,' his mum said, in a soothing voice. 'Are you alright? Do you want me to come in?'

The spasms in his abdomen stopped at last and he sat, breathless, against the wall. 'I'm fine,' he croaked. 'I just want to be on my own.'

His mother fell silent, though he sensed her presence still on the other side of the door. 'I heard about Miss Simpkins,' she said after half a minute or so. 'It's a terrible shock; she was such a lovely young woman.' From downstairs, Jack heard the muffled voice of Mary, calling for their mum to return to the kitchen. 'Come down when you're ready, Jack,' his mum said.

He listened to her footfalls as she descended the staircase, and when he was sure she was back in the kitchen with Mary, he used the hand basin to pull himself to his feet. His pale reflection looked back at him from the mirror above the sink and he splashed some water over his face and rinsed his mouth out to remove the vile taste that lingered.

After he'd dried his face, Jack undid the door latch and walked across to his bedroom where he pulled the sketchpad that contained Miss Simpkins's likeness from the stack in his wardrobe. Sitting on his bed, Jack opened it to the page and gazed at the drawing. She was so beautiful and kind, and Jack vowed that he would keep the picture forever. He traced a fingertip along her cheekbone.

'I love you,' he whispered. 'I'll never forget you.' He closed the pad, placed it under his bed and laid his head back on his pillow. As his exhausted mind began to drift, he heard the front door open and the slow approach of footsteps as they ascended the stairs.

'It's all the same, Jack,' a man's voice said from his bedroom doorway.

Jack tried to open his eyelids, but they were so heavy. 'What is?' he heard himself murmur.

'The past, the present, the future. It's all the same.'

A sudden dread overcame Jack. *Somebody told me that once. When I was old.* No, that didn't make sense. He forced his eyes open for a moment, but everything was blurred, including the man in the doorway. He closed his eyes and sank back into darkness.

It's all the same. Miss Simpkins is alive, and she's dead, and she hasn't been born.

He heard himself whimper and felt something on his shoulder, along with the sensation of rolling from side to side.

'Jack?'

This time he opened his eyes wide, and looked up into his father's face. 'Dad!' He threw himself forward and hugged his father, who was sitting on the edge of his bed with one gentle hand on his shoulder. Jack felt his dad's arms engulf him and breathed in the odour of his aftershave as he buried his face in his neck. He noticed that the room was dim—he'd been asleep for at least a couple of hours. He began to weep.

'It's okay, son. It's good to cry. Just let it out.'

Jack felt himself sway as his dad rocked him, the way Jack remembered he used to when he was little after he'd fallen and grazed his knee or bumped his head. It was comforting, and after a while the deep sobs that wracked his body subsided. He pulled away and wiped his eyes and nose with the handkerchief offered by his father. 'It's a very sad day, for the whole village,' his dad said.

'Why did she go missing? Where did they find her?'

Charles Porter stood from the bed and pushed the door closed. 'I don't want your sister hearing any of this.' When he spoke it was in a hushed voice. 'Mr. Gibbs was walking his dog through the woods down by The Dip. He found her there.'

Jack swallowed. 'How did she die?'

'She was murdered, Jack.'

He had of course considered the possibility that Miss Simpkins had been murdered, as most of the kids at school had in hushed tones at lunch time. He just didn't want it to be true. 'Poor Miss Simpkins,' he whispered.

'Yes.' His dad averted his eyes from Jack's gaze. 'Dinner's ready in ten minutes. Come down. It'll make you feel better than sitting up here alone.'

Jack nodded. He wasn't sure if "better" was the correct word, but he had felt comforted by his father's presence. 'I will.'

Charles twitched the corner of his mouth in a brief, sad smile and opened the door. Before he walked away, he spoke over his shoulder without quite looking all the way around at his son. 'I'm sorry, Jack,' he said. 'I know how much she meant to you.'

3

Matt was glad when *The Flintstones* ended. It wasn't that he didn't like the show but he'd been unable to concentrate.

Something had happened with Georgina and her parents, something worse than usual, and returning to school on today of all days hadn't helped her situation. And there was Jack, who hadn't spoken a word as he and Georgina had walked him home. *Poor Jack.* Matt felt an ache deep inside for his friend, who'd had an enormous—and obvious—crush on Miss Simpkins. *No, it was more than a crush. He loved her.* Yes, the word "crush" made what Jack had felt seem too trivial.

Matt glanced over at Vinnie, still staring agog at the television as the end credits where Fred is dumped on his front doorstep by his pet sabre-tooth rolled. Of the four friends Vinnie seemed the least affected by Miss Simpkins's death, though Matt knew that Vinnie had always kept his emotions hidden somewhere deep. When he considered it, he realised that he'd never seen Vinnie cry in all the time he'd known him, which was since nursery school.

'That was so cool,' Vinnie said when the show was over. 'I wish my mum would get a colour television.'

'You can't rely on other people,' Frankie said.

'What's that mean?' Vinnie asked.

'It means that if you really want something, you'll find a way.'

Matt snorted. 'Yeah, start saving your pocket money, Vinnie. It'll only take you ten years.'

'He doesn't mean that,' Vinnie said. Matt noticed a hint of annoyance in his voice.

Matt looked across at Frankie who was reclined in an armchair with his feet rested on an old oak coffee table. He pulled a packet of cigarettes and a lighter from his pocket, lit one, and offered the pack to Matt.

'No, thanks.'

Frankie shrugged and lobbed the cigarettes and lighter

across the room to Vinnie who popped one between his lips. Matt caught his eye and frowned at him. 'Since when have you smoked?'

'Couple of weeks,' Vinnie mumbled as he flicked the lighter and drew on the cigarette until its tip glowed red. He tipped his head back and blew a thin stream of smoke towards the ceiling. 'You should try it.'

'Yes,' Frankie gazed at Matt. 'You should try everything at least once,' he said. Matt detected a sly undertone in his voice and felt his face redden. Frankie let out a bored little laugh and looked away.

Matt looked around the big, high-ceilinged room, which was decorated in a traditional floral print with dark red velvet curtains hanging open on either side of the main window. It was what Frankie had told them was the *entertainment room*, containing the television, a piano, and a round, green baize-covered card table. Matt had never been in a house like it. Even Frankie had been unable to tell him how many rooms the mansion contained. 'We rarely use any rooms in the south wing,' he'd said at the time.

'I'll never smoke,' Matt said. 'It makes you smell like an old tramp.'

'Well you wouldn't like that, would you?' Frankie took a long drag and puffed a series of smoke rings into the room. 'I heard about your teacher. I don't suppose you get many murders around here.'

Matt and Vinnie exchanged a glance. 'Who says it was murder?' Vinnie asked.

'Oh, I hear things. People say she was a very beautiful woman—bit of a fox. I expect all the boys in your class were very fond of her.' He shot a glance at Matt and smiled to himself. 'Well, most of you,' he muttered.

Matt felt his temper rising. 'What does that mean?'

'Don't get upset. I just mean we all have different tastes.' He looked at Matt's fists, clenched in his lap. 'I didn't mean to offend you, Matt,' he said in an earnest tone.

'We all liked Miss Simpkins, Frankie,' Vinnie said. 'And we're all upset.'

Frankie turned from Vinnie to Matt. 'You're right. I apologise for my insensitive comments.' He rose from his chair and turned the television off. 'Who wants to see something *cool*?' He said the last word in what Matt thought was a mock imitation of Vinnie.

'Okay,' Vinnie said, unaware of the mimicry.

'Follow me.' He stubbed his cigarette out in an ashtray which he passed to Vinnie to do the same before leading them to the big entrance hallway where a wide staircase swept up one side to the first-floor landing.

'Where are we going?' Matt asked.

'To my aunt's room.'

Vinnie shot a glance back at the double entrance doors as they ascended the stairs. 'What if she comes home?'

'Don't worry. She's in London on business. She won't be home until tonight.'

Matt glanced over the ornate dark-wood banisters onto the hall below as they passed along the first-floor walkway. It reminded him of the kind of Hollywood set Errol Flynn would have bounded across in one of his old swashbuckling movies. Frankie led them towards the rear of the house into a passage with half a dozen doors on either side and opened the third one on their left. They followed him into the bedroom, which was dominated by a four-poster double bed. He pulled a stool from the dressing table across to the wardrobe, stood on it and reached up. 'Have you ever seen a naked woman?' he asked.

Matt noticed the glint of excitement in Vinnie's eye and sighed. He just wanted to go home now and sit in the quiet of his bedroom with his copy of *Dr. No*. Frankie hopped onto the floor between them and opened a thin magazine with the title *Glamour Puss* printed on the cover above a colour photo of a bikini clad beauty queen with a blonde beehive hairdo. The pictures inside were in black and white, with just a small caption in the bottom corner of each page.

'Bloody hell,' Vinnie whispered, as he gazed at a photo of the cover girl, sitting cross-legged in a wicker chair with nothing on but a pair of high-heeled shoes. He took the magazine and flipped the page to another pose by the same model, this time relaxing in a foam bath-tub, her breasts protruding from the water like a pair of islands. A frown formed on his brow. 'This is your aunt's?'

'Yes.'

'I thought only men bought dirty books.'

Frankie laughed. 'She's a photographer. She took the pictures.'

'I have to go home,' Matt said. 'You coming, Vinnie?'

'Hang on.' Vinnie had a look of impatience on his face as he flicked through the pages.

'It's all right, Vinnie,' Frankie said, taking the book. 'You can look at it some other time.' He put it back on the wardrobe and led them through the house to the front entrance. 'See you, then,' he said as they left. 'Be careful.' He closed the door before either of them could reply.

The early evening was still bright as Matt and Vinnie's footsteps crunched over the gravel road that joined the grounds of Hope House to the northern approach road. They could have cut through the woods to the field behind Jack's house and saved themselves twenty minutes, but the unspoken fear of Miss Simpkins's murderer had made up their minds.

'Don't you think Frankie's situation's a bit weird?' Matt asked.

'What situation?'

'Well, he's an eleven-year-old kid, same as us, living in a great big house on his own.'

'His aunt lives there as well. You know that.'

'Have you ever seen her?'

'No, but she comes home every night.'

Matt shook his head. 'There's something not right. It's the way he talks, as if he's a grown-up.'

'He's well-educated.'

'Really? I thought he didn't even go to school.'

'Frankie's all right,' Vinnie said. They turned left out of Hope House's grounds and strolled along the grass verge that edged the road. Vinnie nudged Matt's elbow. 'I know what's wrong with you. That dirty book freaked you out. You've never seen a pair of tits before.'

'I see one big tit every day actually; his name's Vinnie.'

Vinnie jumped on his back. 'Hi-ho Silver!'

Matt ran, stumbled and tipped Vinnie over his shoulder as they sprawled across the grass, laughing. Matt was up first and pulled Vinnie to his feet with one hand. 'Listen, Vinnie, Frankie probably is all right. Just be careful, though.'

'Of what?'

'I don't know. But I've got a feeling he's the sort to get you into trouble.'

4

There was no single reason why Georgina began to cut herself again. She had vowed to stop after she was released from the prison of her bed; she had experienced enough pain at the hands of others to make the notion of inflicting any upon herself seem ridiculous. But two months can seem like a long time to an eleven-year-old whose world is a slim space between fear and sadness.

The burial of Miss Simpkins took place after six weeks of autopsies and investigations that whipped the residents of Doom into a frenzy of rumour, innuendo and fear. Just about everyone in the village attended, plus friends and relatives, making it the biggest funeral in living memory for most locals.

It was Frankie that had relayed the details of Miss

Simpkins' death. 'Her hands and feet were cut off,' he'd said, one day on the village green. Georgina had been glad that Jack wasn't there to hear it, and Matt and Vinnie looked at her in a way that revealed they shared her relief at Jack's absence on that occasion.

He chopped off her hands and feet.

She felt sick. There was nothing she could prove, and nobody she could turn to, but it struck her as too much of a coincidence that the mutilations suffered by Miss Simpkins were a match for the ones threatened on Georgina by the butcher. And on the occasions she'd passed by Mr. Poole in the two weeks since the funeral, he'd given her a sly, knowing smile.

But knowing what? That he was the killer? It proved nothing. In fact, if he was the killer, she reasoned, he would not have taken the risk of letting Georgina live with her knowledge of his sick desires; she suspected he would have killed her weeks ago.

She dabbed at the scratch on her left thigh with a piece of toilet paper, soaking the blood. She couldn't take the risk of cutting herself on the arms since her father discovered her injuries, and she only did it if she was home alone. She checked the paper, and satisfied that she had stopped bleeding flushed it down the toilet. She stowed her father's discarded razor blade from the bin in the bathroom to her new hiding place for it, the thin gap behind the toilet cistern, high on the wall.

Three sudden raps from the front door startled her, though she recognised their style in an instant. 'Matt,' she whispered. She ran down the stairs two at a time and jumped the final four before running to the door, where she saw her friend's figure through the frosted top half of glass. 'What're you doing here? I thought you had boxing training.'

'It was cancelled. I got the bus there and back for nothing.'

She had the place to herself and wanted to ask him in, but

was embarrassed. Matt's house was nice, clean and well decorated, as was Jack's and Vinnie's. Georgina was well aware of what a bleak, sparse tip her house was in comparison.

'Can you come out?' Matt asked.

'Yes. Dad's at work and Mum's visiting my Auntie in Durling.'

'Look.' Matt pulled a scrap of paper from his jean-trouser pocket. 'This came through my door when I was out.' He handed it over.

> *Hi Matt,*
>
> *Vinnie and I called to see if you want to come over to Hope House for the day. We will call on Jack on the way, feel free to bring Georgina if you wish. I have something cool planned for which we need at least four.*
>
> *Frankie.*

She studied the small smiley face drawn alongside Frankie's signature that for some reason seemed so familiar.

'What do you think?' Matt asked when she'd read it.

'I haven't been inside Hope House yet. There's not much else to do'

'I suppose so.' They were four weeks into the summer break, and whilst neither of them would describe the long hot summer days away from school as boring, the initial excitement had worn off.

Georgina sensed a hint of distraction in Matt's voice. 'We don't have to go, if you'd prefer not to.'

Matt seemed to consider it. 'No.' He smiled. 'You're right, we haven't much else to do. And you won't believe how many rooms there are.'

'Great!' Georgina slipped into her plimsolls and they headed off. She would reflect, many years later, how such a small decision could wreck so many lives.

5

Jack dropped the handful of weeds into the pile in the wheelbarrow, ran the back of his hand across his brow, and scanned the dirt bed. He'd cleared perhaps half of the overturned soil of unwanted growth in just over an hour, which was a disappointment. When his dad had offered him the chore that morning, with a shilling as payment, Jack had reckoned it to be no more than thirty minutes' work and the easiest shilling he'd ever earn. He now realised just how much he'd underestimated the task, and smiled to himself at his dad's canniness. Not that any of it mattered—he'd have done it for free anyway, but a shilling was a shilling after all.

He bent to pluck an unattractive, gnarled growth as the chime of the doorbell echoed to him through the open back door of the kitchen. He wondered who it might be. It couldn't be Vinnie, Matt, or Georgina—Jack and his friends had developed their own specific knocking-code when calling for each other and would never use the doorbell. He brushed his hands together to remove the loose dirt and crossed through the house to the front door.

'Watcha,' Vinnie said, when Jack opened it. Beside him, Frankie was standing with his hands in his pockets.

'Watcha, Vinnie. Why did you ring?'

Vinnie tipped his head to one side. 'He did it. We haven't given him a knock, yet.'

Jack nodded at Frankie. 'All right, Frankie?'

'I'm well, thank you very much.' Jack and Vinnie looked at each other and laughed at the overly formal reply. Frankie smiled. 'Have I said something funny?'

'No, don't worry about it,' Jack said.

'We're going over to my house,' Frankie said. 'Would you like to come?'

'I'm weeding the garden for my dad.'

'Is he home?' Vinnie asked.

'No. He'll be back in a while. I'm here on my own.'

'Just leave it then.'

'I have to finish it. He's paying me a shilling. I'll be finished in an hour.'

'Come over then,' Frankie said. 'We're there all afternoon.'

'Okay. What are we going to do?' He remembered the book of naked ladies Vinnie had told him about and wondered if he might get to see it.

A faint smile crossed Frankie's lips. 'If everyone's there, something special. Something you'll never forget.'

'Everyone?'

'Yeah,' Vinnie said. 'Matt and Georgina might be there later as well.'

'All right, I'll see you in a little while.'

'Can we cut through your garden?'

'If you like.' He led them through the house and held the loose board open at the back fence for them to pass through into the field beyond.

Something special. Whatever it was, it wasn't looking at nude photos of women if Georgina was going to be there. Not that he was that bothered; he was just a little curious.

Miss Simpkins face, unbidden, popped into his mind, and he felt a surge of guilt over wanting to see the photos at all. He plunged his hands into the soil, ripping at the weeds with a fury. He'd managed to forget the heartache for a little while before Vinnie and Frankie had called as he'd concentrated on the chore set by his dad. He tried to return to that state though he knew it would be impossible.

He pondered what Frankie had said as he worked. *Something you'll never forget.* As it turned out Frankie was wrong. Jack would forget everything that happened that afternoon for almost fifty years.

6

Matt poured another glass of iced homemade lemonade from the jug Frankie had placed on the wood-slatted table and looked around. The garden was almost as big as the village green, its boundary marked by dense foliage and trees so that it almost felt they were sitting in a natural copse.

'This is lovely,' Georgina said, indicating the lemonade.

'It's my auntie's recipe.' Frankie smiled at her. 'She left this jug in the fridge for us when I told her I was entertaining friends today.'

'That was kind of her. She sounds very nice.' Georgina took a sip. 'Does she work, then?'

'Yes, in London.'

'What does she do?'

Matt exchanged a glance with Vinnie who turned away to hide his grin.

'She's a photographer,' Frankie said.

'Oh. Cool.'

Matt shook his head. Even Georgina was aping Vinnie's Americanisms. 'So, what's the big surprise, then?'

'Well, I'd hoped Jack would be here too, but there are four of us. We may as well go ahead in case he lets us down.'

'If Jack said he'll be here, he will,' Vinnie said. 'He's probably on his way.'

There was a hint of defensiveness in Vinnie's voice on his friend's behalf that made Matt feel proud. The four of them had always been a strong unit, loyal to each other, but he'd sensed a wedge being formed between the group and Vinnie in recent weeks, placed there in a subtle way by Frankie, though he knew he could offer no particular incident of proof if asked.

'It's good that you have such faith in your friend,' Frankie said.

'I do. Jack's my best friend. He'd never let me down.'

'And what about you?' Frankie stared at Vinnie. 'Would you ever let *him* down?'

'No.'

Frankie patted his shoulder and stood. 'Good for you.' He looked at the house. 'Actually, I'd like him to be here too. You four really mean a lot to me,' he said. 'If you're so sure Jack's coming, he can join in when he gets here. Come on.' He strode away from the table towards the house.

Matt looked at Georgina who shrugged her shoulders. It was true what Vinnie had said: Jack had always been reliable, but gardening was hard work and could take a while. 'Come on,' he said. 'Jack won't mind us starting without him, whatever it is.'

They followed Frankie across the lawn and into the building. The corridor there led them back to the entrance hall where they crossed to the entertainment room, which was a relief to Matt who'd been concerned that Frankie might lead them up to his aunt's bedroom and the dirty book. He'd already decided he would grab Georgina's hand and walk out of the house if that was Frankie's big plan.

'Do you like board games?' Frankie asked. 'This is the best one ever,' he said, not giving them time to answer. He led them across to the circular card table, which was covered in green baize and set with five chairs. 'It's called an Ouija board.'

Frankie removed the chair intended for Jack that was now spare, and the four of them sat down. A polished wooden board had been set on the card-table's surface, upon which the alphabet had been spelt out in two curved rows of fancy lettering with the numbers from zero to nine beneath, and the words HELLO and GOODBYE at the top and bottom. YES and NO were printed in each of the top corners, the NO accompanied by a half-moon with a face and the YES by a smiling sun.

Matt had read about these boards and knew exactly what they were used for, though he didn't believe in ghosts or demons or any similar nonsense. He looked across at Frankie who'd sat himself opposite. 'This is yours?'

'It's my aunt's.'

Georgina, who had placed herself opposite Vinnie on Matt's left hand side, ran a finger across the smooth wooden surface. 'Is it like backgammon?' she asked.

'Not really,' Frankie said. 'We don't play against each other. We play together, on the same side.'

Matt glanced at Vinnie, whose expression made it obvious that he also had no idea what it was for. 'So what's the point?' Vinnie asked. 'How can anyone win?'

Frankie looked around the table. 'Nobody wins. We just have fun.'

'It's for talking to ghosts,' Matt said. Georgina and Vinnie looked at him. 'If you believe in that crap.'

'Are you saying you don't believe in spirits?' Frankie asked.

'That's right.'

'And how about angels, or God?'

'No.' Matt sensed Georgina watching him. 'Sorry, Georgina, but I don't. I think it's all rubbish.'

'What if I were to tell you I can prove you wrong, right now?'

Matt pushed his chair back. 'Come on, George. Let's go.'

'Hang on.' He felt her hand on his wrist. She looked at Frankie. 'Can we ask the spirits questions?'

'Of course. Anything you like, Georgina.'

She looked back at Matt and spoke in a quiet voice. 'I want to do it.'

'I don't think it's a good idea.'

'Please.'

'Look at it this way,' Frankie said. 'If nothing happens, Matt, you'll be proved right.' He leaned forward on his elbows. 'Whereas if something does happen, you will have the most amazing experience of your life.'

'Come on, Matt,' Vinnie said. 'It'll be cool.'

Matt sighed and pulled his chair back in. 'All right. For five minutes, and that's it.'

'Splendid.' Frankie rose from his seat and took a lighter from his trouser pocket which he used to light half a dozen candles on ledges and tables around the perimeter. He then crossed to the big window where he untied the red velvet curtains and let them drop, the thick material blocking any trace of sunlight. Matt felt the warmth of Georgina's small hand as she slipped it into his under the table.

'Do we have to shut the curtains?' Vinnie asked as Frankie returned to his seat.

'Yes.' Frankie grinned. 'Don't be scared, Vinnie.' Frankie put one of the lit candles on the table and lifted a wine glass from a set of six arranged on a bureau by his side. He placed it, upturned, onto the centre of the board, and touched two fingertips from his right hand on it. 'Do the same as me,' he said. Matt copied his gesture, followed a moment later by Georgina and Vinnie, whose faces looked solemn in the flickering glow of the candlelight. Georgina continued to grip Matt's free hand with hers on his lap.

'Have you done this before?' Georgina asked.

'No. I've watched my aunt and her friends.'

'I ain't scared,' Vinnie said.

'Shh.' Frankie stared at the glass. 'We need silence.'

After a minute or so, when the silence had seemed to take on its own, heavy mass, Frankie spoke. 'If there are any spirits present, make yourself known through the board.'

Matt realised he'd been holding his breath as he focused on the wine glass, and let out a long, quiet stream of air from his lungs. Beneath the table, Georgina's grip was tightening with every passing second. The glass was static. Matt glanced up at Frankie, whose head was tipped forward so that his eyes were shadowed. 'Is anybody there?' he whispered.

Matt felt a tremble beneath his fingertips and felt his heartbeat quicken, only to realise a moment later that the vibration was coming from Vinnie, whose body had begun to shake.

'Don't be scared, Vinnie,' Frankie said, his voice soft. He

tipped his head back and aimed his voice at the ceiling. 'If any spirits are with us, please move the glass.'

The suddenness of its motion startled all four of them as the glass slid in a direct line to the top of the board to settle on the word HELLO. Matt felt a chill work its way through his body despite his scepticism.

'Hello,' Frankie said. He flashed a smile at Matt before returning his attention to the candle-lit board. 'May we ask you some questions?' The glass moved left to YES, alongside the smiling sun symbol. Matt watched Frankie's fingers, trying to discern if he could detect any pressure. Frankie looked across the board at him and raised his eyebrows. 'Perhaps you should ask the first one, Matt.'

'Okay.' Matt thought about it for a moment, taken aback by the unexpected request. If he wanted to catch Frankie out, he knew he'd have to ask a question he was sure that Frankie could not know the answer to. 'What book am I reading?' The glass glided toward the alphabet, and as each of the four letters were indicated his arms broke out in goose bumps.

DR NO.

He kept his head down, could sense the satisfaction emanating from Frankie at the obvious conclusion from Matt's own reaction that *Dr. No* was indeed the book on his bedside table at home.

'Anything else, Matt?'

Matt shook his head.

'Who are you?' Vinnie asked, his voice small. The glass's movement was rapid.

NOBODY—EVERYBODY—MOROS.

'Moros,' Vinnie whispered, and Matt was sure he'd heard the name before. *Or I'm going to hear it.* That didn't make sense, he knew, but it felt true.

'What are you?'

NOTHING—EVERYTHING—MOROS.

Vinnie swallowed. 'Are you good?'

The glass edged towards the moon symbol and NO, then

veered the opposite way to the sun face and YES before once again returning to the alphabet.

NEITHER—BOTH—MOROS.

Even under the yellow glow of the candle flame, Matt could see the paleness that had chased any colour from Vinnie's face.

Georgina cleared her throat. 'I want to ask a question.'

Matt and Vinnie shot a glance at each other, both aware—and fearful—of what they suspected Georgina was going to say.

'Who killed Miss Simpkins?'

The glass remained still for five seconds before moving, much slower than it had before.

CUT—CUT—FUCK—FUCK—NICE.

'That's enough,' Matt said. 'End it Frankie.'

'Who killed Miss Simpkins?' Georgina repeated, louder.

ASK—NEXT—TIME.

The glass moved down the board and stopped on GOODBYE.

7

Jack took a step back and examined the plot. He'd done a good job—he had the aches to prove it—and couldn't spot a single weed in the overturned earth. He wheeled the barrow with the offending growth and parked it in the gap between the shed and the fence. He hadn't been told to dispose of the weeds, or how to, and guessed his father would attend to that particular task. He turned on the outside tap fixed to the back wall of the house and rubbed his hands together under its flow, the mud-stained water splashing in and around the small grille-covered drain below.

He glanced back once more to admire his work and imagined how pleased his dad would be. Jack loved to please his dad. Though he was only eleven he'd sensed a subtle change in their relationship of late, in that his father was treating him as a young man, and a friend, as well as a son. Jack adored his mum, but the connection with his dad was something special. Vinnie was his best friend, and he was very close to Georgina and Matt, but he knew that whatever happened in life, his dad would be there. There was no problem Charles Porter couldn't solve.

He turned the tap off, wiped his palms down the sides of his jeans and was about to go inside and get ready to make his way over to Frankie's house when he noticed the pitchfork he'd used jutting from the grass beside the plot. Jack was tempted to let it stay there but wanted to leave the garden tidy. He hurried back, yanked it from the ground and took it to the shed.

Various garden tools hung from a row of hooks fixed to the underside of a high shelf which supported boxes of nails and screws and a steel toolbox. Jack reached up to hang the pitchfork handle onto a spare hook, and was stepping away as the whole shelf and its contents collapsed in a cacophony of wood and metal onto the floor, sending a cloud of dust that made him cough.

'Oh, bloody hell, that's all I need.' He examined the mess and looked up at the space where the shelf had been and saw that the wooden support had rotted around the screw fixings. There was no way he could mend it, even if he knew how. 'Flipping shelf.' He dropped to his knees and scooped the nails that had scattered back into their box. All he could do was put the tools and hardware in a neat pile against the wall as fast as possible so he could meet up with his friends, who probably thought he wasn't coming by now.

He stood the long-handled tools in the corner and put the other odds and ends in a round tin so that all that was left was the steel toolbox, lying on its side. One half of the double lid was open, revealing a pair of screwdrivers and a hammer that had spilled out. The padlock—which his dad always kept fastened—was open, its body twisted from the U of its arm through the hasp on the lid. Jack tried the lock, which slipped in and out without snapping shut, its catching mechanism broken in the fall.

Should have left the bloody shovel outside. He set the toolbox straight and opened the other lid so that both sides hung on their hinges, and was about to replace the hand tools when he spotted a flash of colour, clean and bright amongst the dull steel of old wrenches and spanners. Reaching in, he moved the tools to one side to reveal what seemed to be a small, yellow rolled up piece of fabric, so fresh it could only have been put there recently.

As he pulled it out he realised that something was wrapped within its folds and the first sense of unease hit him as he recognised just what the yellow material was. *Knickers? Why's there a pair of women's knickers in Dad's tool box?*

A moment later, the unease gave way to confusion, and fear, and a multitude of emotions he'd never be able to describe, as he held the women's underwear open in his palm and gazed at the object that had been hidden inside.

The tremble started in his gut and spread through his body like a ripple on a pond until he could no longer control his extremities, his teeth chattering despite the heat within the shed. He knew what he was looking at, though he couldn't believe it, couldn't think of a sane reason why it should be locked inside his father's toolbox.

You know why. There's only one explanation.

He shook his head as if to clear it of the thought.

Jack heard a deep moan escape his throat as he lifted the pink-framed glasses from the yellow panties and studied them. One lens was cracked, with two red spots of dried blood on its surface, and the arm on that side was bent, but there was no mistaking it; Jack was holding the glasses he'd seen worn so many times by his adored, murdered teacher.

2016—SNOW

1

THE AFTERNOON SKY was as white as the day before, though the snow had stopped falling at last by mid-morning. Jack trudged along the middle of the road, the effort of lifting his feet almost to knee height with every step to clear the virgin snow making him almost breathless. There was no fear of being run down by a vehicle; every road leading in to Doom was impassable. All colour on the trees and bushes on either side had been obscured by the storm so that Jack felt he was moving within a giant orb of white.

He'd been walking for forty minutes on the desolate country road between Georgina's house and the care home, the lunch he'd eaten sitting heavy in his stomach. It was only two miles—he'd have been there by now in normal conditions—but he guessed he still had a little way to go. If it wasn't for the regular coastal hikes in Brighton that Bev insisted on, Jack was sure he'd be on his knees by now. Matt had offered to accompany him, had almost insisted, but Jack would have none of it. He had to see his father alone, despite the fact Charles hadn't said a word in two years.

He had talked long into the early hours with Georgina and Matt, the memories coming back to them even as they spoke, but there was still so much they couldn't recall. Georgina and Matt both remembered up until the séance at Hope House, what they had asked through the Ouija board and the answers they'd received, but that was still days before the fire. Jack's memory of what he'd found in his father's tool box on that summer's afternoon had hit him like a hammer, prompted by Matt's recollection that Jack had not come over to Frankie's because he was working in his garden. He hadn't told Matt and Georgina what he'd remembered, though by the glance he saw his two friends exchange he was sure they had noticed the awful expression that must have crossed his features. It was too much of a shock, and he had to sort it out in his own mind before he told them about his discovery of Miss Simpkins's glasses. And, of course, he was ashamed at keeping such a secret for so many years.

But I forgot. How could I have forgotten something like that?

He didn't know the answer, but he had a feeling that he soon would. It wasn't shock that had wiped their memories, nor smoke inhalation, as they had always told themselves. If the shared amnesia could be blamed on either of those reasons, then why had they all begun to remember such long ago events at exactly the same time, and only up until the same afternoon?

'The memories are coming faster and stronger, as if we're approaching something,' Georgina had said.

'Or coming back on ourselves, in a circle,' Matt had countered, and that seemed right to Jack. Since they had woken this morning, none of them had mentioned the conversation.

He stopped for a brief rest, his breath forming little white puffs of cloud, and looked ahead to where the road took a sharp bend to the right, a hundred feet or so away. Just beyond that, he knew, was the entrance to the Durling and Doom Care Home. In spite of the temperature, he'd worked up quite a body heat within the layers of clothes supplied to him by Georgina, especially in his feet where he'd had to wear three layers of socks to fill the space in Michael's spare pair of Wellington boots.

You chose this.

Jack felt the hair on the nape of his neck rise at the sound of the voice that floated on the crisp air to him from some way behind. It was a child's voice, one that he recognised. He turned to look back the way he'd come and caught his breath at the sight of Frankie, fifty feet away.

He appeared just as Jack remembered him, even his clothes, which were only fit for summer wear. Something was odd—apart from the fact the boy had been dead for almost fifty years—and Jack spotted what it was a moment later. Frankie was standing on the surface of the snow, as if he weighed not an ounce, so that he was at eye-level with Jack. The boy grinned, his open lips revealing a row of sharp, blackened teeth.

Jack turned away from him and tried to run, stumbling through the snow. His pulse throbbed in his ears, and he heard Frankie's laughter, a cold-edged noise that seemed to echo at him from every direction. He pumped his legs, up and down, up and down, until he felt his sixty-two-year-old heart was on the verge of exploding, and had crossed half the distance to the bend ahead when he looked back once more and saw Frankie, still upright on the snow, but nearer, although he didn't appear to be walking. Jack increased his pace, so that he scrambled and tripped and fought his way ahead any way that he could.

'There are no monsters, there are no monsters,' he gasped, and didn't look back until he'd rounded the bend and passed below the sign that read **DURLING AND DOOM CARE HOME**. Frankie, or the thing that resembled him, was no longer there.

2

Georgina dried the last of the dishes and placed it in the kitchen unit. 'He shouldn't have gone,' she said. 'It's bloody madness.'

'He shouldn't have gone alone.' Matt took a sip of his wine

as he wiped crumbs from the work surface with a tea towel. From the living room, he could hear the joint laughter of Michael and Carly over the TV. 'You saw his face last night. He remembered something he isn't telling us. He's gone to visit Charles for a reason.'

'And what about you?' Georgina turned to face him. 'When we spoke about the Ouija board, you looked like you were going to be sick. What did *you* remember?'

'I'm not keeping anything from you, George.' Matt ran a hand through his silver hair. 'It could just be a coincidence.'

She studied his face. 'Matt, whatever it is, you have to tell me. We have to tell each other everything.'

'I know.' He paused. 'I've heard the name Moros spoken once before.'

'By who?'

'By Tom.' Matt looked away. 'It was one of the last things he said, before he died.'

Georgina took his big hands in hers and spoke softly. 'What did he say?'

Matt sighed. 'He was hallucinating. He thought a boy was in the room with us, watching him. Tom called him Moros, and told him to fuck off until he was ready to die.'

Georgina gazed into his dark eyes. 'So who is Moros?'

Matt looked at their linked hands, shook his head, and laughed. 'This is crazy. I don't believe in any of this superstitious shit.'

'Neither do I. But here we are.'

'I looked the name up, sometime after Tom's funeral. It was bugging me.' He raised his eyes to meet Georgina's. 'I found what I was looking for in a mythology book. Moros is the demon god who supposedly drives people towards their destruction. He's also known as Doom.'

'And what else, Matt?'

He sighed. 'Moros controls the Keres. They're demons of violent death.'

'So?'

'They will prey on anyone. But they have a real taste for the battlefield and wounded soldiers.'

3

'How on earth did you get here, Mr. Porter?'

Jack removed his woollen hat and coat and forced a smile for Liza, the young girl who had been so kind to his father and had risen from junior care worker to the rank of assistant manager in the few years that Charles Porter had resided there. 'I walked,' he said, and noted with amusement the look of confusion on Liza's face. 'I don't mean from Brighton. I'm staying in Doom with friends.'

'Oh.' She looked him up and down. 'Still, it's quite a walk in these conditions. You're breathless. And your face is as red as a beetroot.'

'I'm fine. It just feels a little warm in here after being outside.'

'Well go and sit down for a while. Charles is in his room today. He got a bit agitated when we tried to take him to the common area. He just wanted to sit and look out his bedroom window . . . ' She frowned. 'It's as if he was waiting for someone . . . like he knew you were coming.' She put her hands on her hips. 'Go through and I'll get someone to bring you down a cup of tea.'

'Thank you, Liza. That's very kind.' He made his way along the familiar corridors to his father's room and let himself in through the door that had been left ajar. His dad was sitting by the window that looked out onto the approach road from the front gates, his face turned up to the white sky on the other side of the pane. He'd lost weight, and the collar of his buttoned-up shirt was separated from his neck by half an inch all the way around. He'd never been a big man, but the care home staff had suffered a little trouble getting him to eat his meals in recent weeks. Jack and his sister Mary had worried at just how long a man of his age and health could survive like that.

A chair had been placed opposite Charles by the window as if a visitor had indeed been expected, and Jack sat himself down. He looked into his father's eyes, which appeared as kind and loving as they ever did amongst his old, sunken features, and Jack found it impossible to believe that his father had killed Miss Simpkins, keeping her glasses and underwear as a trophy of his crime.

I don't know that he did it for sure. I can't blame him unless he has the opportunity to defend himself. Jack knew that was unlikely to happen now. He leaned forward and studied his father, looking for some clue within his features that he was capable of murder, and was startled enough to jerk back in his seat as his dad broke his long silence.

'I'm sorry, Jack,' Charles said in his frail, aged voice. He turned his desperate, sad eyes to look at his son. 'There was nothing I could do. I know that you loved her.'

Jack felt his shoulders slump. He recalled his father using those exact words years before, when Jack was on a visit with Mary, and had made the mistake in believing that he was talking about Kate. He'd thought then that his father was heartbroken at his son's loss and was merely expressing his own helplessness, empathy and love. The words had a different nuance to them now that Jack suspected they were an apology for murder.

'What did you do, Dad?'

Charles began to weep. It was the first time Jack had seen his father cry since his mother passed away, and a lump formed in his throat at the sight. 'I'm so sorry,' Charles said. He averted his gaze to the window and Jack was afraid he was going to lose him to the silence again before he'd heard what he wanted.

A vibration followed by an electronic ring tone sounded from Jack's hip pocket, and he pulled out his phone. Georgina's name was highlighted on the lit screen. 'Damn it,' he whispered and made the quick decision to turn it off. He didn't want any disruptions.

'Dad. Look at me.'

Charles did as he was asked.

'Dad,' Jack said in a low voice. 'What did you do? I have to know what happened.'

'I killed her, son. I killed Beth Simpkins. But I couldn't help myself—he got inside me. He made me do it.'

Jack felt his own eyes well with tears. The man he'd loved and worshipped, the one person who had never let him down, was not the man Jack had always believed him to be, and the betrayal was like a knife in his heart. 'Why would you do such a thing?'

'We were in my car, as usual, and we were, well, you know.'

'Know what?'

'We were doing what people in love do. We loved each other, son.'

The realisation washed over Jack like a creeping dawn. 'You were having an affair.'

Charles looked down at his lap. 'Yes.'

'Did Mum know?'

'No.'

'But why did you kill her?'

Charles' shoulders shook as he wept.

'Well, you got away with it, didn't you?' Jack spat.

'I didn't want to do it. He got inside me, when we were making love. But that wasn't enough for him.'

Jack felt sick. He'd heard all he wanted to, and was about to leave when his father raised his head. 'Don't be too hard on your old man, Jack. His only crime is a feeble will.'

Jack sunk back into his seat. The voice had come from his father's lips, but it was no longer in the tones of a frail old man. It was deep, and sly, and it had spoken in Jack's nightmares many times. 'Bald Eagle,' he whispered.

'Is that what you call me?' He laughed. 'I have gone by

many names. You probably remember me as the surgeon Barker.' He lifted his thin liver-spotted hands and studied them. 'It's a shame this body has become too old and weak. If it had the strength, I'd like to remove your spleen and sew it tight behind your lips.'

Jack sat frozen in place as he watched his father, whose features seemed to change and waver somewhere between his own and the hook-nosed man who Jack had always thought was just a dream. 'You're not real.'

'Tell that to Beth Simpkins.' He half closed his eyes. 'Oh, it felt good when your father let me in. It was the first fuck I'd had since the Great War.' He licked his lips. 'She was lovely. Cut, cut, fuck, fuck.'

'Shut up.'

He smiled. 'How she screamed and cried, when I dragged her by the hair into the woods. Not the perfect place for a bit of surgery, I admit, but it sufficed. She was still alive, you know, after I'd chopped off her hands and feet. Not for long, though.' He glanced at the open door, where the sound of approaching footsteps clicked off the lino-covered floor. 'Oh well, have to go.' He leaned forward. 'I'll be seeing you and your friends very, very soon, though. Toodle-pip, cunt face.'

'Did I hear voices? Is Charles speaking?'

Jack glanced up at Liza as she placed a tea tray on a side table. 'Just a few words.' He heard the tremble as he spoke and saw the look of sympathy on Liza's face. She patted his shoulder and left the room.

'I'm sorry, Jack,' his father whispered, with his own voice once more. And that was all he had to say.

4

Matt opened the front door and looked along the street for the umpteenth time. The snow had begun to fall again from the purple-tinted sky, and he knew there would be no more than thirty minutes of daylight. 'Come on, Jack,' he muttered.

He felt Georgina sidle up to him, cell phone at her ear. 'For goodness sake, Jack. Turn your bloody phone on!'

Matt put his arm around her and led her back inside the living room. 'I'll have to go look for him. Something might have happened. If he isn't home before nightfall, he isn't going to be able to see a thing.'

'I'll get us a pair of flashlights,' Michael said.

'Thanks, Mike.' He glanced over at Carly who was staring out the window, hugging herself. 'I hope he's okay,' she said.

'I'm sure he is,' Matt forced a smile for her. 'He probably just left the care home later than he intended. Didn't realise how early it was going to get dark.'

'He left there over an hour ago,' Georgina said. "I called. Surely it wouldn't take him that long.'

'It's hard work walking in that stuff. He's not as young as he was. None of us are.'

'Hey, Honey, where are the batteries?' Michael called from the top of the staircase.

'I think I know,' Carly said, and rushed from the room to help with his search.

Georgina lowered her voice. 'Please find him, Matt.' An image of Vinnie flashed in her mind, so sad and desperate as he gazed into the dark depths of the Thames from Waterloo Bridge, the snow floating around him. 'I can't bear the thought of Jack out there on his own.' She pulled him into an embrace and kissed his cheek. 'And please, please, be careful.'

He pecked the top of her head and ruffled her hair. 'Michael's coming with me, George. I couldn't be in safer hands.'

The stamp of Michael and Carly's footsteps preceded them as they ran down the stairs and into the living room, their arms full with coats, boots, and a pair of torches. 'Okay,' Michael said. 'Let's go.'

Georgina and Carly watched them through the window until their figures blurred and became one with the snow. 'Don't worry,' Carly said. 'Everything will be alright.'

'Yes,' Georgina said, in a tone that would not have convinced a two-year-old. 'Everything will be fine.'

5

Jack looked at the dark windows of his old house from the front garden. Nobody was home and no vehicle was parked outside. He could only guess the new owners were away, maybe prevented from returning home by the weather.

He had remembered it all: Hope House, Bald Eagle, who was really some kind of entity that had possessed the surgeon named Barker as well as his own father, and the fire. One mystery remained, though. How had he, Vinnie, Georgina, and Matt survived when Frankie had perished? He thought if he saw his old house it might provoke something deep inside the recesses of his mind, but he felt nothing. There was only one place now that might do that and only one way to return there—the old way.

Jack blew at a snowflake that had settled on the end of his nose which had turned numb with the cold, and made his way to the front door where he uncovered a plant pot on the open porch, smashed a glass door pane, and fumbled a gloved hand to undo the latch. The fading daylight was just bright enough to cut through the shadows inside so that he didn't need to switch the lights on.

He passed through the house, any sense of nostalgia that he might have felt destroyed by his father's revelations. *He couldn't help it. He was possessed.* Maybe, but it was his body, and he knew what he'd done. *His will was weak. He could have shut him out.*

Jack unlatched the back door, slid open the deadbolt, and walked with loping footsteps through the ever deepening snow, his thighs and calves burning. The old loose board was gone, of course, the back fence long since replaced with a newer though no more sturdier version. He grabbed a vertical slat at its top and yanked it away with a snap. Four more slats came away and he passed through the gap he'd created into the field beyond.

'Don't do it, Jack. Stay away.'

Jack started at the sudden voice by his side, and felt his heart race as he looked at the boy who had appeared from nowhere. 'You're not real, Frankie. You've been dead for fifty years.' He fought to keep his voice steady, praying he didn't sound as scared as he was.

Frankie shrugged. 'Don't say I never warned you. Again.'

Jack began the walk across the field to the woods that he knew would lead him to Hope House. Frankie stayed by his side, though he never took a step. Off to his left, twenty feet away, a white coated figure appeared and stalked parallel to him through the snow. Bald Eagle, in the guise of the surgeon Barker, grinned at him and slashed his scalpel through the floating snowflakes, though Jack knew him to be impotent with no physical body to possess. Once or twice he moved closer, only to meet with a black look from Frankie that made him cower and keep his distance.

'He's useful,' Frankie told Jack in a bored voice, 'but he gets out of control sometimes. He's insane, of course, so a little unpredictable.'

It took ten minutes to reach the edge of the wood, where Jack leaned his hands on his knees to catch his breath. The darkness ahead was impenetrable. *Crap.* Jack wondered if he could head in a straight line and find his way through.

'Go back, shithead!' Bald Eagle shouted.

Jack straightened his back and glared at him. 'Fuck off.' He removed a glove and retrieved his phone from his pocket, switching it on. The screen showed a line of missed calls from Georgina. 'Sorry, George,' he whispered, knowing she would be frantic with worry.

He scrolled through his apps, found the one he was looking for and touched the image of a button on his screen. A bright, white light shone from the phone that lit his way as he entered the trees.

'Don't say I didn't warn you,' the surgeon called after him. 'This is your choice, Jack, remember that.'

Jack trudged on, his bones beyond cold, and remembered.

1965—HOPE HOUSE

 1

JACK EXCHANGED A glance with Matt across the table, who gave a slight nod in the direction of Frankie. He knew what message was intended: Matt had warned Jack earlier, before they'd come to Hope House for the Ouija board session that Georgina had insisted upon.

'Watch Frankie,' Matt had told him. 'I can't prove it, but I'm sure he was pushing the glass around the other day.' So the pair of them had made a pact to scrutinize Frankie throughout.

The candles that flickered around the room gave the atmosphere an eerie edge that enhanced the sense of foreboding felt by Jack. He hadn't wanted to come. In fact, for the past three days, he hadn't wanted to do anything. Sleep had become an enemy and food like poison since his discovery of Miss Simpkins's blood stained glasses wrapped in what he guessed was her underwear. He'd returned the items as he'd found them beneath his father's tools, and managed to wedge the broken padlock so that it looked closed and locked on the hasp. His father had made no mention of the snapped lock, but Jack knew it would be just a matter of time before he discovered it.

What then? Will he know I looked inside? His father had laughed when Jack had told him whilst somehow managing to speak in a level voice that the shelf in the shed had collapsed. 'Never mind,' Charles had said as he'd handed his son a shilling and ruffled his hair. 'You did a great job in the garden.'

Jack looked sideways at Georgina, whose face was as

serious as he'd ever seen it. Matt had told him about the question she'd asked three days ago, and the Ouija board's promise to reveal the identity of Miss Simpkins's killer next time. It had made Jack feel sick deep inside his stomach. He had no particular belief or interest in ghosts or the supernatural, though he'd found himself praying in bed the past three nights for his suspicions to be wrong.

'Please, God,' he had whispered, 'please, please, don't let my dad be a murderer. I'll do anything you want, I promise.' He'd also fantasised that the items had been placed in the box by the real murderer, maybe to frame his father, or that his dad had found them and brought them home, not knowing who they belonged to. *Yeah, because everybody picks up knickers and ruined glasses that they happen to find and hide them in their shed.*

Vinnie, who sat to his left between himself and Frankie, looked terrified, but Jack knew why he'd returned despite his fear. Vinnie wanted to know as much as Georgina and Matt if the murderer's name was revealed. That was why, despite him just wanting to lie in bed and never get up again, Jack had to be there.

The room was quiet, the only sound a flock of faraway geese honking as they flew across the country side.

It was Frankie who broke the silence. 'Place your fingers on the glass.'

Each of them rested their fingertips on the upturned underside, and a moment later, before any question had even been asked, the wine glass slid across the smooth polished surface of the wooden board to HELLO. The glass moved to the alphabet as Jack tried to concentrate on Frankie's fingertips, studying them for any sign of pressure. It spelt a name.

VINNIE.

Jack heard a sharp intake of breath from his friend.

'Hello, Vinnie,' Frankie mused. 'Well, well, it seems someone wants to speak to you.'

The glass moved.

YUPPIE—PRICK.

'What's that mean?' Jack heard the waver in Vinnie's voice. 'What's a yuppie?'

BIT—ME—SCREWED—ME—KILLED—ME.

'What's it talking about?' Vinnie's voice hit an unnatural high note of panic.

'Take no notice,' Frankie said. 'Mischievous spirits like to mess around sometimes.' He raised his voice. 'Please leave us. We want to speak to the one we contacted before.'

The glass began to vibrate beneath their fingers so that its downturned rim rattled on the board, and Jack edged a fingertip so that it touched Frankie's, hoping to discern any movement. The vibration lessened, and the glass jerked back to HELLO at the top of the board.

'Moros?' Frankie questioned. The wine glass moved fast.

YES.

Frankie turned his face to Georgina and raised his eyebrows. She didn't hesitate.

'Who killed Miss Simpkins?'

It moved to the alphabet.

C.

Jack began to tremble and hoped it would not be noticeable through his fingertips.

H.

The glass's progress was snail-like across the letters, and Jack glanced at Frankie, his heart pounding. *He can't be moving it. How could he know?*

A.

That was enough for Jack. He hadn't planned it, hadn't thought through what he would do if his father was identified as the murderer, but he knew he couldn't let his name be spelt out in front of his friends. The glass crept along the row of letters, destined, Jack was sure, for the R. It had travelled halfway when he pressed down. The glass slowed, but Jack could feel its power pulling against him. He pressed harder and swerved it away from the alphabet onto GOODBYE.

'What was that about?' Vinnie looked around. 'Who's Cha?'

Matt was the first to remove his fingertips. 'I told you. It's a load of rubbish.' He stared at Frankie as he spoke. 'Maybe Moros doesn't know anything at all. Maybe he isn't even a spirit.'

Jack saw his chance. 'Yeah, Matt's right. This is a waste of time. Let's go home.' He removed his contact with the glass, and Vinnie copied.

'It said it would tell me next time,' Georgina said, her fingers still on the glass base with Frankie's. The glass moved so quick then, that Vinnie, who began to read the letters out loud, had trouble keeping up.

NAUGHTY—JACK.

Jack felt himself blush as the others looked at him and was grateful it would not be noticed beneath the dim glow of the candles.

'Who killed her?' Georgina shouted, and Jack readied himself to swipe the glass clean from the board, but this time, it didn't head for the C.

GO—TO—THE—SOUTH—WING.

'Is that it?' Georgina asked Frankie, who waited with her, but the glass moved no more.

'See?' Matt huffed. 'I told you. That's it, Frankie. No more silly games.'

'This is no game.' Frankie held his hands from the glass, palms out towards Matt.

'I'm not stupid. You were moving the glass.'

Georgina sunk back into her seat. 'What's in the south wing?'

'Empty rooms, mostly. We don't use it.'

'Come on.' Georgina stood. 'Take us there.'

Matt sighed. 'George . . . '

'Come on, Matt,' Vinnie said, already at the door.

Matt stood. 'All right, take us there, Frankie. But that's it. After this, no more Ouija boards or any other nonsense.'

Jack watched the four of them move towards the door and stood to follow, grateful to be leaving the room, but concerned at what may lie in wait. *I'm never stepping foot in this bloody house again.*

He was halfway across the room when he heard a sound from behind that froze him mid-stride; the unmistakable scrape of the glass moving across the board. Ahead, the others were already into the hallway.

Don't look, don't look.

He couldn't help himself. The glass, when he turned to face it, was moving from right to left across the numbers.

6—5—4—3—2 . . .

Jack darted from the room. He didn't want to witness the end of the countdown. He had no idea what the backward counting could mean, but had the strongest of feelings that it was very bad news.

2

The south wing was a long, single-storied extension to the main house. As Frankie led them through the double doors into the passageway that ran its length, Jack was aware that although this was a newer addition to the main building, it had been neglected so that it bore no resemblance to the general splendour of Hope House.

The walls were white painted brick, though off colour, interrupted by eight doors on either side, each with a number on the front. A series of clear glass skylights were set into the corridor ceiling, allowing shafts of afternoon light into the space, where dust motes floated and spun. The low building reminded Jack of the hospital wing in Durling he remembered visiting his mother in when his sister was born. That ward had been clean though, and well kept, whereas this one had been allowed to run into decrepitude.

They walked to the first door on their left—Room 1—and

Matt swung it open on its stiff, rusted hinges. Jack crowded behind him with Vinnie and Georgina, while Frankie stood back, watching.

The room was long with a big boarded-up window on the wall opposite from the doorway, and a small, high window that let in just a little sunlight through its unwashed pane. The only piece of furniture, a dust-covered metallic bed frame, was turned on its side. They made their way along the corridor checking the rooms on both sides, which they found to be in a similar condition. It was Vinnie who voiced the conclusion that they had each come to. 'It's like an old hospital or something,' he said, his words echoing off the walls of the bare wing.

Jack glanced at Frankie. 'Is that what this was?'

Frankie shrugged.

Two rooms remained, and Matt was about to push open the door to Room 15 when he jerked his hand back, as if the door's surface were a hot plate.

'What's wrong?' Georgina asked.

'Shh.' Matt turned to face them. 'I heard something,' he whispered. 'Inside.'

Vinnie shrunk back against Jack. 'What was it?' he asked. His face was as white as the walls.

'I'm not sure. It sounded like somebody groaning.' Matt placed the palm of his hand back onto the door's surface.

'Don't open it,' Vinnie hissed.

'Shh,' Matt repeated. This time, they all heard it. A low, muffled groan of pain.

'Come on, let's go, I want to go home.'

Jack gripped Vinnie's shoulder to comfort him, though he too wanted to turn and bolt from the building just as much as he did. 'What should we do?' he asked Matt.

'If somebody's in trouble, we can't just leave them.'

'Matt's right,' Georgina whispered.

Jack nodded at Matt to open the door, though his insides felt loose. 'Be careful.'

Matt began to push on the door and Jack sensed an immediate difference to the atmosphere within the room from the previous ones. A dim artificial light along with the strong smell of antiseptic cleaner emanated from within. As the door was opened fully he saw an old metallic lightshade hanging from the ceiling that cast a yellow spotlight onto the floor in the centre of the room in contrast to the impenetrable shadows that clung to the interior walls. The floor was clean, unlike the rest of the wing, and as he followed Matt inside, Jack ran a finger over the wall that seemed fresh with relatively new paint. Georgina and Vinnie crept just behind.

'Look at the window. Look at the fucking window!' Vinnie hissed.

It took Jack a moment to realise what he was looking at: not the wooden plyboard he was expecting like in the other rooms, but a sheet of black, moonless sky. He swivelled to look back into the corridor, where the unmistakeable brightness of daylight shone. Frankie stood there, emotionless, staring back at him.

'What's going on?' Vinnie whined, and Georgina put an arm around him in response. The four of them huddled under the spotlight and stared at the impossible night sky on the other side of the window. When the groan came again, louder, more desperate than before, they jumped and grabbed at each other.

'It came from over there,' Georgina whispered. They all peered into the darkness that hung around the far wall on their left.

As his eyes became accustomed, Jack began to recognise shapes within the shadows. 'It's a bed,' he said. And he could see someone was on it.

The moan came again, gruff and muffled as if the person it came from had a mask over his face.

'What the bloody hell's going on, Frankie?' It was Matt who'd spoken, no longer in hushed tones but with an angry edge that Jack had never heard before. He looked over his shoulder at the doorway and huffed.

'He's gone,' Vinnie said. 'The fucking bastard's run off and left us!' He looked at Matt. 'Come on, let's go, Matt. We can get help.' He was close to tears—the nearest Jack or any of them had ever seen him to crying.

Matt put a hand on each of Vinnie's shoulders. 'Calm down. There's somebody over there, in trouble.' A long guttural wail came from the shadowed figure on the bed as if to accentuate his point. 'We'll see if we can help. If not, we'll leave and get a policeman. Okay?' Vinnie was breathing fast, his chest heaving. He nodded his head, unable to speak. Matt released the grip on his shoulders. 'Stay right here with Georgina. Me and Jack will take a look.'

Jack stayed by his side as they approached the bed and the figure of a prone man took shape amongst the shadows. The bed was placed sideways along the wall, the man on his back with no covers on, and the first detail Jack noticed once his eyes grew accustomed to the dimness was that the man was naked. The second detail was the leather straps securing his wrists, legs and head to the bed. The man moaned, in his strange, muffled way, and Jack saw the third detail when they were two feet from the bed. The man, whose eyes were wide with terror, tried to scream at the ceiling but could not; his lips were sewn together, the punctures where the thick thread entered his flesh oozing with droplets of blood and pus.

Jack felt his stomach lurch and managed to swallow down the hot bile that rose and burned in his throat. He looked down the man's body, which was a network of lacerations, stitched and weeping, so many that the flesh between had stretched and split into new, gaping wounds.

'What's wrong with him?' Georgina asked.

Jack looked at Matt. 'We have to get help,' he said in a low voice, hoping for agreement so they could get out of there at once.

'We're taking him with us,' Matt said. 'Before whoever did this gets back.' He stepped forward and spoke to the man. 'Hello. We're here to help you.' The man stared at the ceiling, oblivious. 'Hello?' Matt leaned over him, but the man seemed to look through him as if he were invisible. 'Get the leg straps, Jack.' Matt reached for the man's left wrist and glanced at Jack who had not moved. 'Hurry.'

Jack moved closer and reached for the buckle that bound the man's leg. It was made of thick, dark brown leather, and worked the same as a trouser belt. He pushed the stiff belt-end back through the holding loop and released the brass pin from its hole in the strap, then grabbed the slack and tugged. The whole thing should have come undone, but the strap never moved. *What the hell?* Jack examined the strap, which seemed to be fastened tight as though he hadn't touched it. He shook his head. *I panicked, messed it up somehow.* He grabbed the restraint and undid it again, only to find it tight once more when he expected it to pull free in his hand. He looked sideways at Matt, who had a puzzled look on his face.

'I can't undo it,' Matt said. 'I don't understand.'

Jack rubbed the leather between his fingers and experienced the simultaneous sensation of both its aged roughness and its complete lack of substance. He realized he was actually brushing his fingertips against his thumb. The soft hairs on his arms stood out as if trying to escape their anchored roots. 'It's not really there, Matt.' He pulled his hand away as if it were a rattlesnake he was caressing.

'Somebody's coming!' It was Vinnie who hissed the warning, and a second later Jack heard the slow click of heels approaching from the corridor outside.

'Hide,' Matt whispered. Vinnie grabbed Georgina's hand and led her into the shadowed corner behind the door. The footsteps were just outside as Matt dropped onto his belly and rolled under the bed. Jack felt Matt's hand tug at his trouser leg. 'Quick, Jack!'

He knew it was too late to join Matt in his hiding place.

He'd hesitated for just a couple of seconds, frozen by fear, and now the shadow of the approaching stranger was stretching into the room. Time seemed to slow, and for a moment Jack resigned himself to being caught right there beside the tortured man's bed.

The shadow stopped as the man it preceded stood in the doorway. He was tall and slim, his angular features most noticeable for the hooked nose at their centre and the smooth, shaven head above. He wore a three-quarter length white coat and Jack thought, with relief, *he's a doctor.*

That feeling turned to dread as the man scanned the room and Jack saw the cold look in his eyes. In that moment Jack knew: he was the one who'd cut and sewn the skin of the poor soul beside him. Somehow, the man hadn't noticed Jack, and that gave him the impetus to move at last. He stepped backwards, sinking into the dark corner a few feet from the foot of the bed and breathed with his mouth open to silence his exhalations.

'Hm,' the man in the doorway said. He raised his big nose and flared his nostrils to sniff the air. 'Visitors?' He walked into the centre of the room and turned in a full circle under the light. Jack was sure the man would see either himself or Vinnie and Georgina, but his gaze passed straight by them. He spun on his heels and addressed the man on the bed.

'Has somebody come to see you, Captain Fletcher?' His shoes echoed around the ward as he made his slow way across to the bed. The man—Captain Fletcher—turned his eyes to him and muttered an unintelligible rant that Jack was sure was full with curses. The man in the white coat tutted. 'Well, I know for a fact it can't have been your wife.' He bent over so that his face was inches from the Captain. 'She's in the cellar of your little house in Putney, hands and feet nailed to the floor. Her mouth is sewn, too. Well, I didn't want the neighbours to hear her screams while I was giving her the old pork sausage.'

Jack's breaths were short as he tried to control his fear

and anger as Captain Fletcher screamed into his closed lips and thrashed against his bindings.

'I might pop back again later tonight. I should get a good few days of fun out of her before she starves to death.'

Captain Fletcher's bloodied body convulsed and he shut his eyes tight against the great sobs that could not escape his mouth. Jack felt his heart break for him. An unbidden image of Miss Simpkins as helpless as the Captain or his wife flashed in Jack's mind, and for the first time since his grim discovery in the garden shed, a burning hatred for his father replaced the sense of shame, despair and fear that had clouded his mind.

I'm telling. When we get out of here, I'm telling my friends and I'm telling the police. My dad killed Miss Simpkins.

The bald man reached beyond the head of the bed from where he pulled a slim trolley on wheels that Jack hadn't noticed before. 'I wouldn't mind betting now that you wish the Hun's bullet had finished you off in your trench, Captain.' He leaned across the bed and tugged on a small length of chain that lit a bare bulb protruding from a lamp holder fixed to the wall. The bed area was lit in an instant, and Jack readied himself to be discovered, but the doctor ignored him, preferring instead to examine his trolley, which was adorned with various shaped knives, saws and cleavers that gleamed in the light.

The full extent of Captain Fletcher's injuries became apparent, and Jack noticed that the mattress he'd assumed was on the bedframe was no more than a thick slab of bloodstained wood.

'I applaud your ability to withstand pain, Captain, but I'm afraid it's time to find out exactly where your threshold lies.' The doctor ran a long index figure over the implements, caressing them as if they were favourite pets. He lifted the cleaver and examined his own reflection in it. 'I do hope you haven't grown too attached to your feet.'

He moved with speed, the cleaver slamming through his victim's ankle below the leather constraint and into the wood with a dull thud. The man's foot twisted inwards, separated, then fell, revealing a flat cross section of muscle and bone below his shin.

Jack heaved, and put his hand to his mouth as vomit spilled between his fingers. He felt faint and lurched back against the wall, his legs weak. A scream echoed from the corner, above the squeals from the Captain's clamped lips.

'Stop it!'

Jack wiped the spew from his chin and saw Georgina and Vinnie, still holding hands, in the centre of the room. The bald man ignored them as he replaced the bloodied cleaver and picked up a scalpel that flashed under the harsh light of the bare bulb.

'Stop it!' Georgina repeated, and the realisation that had been creeping up on Jack since his inability to undo the straps blossomed.

We can see them, but they can't see us. They're not really here.

He straightened and stepped forward so that he was within the madman's eye-line. 'They're ghosts, George,' he said, almost unable to believe his own words. 'They can't see us or hear us.' He saw movement low down from the corner of his eye as Matt squirmed from under the bed and stood on the opposite side of the ghost-surgeon.

'I don't care what they are, we have to stop him,' Georgina said.

The man in the white coat pointed his scalpel at the soldier's face. 'What next, eh?' Captain Fletcher's eyelids drooped as he began to lose consciousness. 'How about an eye? That should wake you up a bit.' He moved the knife closer, and both Jack and Matt grabbed for his wrist. Jack felt an electric tingle beneath his palms as they gripped nothing but air.

'Come on,' Vinnie whined, 'there's nothing we can do, I don't want to see any more.'

'He's right,' Matt said. 'I think this happened a long time ago.'

Jack and Matt backed away until they were with Georgina and Vinnie. A sickening squelch sounded as the surgeon thrust his scalpel forward, and Jack was relieved that the carnage was blocked from view by the torturer's white-coated back.

'I SAID STOP IT!'

Jack didn't think he'd ever heard such a loud, high pitched scream from a human before, and he saw the sheer anguished expression on Georgina's face.

'Eh?' The surgeon spun and cocked his head, a bemused expression on his face.

'Oh, crap,' Vinnie moaned. 'I think he heard you.'

'Is somebody here?' A smile flickered at one corner of his mouth. He sniffed the air again. 'Yes,' he hissed. He thrust forward his scalpel, the Captain's eyeball skewered upon its tip. 'I told you we had visitors, Fletcher. Can you see them?' The Captain forced a deep groan in reply.

'Come on,' Vinnie tugged Georgina backwards, a waver in his voice. 'He knows we're here.'

Jack took a step back and grabbed Matt's shoulder.

'He can't see us,' Matt whispered. 'Back out slowly.'

'I can smell your fear. Yes.' He squinted straight at them.

'Fuck,' Vinnie whined as the four of them stepped back towards the door. 'Now he's noticed us.' Jack felt there to be a truth in that: the madman was a ghost from the past, something they should never have seen, and he should never have seen them in return, but they had interfered, made themselves noticed, and that had changed everything.

'Children?' His eyes widened, as did his grin. 'Well, well. I don't know where you came from, but you're in my world now. I'm sure I can find each of you a bed.'

'Run!' Matt yelled. They turned and he pushed the three

of them ahead of him towards the comforting, natural daylight of the corridor. Jack heard the click of the man's footsteps behind.

They turned right, broke into a sprint, and Jack felt the soles of his plimsolls slip away but managed to stay upright. His friends raced ahead of him along the hall, which seemed longer than Jack remembered. He glanced behind and saw the surgeon, bloodstained coat flapping behind him, and noticed that the skylights above the man—*the ghost, he's a bleeding ghost*—turned black with night as he passed below them, so that the darkness washed through the corridor with him like a wave.

We have to stay in the light; he can't touch us in the light.

'I see you, you little shit-fucks.'

Jack looked ahead at his three friends and the doors to safety beyond. *We're going to make it, we're going to make it.*

It was his last thought before the floor connected with his chin like a slammed door, and it took him a moment to realise that he'd fallen. He raised his head, saw his friends at the open door, their mouths forming shocked circles as they looked back at him.

'Get up, Jack!' Georgina screamed.

He pushed up onto his palms as the shadow of night engulfed him. His friends' mouths were working in frantic movements, but their forms were faint as if seen through a veil, and he could no longer hear their screams.

'I'm going to skin you alive, boy.' The voice was vile and too close, and Jack could tell from the pleasure in it that the bastard meant every word. He spun himself into a sitting position and scrambled backwards as the man approached at a slow pace.

'You're not real,' Jack said. 'You're not here. You can't even touch me.'

'Maybe you're right, maybe you're wrong. It's going to be fun finding out.' He grinned. 'Maybe you're the one who isn't real.'

Jack felt his shirt shoulders pulled up and in a moment he was on his feet and being dragged backwards into the daylight, his three friends behind him.

'Go away. You're not real,' Georgina said.

'Oh, how mistaken you are.'

'You're not real here,' Matt said. 'Not in the light. Not in 1965.'

The surgeon creased his brow.

'That's right,' Matt said. He stepped forward, and as he did so the darkness began to recede. 'We're alive. You've been dead for years.'

The surgeon studied the children, looked beyond them at the decrepit state of the hospital wing in the light where they stood as if noticing it for the first time. Jack thought he saw an expression of shock, and maybe even fear, cross his features.

'You're a ghost,' Matt said. 'Now fuck off.'

He was gone. He didn't run, didn't recede with the darkness that clung to him. He just vanished, and the four of them were left in the dusty daylight of the hallway.

'Fuck this,' Vinnie said. 'I'm off.'

3

'They're locked.' Matt stepped back from the big double entrance doors in the main hallway.

'Frankie's locked us in,' Vinnie said as he stepped forward and tried the doors himself. 'What's up with him?'

Jack exchanged a look with Matt.

'He's a wrong'un,' Georgina said. 'I knew we should of never trusted him. He's a bloody weirdo.'

Vinnie peered up at the high windows on either side of the doors, but they were the old-fashioned affairs that didn't open. 'I know there are definitely a couple of doors at the back. Probably more in a place this size.'

'Don't bother. I've locked them all.'

Jack turned and saw Frankie, standing with his hands clasped in front of him at the open doorway of the entertainment room. 'What are you playing at, Frankie? Unlock the door. We want to go home.'

Frankie smiled, but there was nothing pleasant in the gesture. 'I expect you do, Jack. But it isn't over.'

Matt took a step forward. 'If you don't unlock the door, I'll smash your teeth down your throat, and then we'll smash our way out through a window if we have to.'

Frankie held his palms out. 'It's for your own safety. Believe me.'

Matt took a step forward, his fists clenched. 'Wait,' Vinnie said, and grabbed his elbow. 'What do you mean, Frankie?'

'You walked away from the Ouija. If you don't close the session, whatever it is you've let out will stay out. It will haunt you.'

Vinnie's face turned red with anger. 'You fucking bastard. You know what's been let out. You knew all about that fucking bald eagle mental bastard already, didn't you? You little wanker!' It was the first time any of them had referred to the monster as Bald Eagle, and Jack agreed with the description at once. *The shaved head. The hooked nose.* He shivered.

'You can stop it now,' Frankie said. 'You just have to finish what we started.'

'Why should we believe a word you say?' Georgina asked him.

He stood to one side and held one hand out as a welcome into the room. 'Look for yourselves. Or ask Jack.'

Jack recalled the glass, sliding across the board, counting down. 'It was my fault.' He looked at Matt, Georgina, and Vinnie, the frowns on their faces revealing their confusion at Jack's revelation. 'I stopped the glass and forced it onto goodbye.' He walked across the hallway to Frankie and peered into the room, which was still hidden from daylight by the thick curtains. The dozen or so candles on tables and shelves still flickered enough for him to see the upturned wine glass, moving in a slow figure of eight on the Ouija board by its own volition.

He looked back at his friends. 'I'm sorry. I think Frankie's right. We have to finish it.'

Vinnie let out a grunt of annoyance. 'Bloody hell, Jack. What did you do that for?'

'Come on,' Matt said to him. He caught Jack's eye. 'Jack was probably scared and had enough, like the rest of us.' He led Vinnie and Georgina across the hallway and into the room behind Frankie and Jack. 'What's that smell?'

Jack sniffed the air and noticed a pungent, alcoholic scent, a second before he heard Vinnie's whimpers. 'No, no, no,' Vinnie groaned. He was watching the glass, unaware of the uncontrollable tremble on his bottom lip.

'Sit in the same seats,' Frankie ordered as he closed the door behind them.

'What does it mean, going around like that?' Georgina asked as they sat.

'It means we are in the presence of something very powerful.' He lowered his eyes to the board. 'Something magnificent.'

'You know a lot about Ouija boards all of a sudden, for someone who has only watched his aunt and her friends,' Matt said.

Frankie ignored his comment and placed his fingers on the glass. 'Do the same,' he said. They each placed their fingertips beside Frankie's. The glass stopped at once. He turned his face to Georgina. 'I believe you asked a question.'

She cleared her throat, and when she spoke it was in a small voice. Somehow, she knew she wouldn't have to shout this time to get a reply. 'Who killed Miss Simpkins?'

'You don't have to ask Moros, or anybody else,' Jack said as the glass began to move. Tears blurred his vision as he began to weep. He hung his head, unable to face his friends.

The glass moved; C—H—A—R . . .

'I know who did it.' His shoulders shook with great sobs.

L—E—S . . .

'It was my dad.'

They watched in silence as the glass confirmed Jack's revelation. P—O—R—T—E—R.

'Oh, Jack,' Georgina said. He glanced up and saw the tears on her cheeks before looking away.

'I'm sorry, George,' he managed.

'You haven't done anything wrong, she replied.

'That's it now, Frankie.' Matt's voice was soft, resigned. 'No more.'

Frankie nodded. 'Goodbye, Moros,' he said.

The glass moved to GOODBYE.

'I'm sorry,' Jack wept, and covered his face with his palms. He felt arms hug him close.

'It's okay,' Vinnie whispered in his ear. 'We're with you. We'll sort this out.'

Moments later, Jack felt the warmth of Matt and Georgina's bodies as they clung on to him. It wasn't the reaction Jack had expected, and a little piece of his heart cracked at the kindness he felt so unworthy of.

'So, that's that. No more secrets.' There was an ugly hint of glee in Frankie's voice, and something worse, an undertone that Jack felt reeked with cruel intent.

Jack heard Frankie rise from his chair and cross to the opposite side of the room by the drawn curtains of the big window but didn't lift his face from Vinnie's shoulder. Georgina's grip on Jack loosened, and when she next spoke there was a wariness in her voice that chilled him. 'What are you doing?'

Jack, Vinnie, and Matt looked up at Frankie, who was facing them with his back to the curtained window, his arms at ninety degrees to his body with a candle in each hand. 'We are at the end,' he said. 'Or the beginning. That depends on Jack.' He tilted the candles so that the flames touched the velvet drapes which ignited in a whoosh, and Jack realised why the room had such a strong smell of alcohol.

'Are you fucking mad?' Vinnie shouted.

Jack felt the heat from the burning curtains on his face. 'We've got to get out of here.' He squinted against the hotness and saw that Frankie had smoke rising from his shoulders and the back of his head. 'You're on fire, Frankie!'

Matt had seen it too and was across the room, where he grabbed the front of Frankie's collar in one hand and yanked him from the inferno, which had now spread to the carpet and furniture on either side of the curtains. Black smoke swirled from the flames into the centre of the room.

'Get out!' Jack shouted, and they scrambled behind him for the door. He twisted the handle. 'It's locked.' He spun to look at Frankie, whose back was being beaten and smothered by Matt with a chair cushion. 'Where's the key, Frankie?'

Frankie smiled, seemingly oblivious to the danger. Jack's eyes had begun to sting and a sharp, choking warmth was prickling his throat and lungs. Beside him, Georgina was bent at the waist, coughing into her fist.

Matt spun Frankie and gripped the lapels of his shirt. 'Where is it?' Vinnie patted Frankie's pockets before giving in to a fit of hacking coughs. Matt shoved Frankie away and ran at the door with his shoulder, then stepped back and aimed the sole of his shoe at it, but the old, solid wood would not budge a fraction in its frame.

They were all choking now, their chests lurching in great dry heaves as the smoke began to fill every space. Jack slammed his body sideways against the door in time with Matt, but their efforts became weaker with every attempt, until Matt's legs buckled beneath him.

'Matt!' Jack dropped to his knees and rolled Matt onto his back, but his friend's eyes were closed and his jaw slack. He looked around, saw Vinnie, still conscious but wheezing for air, sitting against the wall adjacent to the doorframe with Georgina, whose eyes were glazed, slumped in his arms. The room tilted to an angle, and Jack felt himself slipping into an irresistible slumber as he dropped onto his side close to Matt. *I'm going to die. We're all going to die.* His panicked mind turned to thoughts of his mother, and his sister Mary, and how their hearts would be broken through grief, and even of his dad, despite what he now knew to be true. *You were a good man once. I know you were.*

He moved his burning eyes in their sockets to look at Frankie who was still somehow standing, though his clothes were smouldering. The whites of his eyes were gone, replaced by a total sheen of black, where Jack was sure he saw the flicker of tiny stars. He heard Vinnie's voice, as if from far away.

'Why?' Vinnie croaked. 'Why are you killing us?'

Frankie smiled. 'Because I want to, and I have the opportunity. Because it's exciting. Because, because, because.' He laughed. 'Sometimes, Vinnie, you just have to act.'

The edges of Jack's vision began to darken. 'Please,' he whispered. 'Let us out.'

'Close your eyes,' Frankie said. He crouched and tilted his head, as if examining an insect. 'It's easy, Jack. All you have to do is die. Don't fuck it up.'

Jack closed his eyes.

4

'Smoke inhalation.' The doctor lifted Jack's chin with the tip of his index finger and looked at one eye, then the other. 'Oxygen deprivation. Brain cells will have begun to die.'

Deborah Porter gripped Jack's hand and her voice wobbled. 'Are you saying there may be brain damage?'

'Please, don't alarm yourself, Mrs. Porter.' He tried a smile of reassurance. 'Jack is still as bright as a button. He has simply suffered some memory loss. He is quite fit otherwise.'

246

Charles Porter cleared his throat. 'Will it be permanent?'

'Hard to say. It's been, what, five weeks since the fire? There are no hard and fast rules with this sort of thing, but in my experience, any gaps in Jack's memory that haven't returned to him by now will probably be lost forever.'

Jack noticed his father's exhalation of relief. 'So no further worries over his health?' Charles asked.

'No.' The doctor smiled. 'In fact, I'd say he's ready to go home.'

Jack watched the countryside whizz by from the back seat of his father's car on the way to Doom. He was the last to be discharged by the hospital, and missed the company of his three friends who'd all been deemed fit to return home over the past week. The fire was a mystery. None of them could remember how it started, and the events of that afternoon in Hope House had all but been erased from their minds, except for vague dreamlike images that made no sense. *Like Bald Eagle.* Jack and his friends had spoken of him only to each other during their stay in hospital.

'We were chased by a man in a white coat with a knife,' Matt had said, 'but it feels like a dream.' They each had the same memory of an insane, bald headed, hooked nosed surgeon pursuing them through a run-down hospital wing, though they agreed it couldn't possibly be true. Their memories were patchy for as far back as a couple of days before the event, with Jack's amnesia being the worst; he had lost almost all recollections for the whole of the week leading up to the fire.

Something was wrong, though. Something was terribly wrong.

When he tried to remember the cause of his unease, he was met with a dull ache that began in the centre of his skull before unleashing itself in spikes behind his eyes. So he stopped trying.

They had been frightened at nightfall in the children's ward, for that's when the dreams came. Vinnie suffered most, insisting that Bald Eagle was coming for them, and that they'd abandoned Frankie. 'We left him behind,' he'd cried. 'We left him to die.' For some unspoken reason, Jack felt little guilt or sorrow over Frankie's death, and sensed the same lack of emotion from both Georgina and Matt. And besides, they hadn't left him. The four of them had been found, unconscious, on the front lawn of Hope House by the firefighters when they'd arrived. They were in a line, placed on their backs by their anonymous saviour. For whatever reason, he'd neglected to save Frankie.

Georgina had comforted them. 'There are no such things as ghosts or demons. They only exist if you let them.' She'd crept onto Vinnie's bed one night, when he'd been inconsolable. 'There are no monsters,' she'd said as she rocked him in her arms. He'd repeated the mantra with her, until his breathing became steady at last.

There are no monsters. How Jack wished for that to be true.

2016—DOOM

1

'YOU BASTARD, FRANKIE.' Jack's chest ached and his knee joints burned, but overwhelming that was his feeling of anger. 'You and that ugly bald bastard are fucking evil.'

'It seems you've had some recollections. But I'm not evil, Jack. I just am.'

Jack walked on, and when he emerged from the woods, it seemed to him that Hope House was smaller than he remembered, though no less ominous. The snow had settled in smooth sheets on its angled rooftops above the dark recesses and mottled stonework. The architectural style was what Jack would describe as gothic, though he hadn't even heard that word when he had last visited this place when he was eleven. The building was disused, and Jack marvelled at the fact that no high-flying property developer had purchased and turned it into luxury apartments or a hotel. *Nobody wants it.*

He stood on what he remembered to have been the large circular drive, though he was sure the neat, pebbled ground below his feet was now a neglected weed bed hidden by the knee-deep snow. He looked back at the woods he'd crossed by the torchlight application on his mobile phone. *I made it. Somehow, I made it.*

Another pain hit him then, deep inside his stomach, at the creeping dread that he might not see Bev again, and he felt tired, so tired.

'Why don't you just rest a bit? Lie down in the snow and close your eyes.'

Frankie's words were like a lullaby, and Jack felt his eyelids grow heavy. *Sleep. Yes, I need a rest.* His head lolled forward and he snapped it back with a sharp crack from his neck that made him wince. He glared at the ghost-boy by his side. 'You really don't want me to go inside, do you?'

Frankie turned and spoke to the mad figure in the white coat, who had been circling them at a distance like a predator. 'I believe your ride is here, Keres.

An expression of demented glee crossed the surgeon's hateful features. 'Oh, I've waited for this.' He looked at Jack and slashed his scalpel from side to side before jabbing it back and forth. 'Cut, cut, fuck, fuck. I hope you said goodbye to your friends.'

Jack looked at Frankie, whose eyeballs had turned black. *Your ride is here.* Jack knew what he meant by *ride.* He turned back to Bald Eagle—he couldn't think of him as Barker—but the mad surgeon had vanished. Jack wondered whose body it was he would possess: it would not be Georgina or Matt, they were the objects of his violence, and both Michael and Carly were too strong willed, too good. *He needs somebody weak, or with an evil heart.*

'Maybe you should get back to your friends,' Frankie said. 'You know what he's capable of. He'll torture them and slice them to pieces.'

Jack ignored him and trudged toward the house. For the first time, Frankie didn't follow. Jack lifted his mobile phone, turned off the torch light application, and tapped the screen. The torch had run the battery low and he hoped he'd have enough time to say what he needed to say. Georgina answered on the first ring.

'Jack! Where are you? Are you okay?'

He was still breathless from his exertions. 'I'm fine, just let me talk. This is going to sound crazy, but hear me out. My father killed Miss Simpkins.' He let the silence at the other end hang for a few seconds. 'I think, somehow, you knew that already. We all did.'

'Oh, Jack.' Georgina's voice trailed off as the recollection crept into her mind.

'And Matt was right. Bald Eagle was a surgeon, back when Hope House treated injured soldiers during World War One. His name was Barker, and something got into him back then. Made him go mad and kill those soldiers—same as got into my dad."

Frankie calls him Keres. I just see him as Bald Eagle.

'Jack, where are you?'

'Hope House.'

'Please, come home, straight away.'

He ignored her plea. 'Lock every door and every window. Tell Michael and Matt everything. They can protect you.' He paused for breath; even talking caused him pain. 'Bald Eagle is coming for you. I don't know whose body he'll have, but let nobody in.'

'Jack—'

'Tell Bev that I love her, George.' He heard her weeps and cut her off before his own voice cracked. She would only try to persuade him to turn back, and he was afraid he might comply. He should have said more, like *I love you as well, George, and Matt too*, but there was no need. She knew already.

2

'Do you believe in the supernatural?' Matt brushed snowflakes from his face and shuddered at his own words, could not believe that he was voicing such a question—and with such earnestness—at the age of sixty-two. He'd had a career as an author of fiction, but it had always dealt with the tangible, the possible, a lifetime's meditation on the human condition.

Michael shrugged. 'I suppose so, if we're counting God. I get the feeling you're talking about something altogether different though.'

Matt considered it. *Moros, the demon god, driving men to their own destruction.* 'Maybe, maybe not.' He looked at the man by his side who was even bigger than him, and wondered at how they might look to a stranger, trudging through the snow of a desolate country lane in the dark, like a pair of abominable snowmen with torches. 'Have you ever seen any evidence to justify your belief?'

'I've seen things to make me disbelieve. I've done things to make me disbelieve.'

Matt stayed quiet. Michael had spoken to Matt of his time in Vietnam on just a handful of occasions in the forty years they'd been friends, and Matt knew not to interrupt.

'There was a time I was convinced I was living in hell.' He glanced at Matt. 'I don't mean metaphorically. I really believed it. I believed that I'd died, and was being punished.' He looked ahead into the torch beam. 'I'd done enough over there to deserve it.'

Matt let it hang, waited for more. When it didn't come, he spoke. 'So how can you have faith, after that?'

'Well, I guessed that if I was in hell, there must be a heaven. I clung on to that and it got me through. Still does. When I look in the mirror every morning I see a monster, a killer, and I pray for forgiveness. If nobody's listening, well, then I really have no hope at all.'

A lump formed in Matt's throat that this most gentle and kindest of men had such a hateful opinion of himself, and for what? Trying to survive in a hell-hole created by politicians? He'd had his humanity stripped from him by circumstance, and was as much a victim as those he'd killed. Matt knew he wouldn't thank him for pointing that out though, and merely patted Michael's big shoulder.

'Hey,' Michael murmured. He raised his torch and held it at arm's length. 'I think we've found our man.'

Matt aimed his beam on the figure emerging from the darkness and felt the tension drop from his shoulders. 'He looks fucked. Let's get him home.'

3

'Mum, what's wrong? Is Jack all right?'

Georgina pulled a tissue from her pocket and dabbed her eyes. 'I don't know. He's at Hope House. He didn't sound too good.' She grabbed Carly's upper arms. 'He called to warn us. Somebody may be coming.'

'Who?'

'Someone who means to hurt us.' She saw the bemused expression on Carly's face. 'I'll tell you everything, I promise. Check that the windows upstairs are locked. I'll do down here.' Georgina walked through to the back extension. 'Whatever happens, don't let anybody in apart from Michael and Matt.'

She flipped the latch on the big glass sliding doors as she heard the thud of Carly's footsteps from above. She passed through the downstairs rooms, checked the windows though she was sure they were already secured against the snow storm, and considered what Jack had told her. As much as she hated accepting the idea of any kind of supernatural hocus-pocus, he'd sounded so convinced, so frightened, so resigned.

Georgina grabbed her laptop, sat by the fire in the living room and connected to the internet. From above, she heard the creak of floorboards as Carly moved from room to room, and wished that Michael and Matt would return soon. She typed DOOM into the search engine only to be faced with a page of websites dedicated to a computer game, and had to refine it several times before finding some historical notes on the village. She scrolled through quickly, only stopping to read when she reached the Great War years, and confirmed in moments what Matt had told her and Jack; Hope House had been used as a hospital for wounded servicemen.

We saw one. His name was Captain Fletcher, and that ugly bald bastard tortured him to death.

She wondered how many other victims there had been, their deaths at the insane surgeon's hands blamed on their injuries.

She opened a new tab, typed MOROS, and was directed to the black-screened home page of a mythology site. A column in red on the left listed demons, beasts, spirits and gods alphabetically and she found what she was looking for two thirds of the way down. A click later she had all the information she needed.

> *Moros, also known as Doom, is the demon god who drives mortals to their destruction. He is brother of the Fates, and considered unchallengeable by any other god, demon or being. If any dare to break with destiny once it has been decreed by Moros, they are at risk of introducing Chaos into their world.*

Georgina read the passage several times. Moros was the entity that had made himself known through the Ouija at Hope House, and was the name uttered by Tom on his deathbed. Had Vinnie been driven to his destruction by Moros? If it was true, if Moros had designed Vinnie's doom, then he had done it in the guise of Frankie. Vinnie had long been obsessed with him, claimed that he was haunted by him, and Georgina now allowed herself to believe it may have been more than just the imagination of a mentally scarred drug abuser. Frankie had influenced Vinnie from the moment they'd met, his ideals and influence pushing Vinnie towards the car wreck that his life had become. All those wrong decisions. She wondered if Frankie had been with him on Waterloo Bridge, driving him to his final destruction.

She read on, and just a couple of paragraphs later became aware that she was holding her breath. The intention of her web-surfing had been for information on Hope House and Moros, but now she had it all. Now, she also knew who Bald Eagle was.

Whilst Moros will drive souls to their own self destruction, he also employs use of the Keres, his agents of violence. Demons of torturous death, they are mad, ravenous creatures who satisfy their blood-hunger on the wounded—soldiers in particular —before condemning their souls to the underworld. Although they are female death-spirits, they will take physical possession of any man or woman whose soul is dark enough to accept their cruelty. Moros and his agents exist on all planes—past, present, and future.

Georgina scrolled down, but there was nothing more she needed to know. Frankie had tried to kill them when they were eleven, but somehow, they had been saved. They had cheated their fate, and chaos had been unleashed.

4

Chunks of ceiling plaster, broken pieces of brickwork and other detritus littered the floor in the big hallway. Jack flashed his phone-torch around the space, though its white beam was only capable of illuminating a small area. His back had succumbed to an uncontrollable shiver, and he wondered how close he might be to hypothermia.

He'd been out much longer than he'd anticipated, his original plan being just the return trip to the care home in Durling. He thought of Bev again. *What the hell am I doing here?*

A smell wafted beneath his nostrils, faint but discernible in an instant. *Smoke.* He let his sense of smell lead him to its source, and saw something, another light. The battery on his phone died, and he concentrated on the thin glow of orange ahead. As his eyes became accustomed, he traced its line and realised what he was looking at: a closed door, its oblong shape defined by the glow escaping from around its edges. The odour of smoke grew, and he stepped forward. The door swung in with just the gentlest of prods, and Jack stepped into another world.

5

Matt tried to keep up as Michael loped ahead in the snow that was now blowing down in diagonal sheets, but found it impossible to pump his legs up and down through the snow at the same pace as his friend. Michael held his arms out to the man stumbling towards them, and caught him in his embrace as he lunged forward. Matt stopped a few paces back and rested his hands on his hips. He heard the two men mumble, thought he heard Michael say 'No' with a hint of surprise or even shock in his voice, and felt the first rumblings of unease.

'Michael? Is Jack okay?' *He's been out in it too long, exerted himself too much.* Panic gripped him at the thought that maybe Jack's heart had given out.

He peered at Michael's wide back and shoulders through the dense snow-fall. 'Michael?' he repeated. The big man became smaller, dropped vertically as if he'd fallen through a hole, and Matt realised he'd sunk to his knees. Matt started forward, but Michael fell sideways into the soft snow, where Matt's torch-beam lit a spreading flood of crimson pumping from Michael's torso into the whiteness.

'Surprise, surprise, fucker.'

Matt recognised the voice in an instant and swept his

torch up at the face of the man both he and Michael had made the mistake of believing to be Jack. The man was padded in winter clothes, with a woollen hat pulled down to his brow and a scarf up to his mouth, but the hooked nose and cold eyes were unmistakeable. Matt looked down at Michael whose eyes were glazed, the snow around him turning red, and knew he needed help fast.

'Don't worry about him,' Bald Eagle said as if reading Matt's thoughts. 'I've ripped the bastard from his groin to his throat. He's on his way to hell, and so are you.'

The surgical knife flashed in Matt's torch light as it came at him, Michael's blood flicking from its blade in an arc of thick droplets. Matt leaned back, felt it slice through his left cheek, and uncoiled a right-handed roundhouse, the instinct from his learned boxing skills so many years ago coming back on a surge of adrenaline. Bone crunched beneath his fist as claret spurted from his assailant's nose. He knew he had to finish it quick—had to help Michael—and followed with a left hook into the temple. Bald Eagle staggered and swung the knife back at him, but Matt grabbed his wrist in his right hand and gripped his throat in his left. He squeezed hard, heard the wheeze as his attacker tried to draw breath and tightened his fist. He felt the wrist he held in his right hand begin to weaken, saw Bald Eagle's eyes begin to lose focus.

'You fucker,' Matt growled. 'Why can't you just leave us alone?' As the strength drained from his attacker, Matt noticed his facial features waver and change between the hooked nose ugliness and something else, *somebody else. Of course. It uses other people.* Matt remembered the policeman that had tried to kill him in Yorkshire all those years ago, and watched as the face altered to someone it took him a few seconds to recognise, someone he hadn't seen for years.

'Declan,' he murmured, and remembered the bastard's obsession with Georgina, how he'd stalked her by phone, threatening her until the police had become involved. The image of an abandoned car behind Jack's in The Dip came to mind, and he was positive it belonged to Declan, come to Doom on the day of Vinnie's funeral knowing they would all be there.

A smile crept its way onto Declan's colourless lips and he swivelled his eyes down in their sockets. Matt followed his gaze and felt his heart sink. *Stupid! Bloody stupid!* He'd been too intent on throttling the fucker one handed whilst holding his knife wielding hand away from his face; too sure that Declan was weakening. He hadn't considered what damage his opponent might do with his free hand, and now he saw the scalpel, inches below his throat.

The thrust was fast and violent, the pain instant, and Matt heard the scrunch of snow beneath his knees as he dropped the way Michael had before him. Warmth spread from his throat to his chest and blood oozed between the gloved fingers he held to the wound. A faint buzz echoed inside his head, and he knew, this time, it was all over. Faces swam in his vision, of the living and the dead; Georgina and Jack, Vinnie, Kate and Tom.

Oh, Tom. I did love you.

He couldn't breathe, heard deep gurgling noises from his own throat and looked up at Declan, whose grin was wide with victory.

'This is going to hurt,' he said. He opened his jacket and pulled a meat cleaver from inside as his features morphed once again to resemble the bent nosed killer surgeon.

Matt felt his consciousness slide and closed his eyes to the dark oblivion of forever.

6

It was the entertainment room, of course. Jack had known it before he'd even opened the door, and now, as he stood in the entrance, he felt the heat wash over him as the smoke sucked around his padded clothes into the hallway.

'You shouldn't be here, Jack. This is wrong. You know it is.' Frankie stood in the middle of the room, his clothes smouldering as flames licked at his ankles from the carpet. His eyes were big and black, like two portals into deep space where Jack was sure he saw the twinkle of faraway stars.

Jack looked at the children slumped on the floor. *Frankie's right. I shouldn't be here.* Vinnie sat against the wall to his left with Georgina cradled in his arms. To his right, he saw two unconscious boys lying side by side. One was Matt, and the other, though face down, he recognised as himself.

This can't be.

'Help us, please.'

He looked down at Vinnie, who had turned one half-opened pleading eye up to him.

'Don't do it, Jack,' Frankie said.

'But, if I don't . . . '

Frankie smiled, reading his thoughts. 'That's right. If you don't, you won't live your life. You won't be here to save yourself, or the others. You're an anomaly, Jack, a fucking nuisance. I get one like you every millennia or so.'

Jack's head swam. It had been him, all those years ago, that had carried the four of them from the house. *It's a circle, around and around.* He recalled what Vinnie had said to him the last time they'd spoken.

None of this is over; the past, the present, the future, it's all the same.

They were supposed to have died on that day, but something unnatural had happened, and Jack realised it was just their memories of that afternoon that had all but perished. He looked at Frankie. 'What about our lives? What about the last fifty years?'

'What about them? Were they that great?'

Jack glanced at the flames spreading towards the children across the carpet. 'I can't leave us.'

'Just walk away, and in a few moments it will be over. You won't even be aware of it; you will simply cease to be. Fifty years is nothing to me, Jack. But do you really want to wade through all that bullshit again?'

Jack felt his shoulders slump. It was true—there were times he had wished he were dead, that all that agony could be taken away. But there had been good times too, and at the end of it all he'd found Bev.

He crouched by Georgina, thought of what she'd achieved, how she had saved Carly, the love she had shared with Michael. 'I haven't the right to let anyone die. So what if things got messed up. That's life.'

'Your friends are dying in agony out there right now at the hands of a lunatic, because you let them live. You sentenced them to life, and it always leads to this.' Frankie's voice took on an edge of anger. 'I told you before. If you choose to live, Jack, I can promise you one thing. It's going to hurt.'

Jack slipped his hands under Georgina and stood with her so that she hung from his arms like a rag doll. 'How many times have I been here?'

'Who knows? Once, twice, a thousand.' Frankie glared at him. 'Don't do it, Jack.'

Frankie's voice was full of anger, but Jack spotted something else there, something unexpected. 'Why are you so scared, Frankie?'

The flames had begun to take hold on Frankie's clothes but he seemed oblivious. 'How fucking dare you!'

'If fifty years is such a trifle to you, what does it matter? And if I've saved the children so many times, why didn't you just kill me when I was twelve or thirty or any age to stop it all?' He watched the creature that called itself Frankie, and suddenly knew. He began to laugh. 'Fifty years is a very long time even for you, if it's repeated forever.'

'Put her down, Jack.' Frankie's voice had dropped to a deep baritone, lower than any man's voice Jack had ever heard, and his features began to swim, his face boiling and bulging, changing to something less human. Whatever this thing was, Jack knew it had never really been a boy.

'You're trapped, just like me.' Jack narrowed his eyes. 'You have to let me live, don't you? The only way it can end is if I decide to let my eleven-year-old self die. If I save myself again, we just keep going around for eternity.'

'Please. Mister.'

Jack looked down at Vinnie, begging to be saved. 'You don't give a damn about my friends, but you're not sure about me. I'm an anomaly, like you said, and you don't know if killing me will trap us in this cycle forever.'

The clothes worn by the thing that had resembled Frankie ripped at the seams as the creature's body bulged, and slick black tentacles emerged from the torn material, their tips swaying in the smoke-filled atmosphere as if tasting it. 'You will never understand my power. I will crush you and you will burn for eternity.'

Jack knew what he had to do. He turned towards the door with Georgina. 'I don't know what the hell you are, but I'm the only one with any hope here.'

'No! Put her down! You don't what you're doing!'

'Maybe I don't. But your way hasn't exactly been a fucking success.'

7

When Carly screamed, Georgina felt the blood drain from her face in an instant. It was not just a scream of shock, or surprise, it was an animalistic noise that conveyed pure terror and grief. Georgina rose from her seat by the fire in the living room and ran on unsteady legs through to the conservatory where she saw Carly standing with her back to her, each raised hand grabbing a fistful of her own hair as she peered through the glass patio doors into the back garden which was lit by the motion-sensor halogen lamp. She was hyper-ventilating, her breath coming in short gasps that threatened to stick in her throat permanently, and as Georgina approached on legs that seemed to move of their own accord she saw the shape of two dark mounds set upon the snow-covered garden table.

Is that what frightened her? She grabbed Carly's shoulder in one hand as her mind made sense of the objects, and caught the scream in her own throat before it erupted.

It can't be real. Her mind refused to accept it, tried to find a less horrific, heart-breaking explanation, but the physical evidence could not be ignored. On the table, facing into the conservatory, were the decapitated heads of Michael and Matt. Their features were bloody and drooped, their eyelids half closed over dull pupils, and a ring of red with blurred edges soaked the snow where their torn necks were planted.

Georgina turned Carly from the tableau of horror and embraced her. 'Shh. Breathe slowly,' she whispered, though her own lungs were working at a furious rate. She wanted to scream and cry, to throw herself on the floor and wail, but something took over, some primal survival instinct. *You can cry later. Your priority right now is Carly.*

She averted her eyes from the window as the first, deafening crack rang out, and this time she did scream—along with Carly. They jerked at the sudden shock of noise and looked back at the patio doors. A jagged, diagonal line had spidered its way down the glass. On the other side, meat cleaver in one hand, an apparition grinned at them.

Georgina pushed Carly away. 'Go, run!' She pulled the cutlery drawer open and grabbed the deadliest looking implement within, a wide-bladed chef's knife, and turned to face the killer as the glass door smashed inwards in a thousand fragments. He stepped inside, the wind billowing snowflakes around him into the room.

'Hello, Georgina.' He looked past her and nodded. 'Carly. My, you've grown.'

Georgina gave a quick glance behind. Carly was standing with the base of her back against the dining table, hugging her arms in an attempt to stop the shakes that had overcome her. 'Get out of here, Carly,' she said over her shoulder.

'Too late, no escape.' He stepped closer and waved his blood-stained cleaver. 'Cut, cut, fuck, fuck.' He licked his lips. 'Just like Miss Simpkins.'

'Over my dead body, you sick bastard.'

'You're not dying yet, Georgina.' He leered over her shoulder at Carly. 'I'm going to make you watch, first.'

There was something in his voice, something familiar, and Georgina studied his ugly face. His features resembled those of Bald Eagle, the mad surgeon Barker who'd chased her and her friends through Hope House, but they were wavering, changing shape, not quite settling. She knew how it worked now though; he was an agent of Doom, a Keres, and he needed a body to inhabit to be able to inflict any harm. 'Who are you?'

'I'm the man whose life you ruined, you fucking slut.'

His face flickered, like a television switching between channels at a fantastic rate, and Georgina saw enough to recognise him. She remembered the phone calls, the screaming obscenities, the graphic threats.

'You bastard, Declan. You let him inside you.' She knew it was more than just acquiescence, though. Declan was a sicko, and just like Barker before him, he had welcomed the opportunity to carry out his evil fantasies. She watched the grin spread across his lips and her grief, shock and horror—so fresh and torturous—sharpened and honed itself into a burning spear of rage and hatred. She ran at him, blade first.

She heard Carly scream from behind, felt the whoosh of misplaced air by her left ear, and saw the glass fruit bowl Carly had thrown spin towards Declan. *No, it's some spirit that's useless without him.* She used that thought to focus her fury, and as Declan swung his meat cleaver at the bowl she ducked low and thrust herself forward in a dive. The tip of her blade cut through the padding of his clothes and into his torso with little resistance as her knee came down on the hard floor with a jolt that sent pin-pricks of pain up to her hip. She began to fall sideways, knew she had to thrust deeper to stop him, and saw the cleaver coming back at her in a back-handed swing a millisecond before the nerves in the side of her face exploded. She hit the floor, saw her broken teeth scattered nearby and rolled onto her back. The room tipped, righted itself, tipped again. Her vision shrunk to a pinprick and somewhere, faraway, a girl screamed, but that faded to nothing as she was swallowed by darkness.

8

No, it hurts, please God not that.
But she couldn't talk, couldn't open her eyes, and slipped back into the comfort of oblivion.

9

I've heard that noise before. It was a moaning, but unnatural, constricted.
No, not Carly. Please God, not Carly.
She tried to open her eyes but they were heavy.

10

'Wake up.'
She felt cold, wet, couldn't breathe, water slipping down through her nostrils, choking her.
'Wake up.' Another splash on her face and she tried to shake her head but that sent a universe of agony through her brain that sharpened her senses at last. She opened her eyes

to bright morning sunlight and saw the ugly bald headed fucker's face inches away.

'Good. That's good.' He smiled and she caught the stench of rottenness from his breath. She was sitting in one of her straight-backed kitchen chairs, her legs strapped to the two front uprights, her arms lashed tight behind.

You bastard. That's what she intended to say, but managed no more than a three-syllable hum. *My mouth, I can't work my mouth.*

It took her a few moments to work out the problem, and when she did her heart almost burst at the memory of Captain Fletcher from so long ago. Bald Eagle cocked his head. 'Do you believe in monsters, Georgina? No? Perhaps I can convince you otherwise.'

He straightened and stepped aside. On the kitchen table, tied down by lengths of thin cable, Carly turned her wide eyes to Georgina and tried to talk, but her lips were also sewn. Blood stained surgical implements were scattered on the nearby worktop.

'I couldn't resist starting without you, George,' Bald Eagle said, though the voice was Declan's. 'Don't worry though; I've saved the best until last.' He laughed. 'Mr. Poole would certainly have approved.'

He set to work then, and Georgina squeezed her eyes tight but couldn't shield her ears from the muffled screams and yelps. An eternity later, when the stillness told her that her prayer for Carly's death had at last been answered, he came for her, and she prayed for her own.

EPILOGUE

2017—LONDON

Of THE BRIDGES that spanned the Thames, Tower Bridge had always been Vinnie's favourite. He knew it was regarded by some as a pompous, archaic gateway to a London that no longer existed, but it had character, unlike the sleek, soulless concrete eyesore at Waterloo in the heart of the city. He watched the traffic pass over it from his window table in the Tower Hotel, the dipped headlights cutting through the snow that had begun earlier that evening, and was glad to be in the warm.

'Would you like a drink, sir?'

He glanced up at the young waitress and smiled. 'No, thank you. I'll wait for my friends.' His phone buzzed in his pocket and he read the text:

Give my love to the gang. See you later, Hannah x

Vinnie thumbed a quick reply, returning his love, and pocketed the phone as they arrived. He stood and held his arms wide. 'Happy new year.'

Georgina was first, with a smacker of a kiss on his lips. 'Happy new year, Vinnie,' she said, and moved aside for Matt who crushed him in his big arms.

'Happy new year, mate.'

Vinnie grinned. 'It's good to see you, Matt.'

They sat and ate, had a few drinks, and laughed and filled each other in on their lives since their last annual night out. Matt's latest novel, *Thin Places*, had hit the bestsellers lists on either side of the Atlantic, and Georgina and Michael had recently become grandparents. Vinnie was overjoyed about their good fortune. Georgina and Matt were more than just friends—he loved them like family and they deserved the best. Vinnie was also pleased to share his own good news of recognition at the annual Humane Business Awards. After coffee, with a brandy in hand, Vinnie led the toast that had become a tradition.

'To Jack,' he said.

The glasses clinked and Georgina and Matt spoke in unison. 'To Jack.'

Vinnie felt the tears begin to well, as always, and was grateful when Georgina reached across and stroked the back of his hand. 'Bloody stupid,' Vinnie said as he dabbed his eyes. 'It's been fifty years. Still upsets me, though.'

'Jack was special,' Matt said. 'We all loved him.'

'He should be here. He was only eleven.' Vinnie shook his head. 'I just don't understand why he was left behind.' He wouldn't go through it again. He'd told the story enough times of the strange old man who'd appeared with snow on his clothes in the middle of summer to drag the three of them from the fire. The old man who had seemed to know them. *'Be good, Vinnie,'* the man had said. *'Be good for Jack.'*

'I think the man just ran out of time,' Georgina said. 'Why leave Jack and Frankie otherwise?'

'Damn Frankie,' Matt muttered into his brandy. Neither Georgina or Vinnie objected to his comment—they each remembered enough to know that Frankie had caused the fire.

They sipped their drinks as the snow grew heavy outside and watched the cars as they crawled across the bridge, windscreen wipers on full against the blizzard whipping up off the Thames. When the bill was paid they waited by the entrance for a taxi.

'Looks like the snow's in for the night,' Matt said.

Georgina grabbed both men's hands. 'Come on,' she said. 'Let's walk, like when we were kids. It'll be fun.'

Thick snowflakes drifted slowly on the breeze and Vinnie watched, hypnotized by their haphazard descent. 'Oh, well,' he said, for lack of anything profound to say, and gripped Georgina's hand tight as the three of them stepped out into the night.

Acknowledgements

Thanks to Heather Johnston, whose wealth of knowledge is always shared with such modesty, and all at BWG for their diversity of ideas that bring regular inspiration. Also to Ana-Maria, and her facts on psychotherapy. To Bobby, Harry and Joe, for their contagious youth and support, and to Andrea Dawn, whose fantastic eye missed nothing. And a special thank you to my editor Marc Ciccarone, whose vision, commitment and attention to detail helped me turn this chunk of rock into a polished stone.

ABOUT THE AUTHOR

Raymond Little is a Londoner who now lives in Kent, where he writes dark fiction. His short stories have appeared in anthologies including the resurrected *Horror Library* series and Blood Bound Book's *DOA II* and *Night Terrors III*. He was included in the Dead End Follies article *10 Brilliant Writers You Probably Don't Know,* and his story "An Englishman in St. Louis" sat alongside some of his own literary heroes such as Dickens and Poe in the *Chilling Ghost Short Stories* collection. *Eyes of Doom* is Ray's first published novel.

Discover more about the author on his website: www.raymondlittle.co.uk